Fabulous praise for

Deborah Donnelly's
Wedding Planner Mysteries

"Donnelly rings more than wedding bells with her witty writing and frisky female sleuth." —Mary Daheim

"Deborah Donnelly blends humor and romance with a clever mix of murder and mayhem. The result is high-speed suspense and wicked fun."

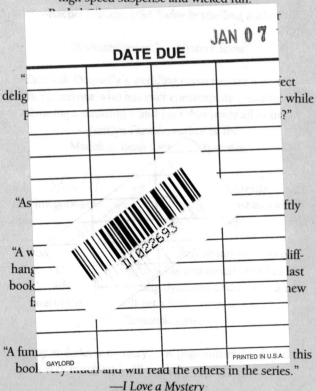

"As ... ftly

"A w... liff-
hang... last
book... ew
fa...

"A fun... this
book ... and will read the others in the series."
—I Love a Mystery

"The descriptions of the scenery are wonderful. . . . The cast of characters is varied and interesting. The bride and groom and her two adorable sons are fun. I enjoyed this book."
—*Mysterious Women*

Death Takes a Honeymoon

"Donnelly's funny tale is full of arguments, conflicts and endless bickering. With the body count rising, tension mounts, leading to surprising revelations and a hot, cliff-hanger ending." —*Lansing State Journal*

"Plenty of humor and a bit of romance, [plus] a puzzling mystery and the excitement of danger. If you like intrepid heroines who solve problems with flair, you'll love Carnegie Kincaid." —*Romance Reviews Today*

"A cozy mystery, and a delight to read." —BookLoons.com

"Read along and enjoy yourself as this delightful writer takes you 'down the aisle' with romance and mystery."
—*Rendezvous*

"*Death Takes a Honeymoon* is the best entry in the Wedding Planner series so far. Carnegie is, as always, just the right amount of snarky and humorous . . . a wonderful package, one well worth reading." —*I Love a Mystery*

May the Best Man Die

"Joy to the world! Donnelly returns with long, tall Carnegie Kincaid, who spends Christmas juggling Bridezilla's wedding, three ardent suitors and a new professional rival, as she shakes up Seattle in pursuit of a killer. Stuff this one in your stocking!"
—Marcia Talley, award-winning author of
Occasion of Revenge

"Fun for readers of mystery and romance." —*Oregonian*

"Charming, funny, fast and fresh, with an interesting cast of characters and a bubbly mystery swimming throughout."
—*Mystery Reader*

"A bubbly blend of farcical humor and madcap mystery . . . The book's nonstop action and judiciously doled out clues will keep both romance and mystery lovers riveted until the Dickensian denouement." —*Publishers Weekly*

Died to Match

"Offers droll humor, interesting background, cunning whodunit misdirection, and what amateur-detective cozies so often lack: real detection from fairly presented clues."
—*Ellery Queen Mystery Magazine*

"Like a slide down the rabbit hole, this compulsively readable mystery gains speed with every turn of the page, culminating in a chaotic conclusion that leaves enough threads dangling to keep readers coming back for more."
—*Publishers Weekly*

"Donnelly delivers a delightful mix of brides, bodies and mayhem that's a treat to devour." —*BookPage*

"Always a bridal consultant, but seemingly doomed to never be a bride, Carnegie Kincaid is the kind of woman anyone would want for a best friend."
—April Henry, author of *Learning to Fly*

"Donnelly is a writer who knows her stuff. This is a great mystery and I highly recommend it."
—*Romantic Times* (Top Pick)

"Another tasty confection in what is fast becoming my favorite cozy series." —*Mystery Reader*

Veiled Threats

"Reminiscent of Donna Andrews's *Murder, with Peacocks,* this zany mystery is a bubbly blend of farcical humor, romance and intrigue. First-time author Donnelly will beguile readers with her keen wit and mint descriptions, but it is her characters that make this a stellar debut."
—*Publishers Weekly*

"Donnelly's fast-moving story and likable sleuth will please readers who like romantic soft-boiled mystery."
—*Booklist*

"*Veiled Threats* is a solid start for what could be an entertaining addition to the cozy ranks. With her charm, intuition and the unpredictability of weddings, Carnegie could find herself a very busy sleuth." —*Mystery Reader*

"A nice mix of romance, suspense and humor . . . Like Elizabeth Peters, Donnelly offers a solid read, lively and entertaining, with a spunky, independent heroine."
—BookLoons.com

"An exciting and highly entertaining ride through danger and suspense with a dash of sensuality along the way."
—*Romance Reviews Today*

Bride

and

Doom

DEBORAH DONNELLY

A D E L L B O O K

BRIDE AND DOOM

A Dell Book / January 2007

Published by Bantam Dell
A Division of Random House, Inc.
New York, New York

ISBN 978-0-440-24285-7

Printed in the United States of America
Published simultaneously in Canada

www.bantamdell.com

OPM   10 9 8 7 6 5 4 3 2 1

*This is still dedicated
to the one I love.*

Acknowledgments

Seattle baseball fans will note that I've changed their team from the Mariners to the Navigators, the better to emphasize the fact that all the sports figures in this story—and their misdeeds—are entirely fictional. Snow Lake is quite real, however, and quite heavenly.

Caitlin Alexander has always been a mainstay as my editor, but she was especially so with this book. Thanks, Caitlin. My thanks also to Gemma Utting, who coached me through some tough stretches, to Diane Hall-Harris of Diane's Designer Cakes, and to Frederick K. Dezendorf, Patron of the Arts. And special gratitude to Emma, the elderly corgi who has slept serenely beneath my writing desk ever since she was a pup. *Good* girl.

Bride and Doom

Chapter One

Boris the Mad Russian Florist held me close. As his massive arms enfolded me from behind, a warm whisper teased at my ear and sent goose bumps rippling down my spine.

"Gr-rip with fingers, my Kharnegie," he breathed. "Not with palm."

I obeyed. I'd done this before, plenty of times, but tonight was different. Tonight I was in the hands of a master.

"Perr-fect." He tilted his head aside to get a better look at my legs, and his voice rose with authority. "Be ready to move heeps. First heeps, and then—"

"Enough about her hips!" Aaron Gold called out, amid hoots of male and female laughter. "For crying out loud, Nevsky, let her hit the ball already."

With a huge and comical shrug, Boris Nevsky lifted his hands from me and stepped out of the batting cage that arched like a giant clamshell over the home plate of Seattle's Yesler Field. Whether or not Boris had pinch-hit for the Red Army as he claimed, he was almost as good a coach as he was a floral designer. And that was saying something.

I cocked the bat over my shoulder, blew a kiss to my fiancé Aaron—our engagement wasn't public yet, but how I savored that word *fiancé*—and nodded to the pitcher that I was ready.

If this had been major league batting practice, the pitcher would have been way back on the mound, protected by a shield in case the ball was belted back to him at a dangerous speed. But he was in no danger. The regular season was over—the World Series opened tomorrow in Minneapolis—and this was just a major league engagement party.

Of course Gordo Gutierrez, the bridegroom and our catcher tonight, wasn't "just" a baseball player. He was the Home Run King, the man who had just smashed the all-time record for home runs in a single season with a spectacular seventy-five. The Navigators might have drifted out of Series contention after the All-Star break back in August, but their season had ended on a higher-than-high note with Gordo's feat.

The Navigators' owners, cannily sensing yet another PR coup in Gordo's engagement, had decided to play fairy godfather. The franchise was footing the bill for the wedding and making it an open-to-the-public extravaganza. And they were hosting tonight's engagement party as a media event—with batting practice as one of the party games.

So tonight the pitcher's windup looked impressive, but that was just for show. He was taking it easy on the guests, and when he released the ball, it lofted toward me quite gently. Also quite deceptively—my bat fanned the air, and the ball plopped into Gordo's catcher's mitt unscathed.

"Strike one!" he called, then said to me, "Good try, though."

This big-league baseball wedding, taking place in just over a week on this very diamond, would normally be out of my league altogether. I'm Carnegie Kincaid, owner of Made in Heaven ("Elegant Weddings with an Original Flair"), but I was on duty tonight as a temporary employee of Beau Paliere, celebrity wedding planner and my occasional rival.

Beau and I had certainly had our differences in the past. But when he suddenly needed a local assistant for this wedding, I just as suddenly needed his hefty commission to finance my own nuptials. My partner Eddie Breen had grumbled, but then he always grumbled. It was one of his job skills.

I told Eddie I'd get back to work for Made in Heaven the day after Gordo's ceremony—after I'd made myself a nice pile of cash. My wedding plans were still vague—Aaron and I hadn't even picked a date yet—but people would expect the owner of Made in Heaven to put on an unforgettable event. Something elegant, something grand . . . something extravagantly expensive.

Though nowhere near as expensive as the union of Gordo Gutierrez and a very hot, very young rock singer—so young that Beau had directed me to keep an eye on her. Baseball fans would attend the wedding because of Gordo. But some other Seattleites, who couldn't tell a bunt from a batting helmet, would come just to see the bride. She had just released her first album, and she went by the name of Honeysuckle Hell.

Still others—female baseball fans—would be here on Sunday to sigh over Rob Harmon, Gordo's best man and our pitcher tonight. Recently retired from the Navs, Harmon was a sure bet for the Hall of Fame when he became eligible next year.

Originally from Virginia, Charmin' Harmon had a soft drawl and thick fair hair and a power of concentration like a laser beam. They said he could X-ray batters right from the mound and decide how to pitch to them in the time it took to pull back his formidable arm. They said if Harmon stared at you, you'd be the one to blink.

But his athletic skills were matched, if not surpassed, by his good looks and southern charm. Those unblinking eyes were so blue you could swim in them, and every time he started for Seattle, the stands were packed with women and girls. I myself had gotten his autograph once, about ten years ago, and the way those unblinking blue eyes looked into mine...

"Oh!"

The second pitch sailed by, jerking me out of my reverie.

"What was wrong with that one?" demanded a male heckler in an arch, plummy voice. "Not good enough for the girl?"

"Take your time, Stretch," Aaron countered from the other side of the cage. "Look 'em over."

Instead I looked around at the crowd outside the batting cage. The guests drifting back and forth between the diamond and the owners' luxury suite tonight made quite a see-and-be-seen assortment: ballplayers, rock musicians, sportswriters, general-assignment reporters like Aaron, management types, baseball groupies, big names from the city's football and basketball teams, and various friends and family.

At least a hundred people in all, a motley mix but an impressive one—and they were certainly trying to impress each other. But even the VIPs wanted to play fantasy baseball, it seemed. It was hard to say which was the bigger draw, the lavish buffet and bar upstairs, or the chance to come down on the diamond and bat against yesterday's star Rob Harmon, with today's star Gordo Gutierrez catching.

It was pretty casual batting practice. The Navs were staying out of it, leaving the fun to the civilians, so Gordo wasn't in full protective gear and Harmon wasn't at risk of a belted ball. None of the other guests were likely to hit very hard, if they even connected at all.

Certainly I wasn't. I'd only offered to bat first to break the ice for the guests. Or so I told myself as I got ready for the next pitch. I really should have been upstairs in the suite babysitting the bride, but I just couldn't miss this opportunity. Not only had I followed the Navigators for years, but I'd once had a terrific crush on Rob Harmon.

I took my stance carefully, recalling Boris's advice and determined not to embarrass myself in front of my onetime idol—not to mention all these glamorous and important onlookers. I was about to nod at Rob that I was ready, but then the same heckler called out again.

"Come on, dear, speed it up, and let the men have their turn!"

Oh, yeah? Pointedly defying him, I signaled for a time-out and stepped out of the batter's box. Just as I did so, a train whistle sounded from out behind center field, probably an Amtrak run coming into Union Station. As if in response to the whistle, the stadium lights sprang on, outshining the October twilight above us and weirdly transforming all the colors.

Suddenly the infield was a violent green, the baselines so bright white they were almost blue, and the foul poles at either corner of the outfield turned a quivering acid yellow. The faces of the party guests were illuminated too, clustered among all that green.

With the stadium's retractable roof open and its forty thousand seats empty, we made a little island of gaiety in that vast emptiness. I could hear the tinkle of ice cubes in glasses amid the bantering voices and smell the perfume of the women that mingled with the green scent of dewy grass.

The glasses were plastic, of course. No breakable glass, no smoking, no high heels on this precious turf. The design of Yesler Field was a tribute to the ballparks of yesteryear. Even the name, instead of being a paid advertisement for some corporation, was a reference to an early Seattle ballfield and an even earlier city pioneer. And just like back in Henry Yesler's day, baseball here was played out in the open air, on real live grass.

And what grass! The infield was precisely mowed into cross-hatched strips that showed electric green in this artificial sunlight. Rob's white shirt gleamed against the green, and his white teeth gleamed in that well-known smile. It was a knowing smile, the kind that invited a woman to come just a little closer . . .

Down, girl. It was heady stuff, standing at home plate in a big-league ballpark, let alone in the presence of Charmin' Rob Harmon. But I tried to shut it all out as I stepped back in the box, rolled my shoulders, and dug in for the next pitch. *Steady now, eye on the ball.*

Of course my performance at the plate hardly mattered tonight. The success of the party was far more important, and so was my image as a gracious, competent, in-control wedding planner. So what if I couldn't get a hit? I told myself to just make a reasonable try, laugh off my strikeout, and walk away with my dignity intact.

That's what I told myself, but I guess I wasn't listening. Suddenly the visceral cues of the bat in my hands and my feet in the dirt transported me even farther back into my own history. I was in high school again, gawky and vulnerable and hell-bent on a home run.

Smash it, my high school self insisted. *Surprise them all. Smash it hard.*

The ball floated toward me quite gently, a nice fat pitch right over the plate. Leading with my wrists, I brought the bat around with all my might—all the way around, as I spun full circle and fell flat on my butt.

Chapter Two

"Good effort," said Gordo, over the laughter of the onlookers. He helped me to my feet and brushed me off with his broad brown hands. At least I was wearing slacks. "Good strong swing."

His hands didn't linger on my backside, the way Boris's would have. Gordo was a gentle giant, a shy and quiet *Dominicano,* one of the drove of talented baseball players who'd come to the States from the Dominican Republic. How he'd gotten himself engaged to a Goth rocker who called herself Honeysuckle Hell was something I had yet to discover. Meanwhile, though, he was a sweetheart of a groom.

"Take another try," he said, in a light tenor voice with a heavy Spanish accent. "We're not counting strikes tonight. You'll get it this time, no worries."

But I'd come to my senses. My professional worries were up in the luxury suite, and now that the party was rolling down here, I needed to attend to them. And I didn't care to mortify myself again.

"Thanks, Gordo, but I'd better get back upstairs. Have fun."

I waved my thanks at Rob, handed the bat to Gordo's uncle Julio, next in line, and headed toward the dark gap in the empty stands that would take me to the suite's private elevator.

I glanced around for Aaron as I went, but instead I encountered the plummy-voiced heckler, who planted himself right in my path.

"Quitting so soon?"

Digger Duvall was a big man, muscle running to fat, with a tight helmet of curly silver hair and a broad florid face surrounding oddly small, almost babyish features. He wore a white dinner jacket and a heavy dose of cologne. And speaking of babes, he had a blonde on his arm whose eyelashes were longer than her skirt.

Apparently the high-heels ban on the party invitation hadn't gotten through to her—or maybe wearing flats in public was too much of a hardship—because she had taken off her stilettos and come barefoot across the grass. The shoes dangled from her hand in a lethal tangle of straps and spikes, while the other hand hung quite possessively onto Digger.

According to the hype on ESPN.com, Digger Duvall was a sports commentator extraordinaire, with a huge audience for his online columns and his weekly radio show. The Sage of Summertime, they called him, a shrewd analyst of baseball and the men who played it, a power broker, a maker and breaker of careers.

According to Aaron, who once worked with him on the *Boston Globe,* Digger was an old-school womanizer and a four-season pain in the ass.

"You know what they say, little girl," said Digger, pursing rosebud lips. " 'Quitters never win, and winners never quit.' "

"Is that what they say?" I gave him and the blonde a tight

smile. At six feet in heels, I'm hardly little, and being patron-ized makes me feel anything but girly. "I always wondered what they said."

"You've got that redhead's temper, eh?" Digger blinked slowly, like a toad, then glanced around as someone touched his elbow. It was a paunchy man with a face like a basset hound, mournful and apologetic.

"Here's your drinks, Digger," said the man, and handed each of them a tumbler of something dark on ice.

"About time," Digger muttered. He returned his attention to me as the other man shambled away. "Females simply don't have the upper body strength to swing for the fences," he said. "Next time just try to *tap* the ball."

He tapped my admittedly scrawny biceps as he said it, and I tried not to show my distaste at his touch. Beau had informed me in no uncertain terms that the Navs' owners wanted Digger treated with respect, after they'd cajoled him—if not bribed him—into covering this party and taking a red-eye to Minneapolis afterward. And the owners were the client here, not the bride or the groom.

The client is always right, I told myself, and manufactured an-other smile. Then the smile turned genuine as I spotted a rangy, boyish brunette in jeans and sneakers coming toward us.

"Hey, Carnegie," she called with a mile-wide grin. "My hero!"

Holly Crider covered sports for the *Sentinel,* Aaron's paper, and she seldom wore anything but jeans. Except for her wed-ding, which I'd helped her out with a few weeks ago. Not as an official wedding planner—Holly's budget was minuscule—but just as a friend lending her expertise. I hadn't seen her since the honeymoon.

"So how was San Francisco?" I asked. "Did you kiss on a cable car?"

"You bet. We did all the corny tourist stuff. And that package deal you found us saved a ton of money." She turned her grin to Digger and Co. "Hi, there."

Duvall deigned to nod at her but didn't introduce the blonde, and after an awkward moment the two of them moved away. Holly rolled her eyes.

"What *is* it with him? We're in the same line of work, and he treats me like pond scum."

"Don't quote me," I said, "but could it possibly be gender bias? Just a theory."

Holly made a crude suggestion about what Digger could do with his biases, and we were still laughing when Boris joined us.

"Kharnegie, you forget heeps!" Boris shook his shaggy head mournfully and heaved a vast vodka-scented sigh through his black thornbush of a beard. "We practice more, you will improve. Here, I show you."

The massive arms encircled me again, but I slid out from under them. Lately Boris kept finding excuses to get physical, and I kept sending signals for him not to. We had dated once, until I bailed out, and since then we'd been strictly colleagues, though with some cumbersome flirtation on his part.

As the most creative florist in town—not to mention the only one who invited himself to all his clients' events—Boris made me look good with my brides, and he was great fun to work with. But I'd have to start sending louder signals.

"Don't, Boris. I've got work to do."

"Always working, my Kharnegie!" He clamped an arm around my waist and planted a proprietary kiss on my cheek with a loud Slavic smack. "She is best wedding planner but works too hard! I must teach her to play!"

Just at this inopportune moment Aaron came threading his way through the crowd. He wore a herringbone sports coat and gray slacks, and he was sliding his reporter's notebook into his pocket. Crow-black hair, deep brown eyes with laugh lines, a fine jawline—and a nasty scar on his right cheek, souvenir of a run-in with a forest fire this past summer.

Lately Aaron had almost lost his self-consciousness about the scar. He certainly seemed unaware of it tonight—and all too aware of Boris Nevsky. He cocked his head and gave me a quizzical look.

"There you are, Stretch. Doing a postgame wrap-up with your coach?"

"Not exactly." I moved away from Boris. "Aren't you going to bat?"

Aaron had been quite a pitcher himself in college and was a lifelong follower of the Boston Red Sox, with a sideline as a Navigator fan.

"Nah, the line's too long."

He shrugged, and a lock of hair fell across his eyes. I reached out to lift it into place with my fingertips. Aaron Gold was a little shorter than me, and a lot more cynical, and much given to wisecracks when I wanted to be serious. Oh, and when we first met he neglected to mention that he was married, with his divorce not quite final.

But it was final now, and Aaron was also charming and sexy and whip-smart—and almost as short-tempered as I was. We'd been bickering even more since he proposed, but surely that was just prewedding nerves. I'd gone down for the third time over this guy, and I didn't plan on coming up again. Ever.

"So," he was saying, as he smiled at Holly and raised a suspicious eyebrow at Boris, "I thought I'd go get some dinner."

"I'll go with you," I said. "I'm starving. I've been here since breakfast and— Hi there, Beau."

My temporary employer was bearing down on me like a well-tailored Parisian freight train. With his dark wavy hair and bottomless blue eyes, Beau Paliere was even handsomer than Rob Harmon. But infinitely less agreeable.

"You think you are a guest?" he hissed, his handsome nostrils flaring theatrically. "You work for me!"

Some of the guests waiting to bat turned to look at us. Beau clutched my elbow almost painfully and marched me down into the home team dugout, where the long wooden players' bench was empty.

"I tell you to watch 'Oneysuckle," he said, his voice low and furious, "but instead you come down and play games!"

"Honeysuckle's fine, dammit!" I yanked my arm away. I was tired of being manhandled tonight. "She's up in the suite with her friends from the band. Everything's under control."

Famous last words.

" 'Scuse me, Mr. Palliser?" Eugene, a gray-haired security guard, peered down at us from the dugout railing. "There's a young lady in the suite making kind of a fuss. I wonder if you could come up and— That's her, that's the lady!"

He whipped his head around as shouts and shrieks of laughter echoed from across the diamond. Beau and I scrambled up the steps to look, just as three figures burst from the darkness of the hallway and sprinted into left field.

Cries of amusement and alarm rose from our little crowd, with Gordo hollering loudest of all as one figure took the lead. This was a young woman with short-cropped hair and an even shorter skirt puffing out beneath a strapless black bustier. The bustier was cut dangerously low, so the girl's cleavage shone white in the stadium lights, and as she ran her thighs flashed pale above tall black boots.

"Can't catch the wind!" she screamed.

She paused to taunt her pursuers, two young men in scruffy leather and denim. But as they closed in on her, she darted away again, laughing shrilly. Then she began to whirl in circles, face raised to the sky and arms outflung in ecstatic high spirits.

The ecstasy didn't last. All of a sudden the girl crash-landed, dropping to her knees with such a jolt that her breasts popped right out of the bustier.

"Mon dieu!" cried Beau, horrified.

It got worse. Oblivious to her wardrobe malfunction—and the rapt attention of some twenty or thirty spectators—the girl arched forward convulsively. A moment's hideous hesitation, and then she puked up a mess of expensive hors d'oeuvres onto the sacred grass of Yesler Field.

"That was no lady," I said, wincing. "That was my bride."

Chapter Three

"Her r-real name is Rose."

The bride's father, a tall, stooped, watery-eyed man with a cheap suit and a slight stammer, regarded his daughter like a sparrow with an unexplained peacock in its nest. He stroked tenderly at her hair, chopped short and dyed midnight purple, but when she stirred on the couch, he snatched his hand away with a guilty start.

"Rose is a nice name," I said, trying to be comforting, and continued to dab at the girl's feverish forehead with a moistened towel. "Rose McKinney. Very nice."

Rose McKinney was a sadly disheveled peacock at the moment, slumped on a couch in the office of the Navigators' general manager. Her short tulle skirt, ballerinalike except for being jet black with a belt of silver skulls, was creased and grass-stained, and her black leather bustier showed unpleasant damp stains.

A couple of her green-painted fingernails were broken too, and her fishnet stockings were torn in spots, but then those might have been fashion statements. Goth was Greek to me.

There was something anomalous about Rose's appearance, beyond the bizarre costume, but I couldn't quite place it. Maybe it was just how young and vulnerable she looked with her eyes closed. She wasn't unconscious—the team doctor had verified that—just too miserable or perhaps too embarrassed to face anyone after the fiasco on the field.

Apparently it wasn't her first fiasco.

"She does this sometimes," Gordo had confided to me a few minutes earlier, as we helped the stumbling girl off the grass and into the elevator. "She gets nervous or something, and then she drinks a little too much. She'll be OK tomorrow."

"Sure she will."

The groom looked at me plaintively. "Mr. Theroux wants me to stay out there with Rob. He promised all the big shots they could bat. You'll take care of her?"

Leroy Theroux was the team's general manager, a bantamweight black man with a notoriously short fuse. Even the great Gordo had to toe the line for the GM. Rob Harmon had retired the year Theroux arrived, but he treated him now with grave deference.

"Absolutely," I told Gordo, as I berated myself for not sticking with my bride in the first place. "I'll find her father, and he can drive her home."

The bride's father was Walter McKinney, the assistant equipment manager for the Navigators—although with his wire-rimmed glasses and thin hunched shoulders, he looked more like an assistant bookkeeper. And it turned out that he was obligated to stay till the end of the party, to supervise the disassembly of the batting cage and other matters.

So now we were waiting, rather awkwardly, for a taxi.

"Her mother used to call her Honeysuckle R-rose," he went on. "Like in the song? I d-don't understand the Hell part."

The office door opened then, and Leroy Theroux looked

in, scowling. Some people have laugh lines, but he had scowl lines.

"She all right?"

"She's fine, Mr. Theroux." McKinney was blinking nervously. "I'll send her home and—"

"You damn well better! Making a show of herself like that, at a time like this. Unbelievable. *Un*believable."

I wanted to intervene, but the man had a point. And besides, he'd already shut the door, leaving McKinney and me to our uncomfortable silence.

"You were saying something about Rose's mother...?" I probed delicately. Damn that Paliere, he'd promised me a file of information on the wedding party but never produced it. You can't tell the players without a scorecard.

"My wife p-passed on," said McKinney, with a wobble in his voice.

"I'm so sorry. It must be difficult, raising a daughter by your—"

"Fuck *sorry*." The bride's eyes popped open and she glowered at me. Even bloodshot and smudged they were extraordinary eyes, luminously green and tilted like a cat's. Her mouth tightened into a curl of dark-fuchsia lipstick. "And fuck you! Who are you to be asking about my mother?"

"Rosie, don't," pleaded McKinney, and turned his watery eyes to me. "She doesn't mean—"

"Sure I do, old man," said the girl. She swung herself upright on the couch, her hair askew and the pattern of the upholstery imprinted on one cheek. "I don't need some nosy...uhhh..."

Her pale face went abruptly paler, and she clamped her lips tight.

"Walter," I said hastily, "could you go check on that cab? We'll be downstairs in just a minute."

He wasn't sorry to flee the room, and as the door shut behind him, I dragged over a wastebasket and held Rose's head while she emptied her stomach the rest of the way. Then I slapped a water bottle into her hand, dumped the towel in her lap, and stood up, fists on hips.

Inside the fists, my nails were digging into my palms. I was angry about Beau and Boris and Digger, but mostly about this poor man who dared to stroke his daughter's hair. My own father had died when I was about Rose's age, and I'd have given the world and everything in it to have him back.

"Are you done?" I demanded.

"Yeah." Rose dragged the towel across her mouth and took a slug of water. With the resilience of youth, she seemed to be sobering up already, now that the toxins were out of her system. At least she sat up straighter, and her sullen glare was more focused. "It's probably food poisoning, you know. That stinkin' sushi was probably—"

"Shut up."

"What?"

"I said shut *up*. You were drunk, and you know it."

Rose opened her mouth in outraged protest, but I held up a hand like a traffic cop and then cocked my finger at her face.

"I don't want to hear a word from you unless it's an apology. You just made a fool of yourself at an event that's very important to your fiancé, and then you were disrespectful to your father and extremely rude to me."

"But—"

"Look, if you don't want to marry Gordo, then fine, don't."

"But I do!"

"All right, then grow up a little. Is that clear?"

Thunderstruck, she just nodded her head and gulped. I crossed the room and hauled open the door.

"Can you walk? Good. Let's go."

I led the way along an indirect route that no one else was likely to use tonight. The hallway was curved to follow the shape of the stadium and lined with Navigators memorabilia. In stony silence we passed magazine covers and blown-up photographs, a few framed jerseys, and a wooden cradle bearing the bat that hit the first home run in Yesler Field.

I steered clear of the commemorative bat—it had been knocked to the floor once already as the caterers wheeled in the liquor—but I gazed at the headlines and the faces as they went by, one young male face after another. Rob's chiseled features appeared several times, and Gordo's round jolly ones as well. Why on earth was he marrying this petulant girl?

In the empty hallway the footfall of my lace-up flats, still dusty from my tumble at home plate, was obscured by the hostile clomping of Rose's boots. These were knee-high Doc Martens zipped up the outside, with full-sized handcuffs as zipper pulls. Cute.

But beneath the Honeysuckle Hell getup, Rose McKinney was just a girl—that "I do!" had sounded quite young and quite sincere—and I began to regret my harshness. She shoved her way through the double doors at the end of the corridor, and I hurried to catch up with her. As we came out onto the gallery above the stadium's entrance rotunda, I stopped her with a hand on her elbow.

"Why don't I call you tomorrow afternoon," I offered, "and we can talk about your dress."

Coming late to planning this wedding, I hadn't been involved in choosing the bridal gown. That was always one of my favorite tasks—but possibly not with this bride. She didn't reply.

"Beau told me that your gown came in at Le Boutique," I continued, "but now there's some question about the style?"

More stubborn silence from Rose, though I could hear her angry breathing in the echoing hush around us. The escalators down to the main doors were shut off for the night, and so were the flashing lights in the huge chandelier suspended above our heads. This rotunda was where the wedding reception would take place, a grand space for a grand occasion.

The chandelier was an extraordinary construction, more than a thousand translucent baseball bats in a glittering spiral that mimicked a batter's swing. Yesler Field was full of baseball art—even the terrazzo floor where we stood was inlaid with an enormous compass rose, the Navigator logo—and it was a perfect venue for a festive baseball wedding.

If only this imperfect and temperamental bride would cooperate. I gazed up at the bats and down at the compass, reining in my own temper, and tried one last time.

"If there's an issue with the dress that I should know about—"

"There's no *issue*," she snarled. "Just that my friends say it's totally lame."

"Oh. I thought it sounded lovely."

"Like anyone cares what *you* think, you're just some flunky. Why don't you leave me alone?"

With that she went pounding away from me across the gallery and down the main staircase. I followed with a sigh across the compass rose, then down the stairs. But I breathed a sigh of relief when we emerged into the chill of the October evening and spotted her father and the taxi.

Yesler Field is just south of Pioneer Square, the historic precinct of downtown that's now packed with shops and nightclubs, and even on a weeknight with no ballgame there was plenty of traffic going by. As Rose's cab rolled away up First Avenue, Walter began to speak to me, but his voice was too soft to make out above the noise.

I gestured us back to the entrance and unlocked one of the swinging doors with my passkey. Once inside I should have checked to make sure it locked again behind us, but Walter was already on his way up the stairs.

"What were you saying?" I asked as I caught up to him.

"I just hope Digger doesn't write about this," he muttered.

"Do you really think he would? It's got nothing to do with baseball."

"No, it doesn't. But that wouldn't stop him."

Although I rarely read Duvall's online column, I made a mental note to look for it this week. Beau welcomed publicity for his brides, but not that kind.

"I don't think you need to worry," I said. "Remember, Digger's got the World Series to write about for the next week. He'll forget all about this."

"He'd better," said Walter McKinney. His gentle features twisted into something remarkably like hatred. "He had just b-better."

Chapter Four

Back upstairs in the owners' suite, the clamor of voices and laughter was louder than ever. This crowd was so focused on baseball that the bride's departure hadn't dampened the party all that much. Some of the Fiends—that was her band, Honeysuckle Hell and the Fiends—had left without even checking on the condition of their lead singer. But the rest of the guests were still eating beef, drinking bourbon, and lionizing Charmin' Harmon.

Batting practice was over. Rob Harmon, now wearing a Navigators warm-up jacket, was standing at the circular bar that dominated the suite with a knot of foxy women and cigar-puffing men hanging on his every word. Several reporters were taking notes, and a few even had tiny tape recorders going.

But I didn't see Aaron anywhere, so I kept scanning the room. Over in a corner Digger Duvall was deep in conversation with one of the two young men who had chased Rose on the diamond. *Must have parked the blonde somewhere else,* I thought.

The young man, despite his macho leather getup, had a soft weak-looking face underlined by a pathetic little wisp of beard. He was speaking quickly and earnestly, but when

Digger suddenly burst into scornful laughter he stopped, his mouth quivering like a scolded child's.

"Yo, JD!" said someone behind me. "Let's blow."

It was Rose's second pursuer, who looked anything but childlike—his head was entirely shaved except for a long hank of hair combed forward to a point between his eyebrows. As I watched, he pushed through the crowd to Digger's corner and disengaged his comrade.

Wispy JD seemed to argue with him about leaving, but then Leroy Theroux stepped in to claim Digger's attention, and both the young men left. Theroux didn't sit down but leaned his gnarled black fists on Duvall's table and glowered as he spoke. The sportswriter glowered back, and I wondered what the problem was. *So long as it's not about the wedding.*

Then my observations were interrupted by an imperious tap on the shoulder and Beau Paliere's voice.

"She is gone, *la pute*? You got rid of her?"

"She's the bride, Beau, or hadn't you noticed? At least call her by her name." I wasn't sure what *pute* meant, but it sounded nasty. "Rose is on her way home, but I'm going to talk to her in the morning and see if I can find out what's going on. She seems awfully unhappy."

"*She* is unhappy? Monsieur Theroux is unhappy! And he is—"

"The client, I know, I know. Listen, I haven't eaten since this morning, so I'm taking a break, all right?"

Beau's expression darkened. First an exhibitionist bride, now an assistant who dared to require nourishment.

"Very well, a *brief* break."

"I'll just swallow, I won't chew."

He sniffed and turned away, and I went in search of food

or Aaron or preferably both. But I didn't get three steps before Digger Duvall, flushed with drink, confronted me again.

"And how is the blushing bride? Blushing a little extra tonight?" Digger had his reporter's notebook, much like Aaron's, in one hand, and the other hand slid around my waist as he put his cheek near mine. His breath was foul. "How about a quote, Red? Did she show off her tits on purpose? All the world's a stage for some people."

"And a sewer for some others." I'm just not myself when I've skipped a meal. Or maybe I'm more myself. I glared at him. "Sure, here's your quote. 'If you don't take your hand off me, I'm going to cram that cigar up your ... nose.'"

Digger was still making blustering noises as I stalked away—and bumped into Gordo, whose normally cheerful round face was puckered with concern.

"You were gone when I got up here," he said. "Is Rosie all right?"

"She'll have quite a headache in the morning, but yes, she's all right. She took a taxi home."

"Thanks a million, Carnegie." He pronounced it *mee-leon*. "It's really nice of you to take care of her. I'll go see her later on. Come have a drink with me and Rob?"

I hesitated—especially when I saw Rob beam his smile at me from the bar—but I really was starving.

"I'd better eat first. Catch you later."

The buffet table was pretty well picked over—something my friend and favorite caterer Joe Solveto would never have allowed. But I managed, making a sandwich from scraps of prime rib and a couple of mangled half-rolls, adding the radish roses no one wanted and the grape garnish from the long-gone Brie.

Behind me Rob concluded some anecdote, and his audience howled with laughter. I turned to look. Even with today's Home Run King on hand, the party was coalescing around yesterday's star pitcher. Rob had that kind of charisma.

I noticed the basset hound fellow, the one who had brought Digger his drink, standing at the fringe of the crowd with his folded arms resting on his belly. He was gazing with a strange intensity at the man of the hour, and I wondered if he'd ever dreamed of fame for himself. Then I spotted someone else gazing at me and forgot about Rob and the basset fellow both.

In the far corner of the suite, beneath a huge blow-up of a Babe Ruth baseball card, Boris Nevsky was sharing a table with a bottle of Stolichnaya. He waved hopefully at me, but I just gave a vague smile and kept going, determined to keep my distance and dine undisturbed.

The owners' suite had a connecting door to the stadium's "press box," so I went over there. It's an old-fashioned name for an up-to-date area, with tiers of swivel chairs and desktops instead of spectators' seats. Each place had an outlet and phone jack for the sportswriters' electronics, and the ones in front with the best view of the action bore name cards for specific newspapers or magazines.

Down in the front row, reading the name cards, were two dear and familiar figures, one Petite and the other Extra-Large.

"Buck!" I said, surprised. "Betty!"

"Oh, you *are* here!" little Betty Buckmeister twittered, her patent-leather-black curls dancing and her apple cheeks as rosy as ever. "I was so hoping you would be, dear."

"Course she's here, Mother," rumbled her burly husband

Buck. He wore a tomato-red bandanna tied pirate fashion around his bald head—Buck had dozens if not hundreds of bandannas—and beneath it his face was one big grin. "Monsoor Paliere told us you were givin' him a hand with this shindig. How you been keepin' yourself, little lady?"

Unlike some people, Buck Buckmeister, the retired hot tub king of El Paso, was welcome to call me "little lady" all he wanted. Eddie might refer to them as the Killer B's, but Buck, Betty, and their daughter Bonnie were the nicest Yuletide fanatics you'd ever want to meet. I'd done a lavish wedding for Bonnie this past Christmas, but I hadn't seen the family since. And I certainly didn't associate them with baseball.

"How wonderful to see you!"

I gave each of them a hug. My arms went almost twice around little Betty but could only take in half of bulky Buck. Their absent daughter Bonnie was sized in between them, so when the trio came together, they looked like those Russian dolls that fit one inside the other inside the next.

"What are you doing here?" I asked. "Do you know Gordo or Rose or what?"

Buck gave a basso profundo chortle. "Only met the fella tonight, and we still haven't met the girl. I heard she went home already?"

Oh good, I thought gratefully. *Not everyone was watching.* "Yes, she wasn't feeling well. But then why—?"

"Why're we here?" completed Buck. "Why, because as of last week I'm the bone-a-fide minority owner of the Navigators!"

"You're not the only one, Father," Betty added, determined to be accurate. Her eyes twinkled. "But he surely is the biggest!"

After we shared a chuckle about that—the Killer B's were big on group hugs and group chuckles—I invited them to join me.

"You go ahead and finish your supper," Buck told me. "We're gonna go get ourselves an autograph from Mr. Harmon there. Ain't it something, having him right here in person? I'm gonna enjoy this owner business."

I ate quickly, then returned to the party to see the Buckmeisters beaming at Rob, who was pulling baseballs from his jacket pockets and signing them left and right. Then I looked past the bar to the corner, where Boris had been joined by Digger Duvall. Boris was doing all the talking, while Digger just kept nodding sympathetically and pouring him more Stoli.

"Can you drink on duty, Stretch?"

I looked around and smiled. Aaron had a glass of wine in each hand.

"You bet I can! Come sit down and be nice to me before Beau pounces again. It's been a hell of a night."

"No kidding. Do many of your parties feature strip-teasing brides?"

I dropped into a seat at a table for two and groaned. "I suppose everyone's been sniggering about it."

"They started to," he said, setting the glasses down, "until Harmon distracted them with a demonstration of his different pitches. And *then*, get this, he pulls all the press guys together and makes this little speech about how we all have our moments, and he knows we'll be gentlemen and not print anything nasty about Gordo's bride!"

"And you all agreed?"

"Yeah, we did. Everybody likes Gordo, and they sure as

hell respect Rob Harmon. When a guy can throw a hundred-mile-an-hour fastball, you listen to him. Of course, *you'd* listen to him anyway, wouldn't you?"

I'd made the mistake of telling Aaron about my onetime infatuation with the famous pitcher, and he'd been teasing me about it ever since.

"Never mind that," I said sternly. "You really think no one will write about what happened?"

"I think your girl's reputation is safe, for now anyway." He sipped his wine. "She looks like a real piece of work."

"You're telling me."

We were both so intent on our conversation that we didn't notice Boris until he lurched up against our table. We do all have our moments, and the Mad Russian was having one now.

"Khar-rnegie!" he said, in a kind of lovelorn bellow. "You avoid me, why is this?"

"I'm not avoiding you," I began, but then Aaron spoke up.

"Listen, Nevsky, you've had a little too much, you know? Why don't you—"

"I talk to my Kharnegie, not to you!" The bellow was belligerent now. Heads turned along the bar, and the room fell silent.

Aaron kept his voice low and even. "All I'm saying is, you should go sit down for a while."

"*Nyet!* Who are you to tell me what to do?"

Boris was the taller of the two by a head, but when Aaron rose to his feet with a stony glare, the Russian fell back.

"I'm her goddamn fiancé, that's who," said Aaron, much louder. "Now back off!"

Well. As I said, our engagement wasn't public yet, but that

was because I wanted to announce it at a charming little dinner party and then send out charming little invitations. Not
because I wanted to pole-ax Boris Nevsky and create a scene
straight out of a prime-time soap opera in front of all these
people.

Somebody muttered something, and somebody else
shushed him. Cigars stopped puffing, false eyelashes flut-
tered in anticipation, and drinks were held suspended. The
whole bloody room was on tenterhooks waiting for the next
line in this farce, when who should speak up but Digger
Duvall.

"My, my," he said roguishly, and loudly, from just behind
Boris. "Here my Slavic friend is madly in love with the redhead, and she's secretly engaged to another man! Isn't she a
sneaky little minx?"

Boris Nevsky's English was pretty good, but—as Digger
was about to learn—it didn't cover the finer points of collo-
quial usage. Such as the fact that *minx* is not an obscenity.
With a thundering roar, Boris erupted.

"How dare you call my Kharnegie such thing!"

Then my dinner plate went flying, along with my table
and several chairs, as the Mad Russian wound up like a
Hall of Fame pitcher and lunged to punch the Sage of
Summertime square in the face.

Chapter Five

On game nights in summer, the outdoor concourse of Yesler Field is a great place to grab some nachos (or clam chowder, this being Seattle) and watch the sun go down from four stories up. The view is a show in itself, and the open-air plaza is always populated by hungry fans, cavorting children, and picture-snapping tourists.

But not tonight. Tonight the concourse was deserted, just the place for me to escape the ruckus in the owners' suite.

Strictly speaking, I should have stayed at the party. But it was soon obvious that Digger wasn't hurt—Boris's drunken punch had barely grazed him—and even more obvious that there were plenty of people on hand to grovel and placate and pacify the great Digger Duvall. I just couldn't bring myself to be one of them.

So, suddenly weary of male voices, male ego, male everything, I had seized my wine glass, shrugged at Aaron, and fled. Beau was the boss here—let him do the groveling for both of us. And if Digger wanted me fired, I was in no hurry to hear about it.

The concourse was dark, with just a muted glow from the entrance to the main hallway behind me, and I thought at first that I was alone. But as I approached the perimeter rail, a dim form detached itself from the shadows and turned toward me.

Startled, I tensed up, but the voice that emerged from the gloom was reassuringly mild, and I recognized the pot-bellied figure.

"Oh, hello," said the hound-faced fellow who'd been staring at Rob earlier. "I was just, um..."

He trailed off awkwardly—he seemed to be under the influence—so I stepped into the breach.

"I'm Carnegie Kincaid," I said, extending my hand. "I'm helping with Gordo's wedding."

"Tibbett." He made to shake hands, but his right palm was filled with the torn-off half of a dinner roll. "I, um, been feeding the birds."

Sure enough, a pair of seagulls passed over our heads and then wheeled back on tilted wings, their cries sharp and piercing above the hum of traffic on First Avenue far below. With a mischievous smirk, Tibbett flung the bread over the railing. Instantly the gulls dropped into a shrieking, spiraling dive, pursuing their prize almost down to the sidewalk until one of them plucked the fragment from the air and made off with it.

We watched them go in companionable silence, then turned our gazes to the larger panorama. To our right, the lights of downtown and Queen Anne Hill begin to wink and sparkle, while to our left, south, the giant ship-loading cranes of Harbor Island stood silhouetted against the sky like giant insects. In between, on the dim surface of Elliott Bay, a long freighter went creeping past the dark hump-backed islands.

Tibbett was peaceful company. We stood quietly for a

while, and I began to ask him about his role with the Navigators. But we heard footsteps approaching.

"So this is where you're hiding." Aaron grinned at me and nodded at my companion. "Hey, Nelly."

Tibbett nodded back, then gave me a half-smile and went inside, weaving a little. I waited till he was out of earshot.

"Nelly?" I asked.

"As in Nervous Nelly, his baseball nickname. He was in the majors once, back when Rob Harmon was pitching for the Red Sox. I remember the way he kept fouling off pitch after pitch, like he was afraid to let the ball go by. The Navs made him an assistant batting coach as a favor to Harmon, and he's been doing it ever since. Or he was, poor guy."

"What do you mean?"

Aaron shrugged. "He drinks. He used to help steady down the rookies, but now he's sloshed half the time and not too useful the other half. He's not coming back for spring training, he just doesn't know it yet."

"So how do you know it?"

"Duvall told me." Aaron grimaced. "I can't stand the guy, but he always knows what's going on before anybody else. You listen to him because you're curious, then you end up feeling disgusted with yourself. Too bad Nevsky didn't hit him harder."

I thought about Tibbett gazing at Rob Harmon there at the bar. The has-been and the superstar. Sad. Then I returned to my own problems.

"Has Digger left yet?"

"Is that why you're skulking around out here?" Aaron slipped his arms around me. "Yeah, he's gone. But Leroy Theroux's on the warpath, big time, and Paliere keeps asking where you are."

"They can both wait." There was a pause as I kissed him, and a longer pause as he kissed me back. Much longer. Then I pulled away. "Seriously, what's been happening in there?"

"Mostly people sucking up to Digger, till he finally left to catch his plane."

"Is Boris still around?"

"Are you kidding? He took off the minute he realized what he'd done. And now that the show is over, people are getting ready to leave. Hey, your friends the Buckmasters are here!"

"Buckmeisters. I know, I saw them." I sighed and combed my long disorderly hair into place with my fingers. "I suppose I should go face the music. I know you're busy tomorrow, but are we still on for dinner?"

"Sure. The game starts at six."

We'd begun strolling back across the concourse, hand in hand, but now I halted. "The game? I thought we were going to sit down with a calendar and pick out our wedding date!"

"We can do that with the game on, can't we? Come on, Stretch, it's the World Series."

"Ohh no, wait just a minute. You told me that if the Red Sox didn't go to the Series, you'd be done with baseball for the year. You said that weeks ago."

I enjoyed baseball myself—in moderation. But Aaron was raised Red Sox Orthodox, and he'd obsessively followed his beloved Boston team all the way through the playoffs this fall. Day after day, on the car radio or his television or mine, the games had been a constant soundtrack to our time together.

I'd tried to be a good sport, but we had already been separated all summer while Aaron recuperated from his fire injuries at his sister's place in Boston. Now that I had him back—now that he'd proposed—I was weary of baseball and anxious to talk about the wedding.

But with Aaron back in his old job at the *Sentinel*, and me working most weekends, finding the time had been difficult. And having a conversation without a ballgame on the radio had been almost impossible.

"Besides," I went on, "I'm seeing Joe Solveto for coffee on Sunday. We're going to brainstorm menus, and I was hoping to give him our date so he can work it into his schedule. He books almost a year ahead, you know."

Aaron made no reply, just went on walking, but I tugged at his hand.

"You promised, Aaron. You promised that this week we'd pick a date and make up a guest list and—"

"And we will!" He looked back at me, his face in shadow. "As soon as the Series is over."

"But you said—"

"I know what I said," he snapped, and I flinched a little. Aaron took a deep breath and switched to a patient, tolerant tone, as if speaking to a child. "But I said it before the Cubs won the pennant. How was I to know they'd get this far? The Chicago *Cubs*, Stretch. The Cubbies haven't been in a World Series since 1945, and they haven't won it in almost a hundred years."

I hated that tone. "I don't care if it's been three hundred years! I'm sick to death of talking to you between innings. You've never even been to Chicago."

"That's not the point. Now that the Red Sox have broken their curse with the Series, it's the Cubbies' turn. They're the underdogs of all time! They're—"

"The *point* is that we have a wedding to plan, and you act

like you're not even involved! We've both been working so much lately that I never see you except during a game, or a pregame analysis, or a postgame wrap-up." An alarming thought occurred to me. "You're not going to pull this on Friday, are you? Mom and Owen are only in town for that one night."

Owen Winter was my mother's fiancé. Mom and I had become engaged within a week of each other, and now she was living with Owen up in the San Juan Islands. At first I'd had doubts about their romance, but now I could see that after all her years as a widow, my mother was truly happy.

They'd be passing through Seattle soon, and Owen had arranged weeks ago to treat the four of us to dinner. If Aaron tried to cancel—

"Friday night is still on, Stretch. You think I'd screw up something that important to you?" He grinned. "Besides, it's a travel day. No game."

"Very funny. But what about our planning?"

"Hey, I'm just the groom here, remember? You make the decisions, I shave, shower, and show up. Right?"

He was trying to cajole his way out of the argument by getting me to laugh. I hated that too.

"Wrong. We agreed to plan this together, and we decided to start tomorrow night."

"Fine. But I'll be watching the game."

Aaron jokes a lot, but he's a stubborn man, and I knew better than to push him too far. I also knew better than to bicker with him when I was upset about something else. But it was too late for knowing better now.

"Fine," I said. "But you're not watching it at my place."

He dropped my hand. "Suit yourself."

And with that my fiancé strode back inside, almost colliding with Beau Paliere on the way. I might have called out after him, but Beautiful Beau was boiling over.

"Again, like a guest! Everyone leaves, you should be present to help with the coats, to—"

"I'm *coming*," I told him through gritted teeth. "Just give me a minute, would you?"

"There is not a minute," he said icily. His eyes traveled from my disheveled hair to my dusty shoes and back again. "The cleaning company has arrived early, and they have no key. You will wait at the service entrance and let them in, *tout de suite*. And do not use the main 'allway. You are not fit to be seen."

So for the second time tonight I headed down the corridor of memorabilia, striding so furiously that my footsteps were almost as noisy as Rose's boots had been.

"Goddamn Frenchman!" I said aloud as I stomped along. "Goddamn baseball, goddamn cleaners."

I checked my watch. Ten o'clock, definitely too early for the cleaners.

Why do I bother writing up schedules if people won't—

From somewhere down a side passage, I heard a door close. *Damn.* Was that some wandering guest, and had he or she heard me swearing to myself like a madwoman? I waited, wincing, to see if they were coming or going, but all was silence. Going, then. Good.

I continued on my way along the curve of the corridor, mouth safely shut, staring at the photos and plaques and headlines as I went. But when I came to a point where I could see down to the end of the hallway, I stopped.

A man lay sprawled grotesquely on the floor, and he wasn't moving.

The dark leather soles of his shoes were facing me, and as I heard myself breathing in short, shallow gasps, beginning to hyperventilate, I focused on the shoe soles and tried not to see anything else.

But I couldn't help it. As my eyelids quivered in shock and my gaze flickered upward, I could tell that the sprawled figure was Digger Duvall. And that the man standing over him was Boris Nevsky, gripping a blood-smeared commemorative baseball bat in one massive hand.

Chapter Six

"He was coming back to apologize!" I paused to gulp at my coffee, rapidly cooling in the morning breeze, then returned to pacing up and down the narrow deck of my houseboat. "I kept telling that idiot detective, Boris was on his way back to the party to apologize. He only picked up the bat to move it so he could see if Digger was still alive."

"That's what Boris told you," said Lily, sipping from her own mug. She was bundled in a fuzzy purple sweater and perched sideways on a lounge chair that I hadn't yet stowed away for the winter. "You didn't see it yourself, so it's hearsay."

"Hearsay!" I yelped. "You're saying Boris was *lying*? And besides, what about that door I heard closing? That was probably the real murderer getting away!"

"Calm down, Carnegie, please. It won't help to—"

"I will not calm down!"

Lily James was my best friend and a reasonable woman, but I wasn't ready to listen to reason. I'd been up half the night being grilled by cops and smoothing the ruffled feathers of VIPs whose big event had been so rudely interrupted by murder. Beau had removed himself from the stadium the minute he could, leaving me with the fuss, and now it was a toss-up who I was madder at this morning, him or Detective Sergeant Kenneth Starkey.

But of course that was no reason to bite Lily's head off. I looked at her contritely.

"Sorry. But you don't really think Boris Nevsky is a cold-blooded killer. Do you?"

"Of course not. I'm just trying to see things from Ken Starkey's point of view."

Lily was familiar with a homicide detective's viewpoint, being married to one herself. Michael Graham, the world's most sensitive police officer, was her husband of only a few weeks. He was also Starkey's boss.

"It wouldn't have been cold-blooded," she continued. "It could have been a sudden angry impulse during an argument. You did say Boris was drinking a lot."

I quit pacing and leaned on the rail of the deck, picking at a splinter that stuck up from the weathered wood. Sweet old Mrs. Castle, my landlady, wasn't big on repairs, but at least she kept my rent down. I pried the splinter free and dropped it into the deep cold water of Lake Union. As it drifted away I drew in a mouthful of salt-tasting air, cool and moist. I was home, and Boris was in a jail cell. Lily watched me and waited.

"That's the line the police are taking," I said at last. "A drunken argument that turned nasty. But they're wrong. I know Boris, and I saw his face. He was just as much in shock as I was to see a corpse lying there. He was horrified."

I chewed at my lower lip, remembering Starkey's reply to that. *So would you be horrified, miss, if you'd just killed a guy.* His gruff manner and cynical attitude were worlds away from Mike Graham's quiet thoughtfulness. But Mike wasn't on this case, and Starkey was. When I'd made the mistake of mentioning my friendship with Detective Lieutenant Graham, Starkey had turned even gruffer. *That's very interesting, miss. Now just answer the questions and let us draw the conclusions.*

"Boris didn't do it, Lily. I know he didn't. I tried to stay calm and explain that last night, but—" I shivered, suddenly chilled to the core. "God, it was so awful. Digger's head was . . . it looked like . . ."

My best friend was at my side at once, detaching the coffee cup from my trembling hands and folding me into a hug. Lily is a statuesque black woman, even taller than me, and it was comforting to lean into her shoulder and let myself cry.

"It's all right," she murmured. "It'll be all right."

"But what if it's *not*? What if they use my testimony to convict Boris?" Snuffling, I searched in my pockets for a handkerchief. I carry three when I'm working but couldn't find one now. "I want so badly to help him, but I don't know what to *do*."

"You can't do anything right now," said Lily, in the level but commanding voice that she used with Marcus and Ethan, the two little boys from her first marriage—and sometimes with her patrons at the public library. "He's not even arraigned yet. I'm sure Boris will call you if he needs help finding a lawyer or whatever, and meanwhile you're freezing out here. Come inside and get warm."

My houseboat is moored at the end of a dock with a million-dollar view of the lake, from downtown Seattle at the south end to Gas Works Park at the north. I can see it all: one wall of my living room is glass, with sliding doors out to a narrow deck. From the deck a planking ramp leads down to a little floating platform, right at water level, that's perfect to swim from.

I used to barbecue down there in summer—until one day the lake got choppy, the platform rocked, and my grill went over the edge and straight to the bottom. Boris was with me that day, and how we'd laughed . . .

"Come *on*." Lily scooted me through the sliding doors and slid them shut behind us, then gave me a nudge toward the couch.

As I sank into the cushions, I noticed her canvas tote bag lying there. When she'd shown up for our Saturday morning coffee date, I'd been too distraught to notice anything. The bag, one side of which proclaimed that LIBRARIANS ARE NOVEL LOVERS, was spilling over with glossy magazines.

"What's all this?" I asked dully.

"We were going to look at wedding gowns today, remember? Before we start browsing the shops at lunch on Monday?"

"Oh, that's right. I can't even think about that now."

"Of course you can't," she said. "More coffee?"

I nodded, and as she headed for the kitchen, I chafed my chilly fingers and gazed at the topmost magazine. The cover model had huge pillowy lips and that typical blank high-fashion stare, the one that looks like the girl's been smacked in the back of the head with a two-by-four. *Or a bat* . . . I shuddered and looked away.

"What does Aaron think?" said Lily, returning with refills.

"I didn't get a chance to talk to him last night, with the police there and everything. I mean, they kept me later than anyone else. And he's out doing interviews today. He's on deadline, so he's really busy. He'll probably be working tonight too. Definitely tonight, in fact . . ."

I heard myself babbling and trailed off. Lily was grinning at me.

"Was it bad?" she asked.

"Was what bad?"

Her eyes sparkled over the rim of her mug. "The fight that you and Aaron had last night."

"What makes you think we had a fight?"

Lily has this amazing laugh. It's deep and throaty, and you can't help laughing along. Or at least smiling sheepishly, which is what I did now.

"Am I that obvious?"

"Girl," she said, "you are an absolute pane of glass. And you two are as prickly as a pair of cactuses lately. So what happened this time?"

I told her about the plan to choose a wedding date tonight, and Aaron's ridiculous fixation with the ballgame. It was better than thinking about my inability to help Boris.

Lily set her mug aside and frowned. "You want Aaron to miss the World Series?"

"Don't you start on me! I've listened to nothing but baseball since he came back from Boston, and he promised—"

"Carnegie, it's the Chicago Cubs. I don't even follow the game, and I've heard about the Chicago Cubs." She shook her head. "Besides, what are you going to do when you're married—banish baseball?"

"Of course not." Lily might still be a newlywed, but she'd been married once before. She knew about the ups and downs of marriage, the give and take. I only knew about gowns and cake. Avoiding her eye, I flipped open the magazine with the pillow-lipped model. "I just want to enjoy being engaged, that's all. I've worked for enough other brides—now I just want to *be* one. This bias-cut number is kind of cute . . ."

Lily joined me on the couch. "But do you want to go that slinky? You're so nice and slim, you could carry off a Princess Di style. Look at that white satin—it's got just a hint of blue in it."

"You don't think that's too cold a shade for me?" I turned a page, from one fantasy to the next. "Ooh, flutter sleeves. Chiffon is so romantic."

"Kind of bare for a winter wedding, though." She tapped a purple-polished fingernail on the glossy page. "If it's going to *be* in winter. How long will you need to pull this together?"

"Depends on our venue. I thought about having it on board the *Virginia V* or some other cruise boat, but that means summer, and summer's so far off. Of course all the really nice places book up months ahead anyway. If only Aaron would focus—"

"He will when he's ready," she said. "Just give him some space. Tell me, do wedding planners work faster or slower on their own weddings?"

"You're playing peacemaker, you know that?"

"Sure I know it. Now answer the question."

I laughed. "*That* will depend on how many other brides I've got coming up. I know the vendors I want already. Joe Solveto for the catering, and Boris for the—"

I caught myself, and we looked at each other in dismay. Boris might never create another bride's bouquet. He might never—

The phone interrupted this dreary thought, and speak of the devil, it was my latest bride. Or rather, Beau's and mine. Rose McKinney sounded like a different person from the hellion at the party.

"Carnegie?" she quavered. "I, um, don't exactly remember

what I said last night, but I guess I'm sorry. I mean, I am sorry."

"That's all right," I said, surprised and disarmed. "How are you feeling today?"

"Not too good. But I'm supposed to have a final fitting at that dress place downtown." She hesitated. "I sort of wondered if you could come? Beau said he could be there if I want, I guess he's big buds with the owner or something, but it seems kind of, you know . . ."

"Kind of strange to have a man helping with your gown?" I filled in.

"Yeah."

"I'd be happy to be there, Rose. What time?"

"Well, now, I guess."

"Now?" I rolled my eyes at Lily, who was following the conversation with interest. She grinned and took our coffee cups back into the kitchen. "Give me half an hour."

I hung up and called Beau. He always stayed at the Alexis, a small deluxe hotel right downtown between Pioneer Square and the Pike Place Market. It made a convenient and prestigious base when he was working and of course a comfy little nest for his various *amours*. But he didn't answer his room phone or his cell, so I left a message that I would take care of the dress fitting.

"I took care of the cleaning crew last night too," I added sardonically, "since you weren't around. Oh, and I gave the police your room number in case they need you. Have a nice day."

It was only as I was walking Lily out to her car, before climbing into my own van, that I realized something odd. Rose McKinney didn't seem to know that her engagement party had ended with violent death. Which meant that I was going to have to tell her.

Chapter Seven

Le Boutique was an exclusive bridal shop in the heart of downtown, and Beau Paliere was indeed big buds with the owner, an utterly un-French woman named Hazel Cohen. Hazel barely acknowledged my existence, but then I didn't bring her bouquets of roses or vials of French perfume—or lucrative orders from celebrity brides.

Seattle was enjoying a remarkably balmy October, and downtown was full of grateful tourists and Saturday shoppers. I found Rose on the Seneca Street sidewalk, fixed in place like an obstinate little rock with the chattering stream of pedestrians parting and re-forming around her. She was clad entirely in black leather, including the spiked collar around her neck. It contrasted nicely with her hangover.

Up in its haughty second-floor location, Le Boutique had a row of display windows peopled with white-gowned mannequins. Rose was squinting up through the sunshine at them.

"I'm never going to look like that," she said, with an odd mixture of defiance and wistfulness. "Never."

"I don't suppose you will," I retorted. "Not being made of plastic."

A scrap of a smile tugged at her lips. "Thanks for coming."

"Don't mention it."

I had debated with myself on the way downtown whether

to tell Rose about Digger Duvall before or after her fitting. There'd been nothing on the news this morning—the police were keeping a lid on the murder for some reason—so I'd decided on after. Why spoil the moment?

As we went around the corner to the building entrance, Rose lifted her face to the sun.

"God, what a day. Makes me want to get up in the mountains."

"You?" I said, startled.

"Why not?" she said, grinning. "You think I spend all my time in gloomy clubs? Actually, the Fiends do that. They think it's weird that I like to get outdoors."

"Oh."

I pondered that as we walked—and also something that I'd been wanting to tell this particular bride before we went any farther. As we entered the building, before we reached the stairs up to Le Boutique, I drew her over to a bench in the lobby.

"Let's have a talk, shall we?"

"What about?"

Rose's dark brows drew together, and her lips set in a stubborn line. She was expecting another lecture, but I was about to surprise her.

"About you and Gordo. Rose, sometimes the preparations for a wedding can take on a life of their own, until the whole thing seems like one huge unstoppable process. And that could be especially true for this wedding, with the Navigators management running things. But it's not unstoppable, and your wedding day is just one day out of your whole life. It's not the wedding that's important, it's the marriage. So if you—"

"What are you talking about?" She was staring at me with

her head aslant, puzzled and indignant. "Are you saying I shouldn't marry Gordo?"

"It's not up to me, is it? It's up to you, Rose. Do you want to marry him?"

"Of course I do!" A transformation came over her face, a melting and a brightening together. "He's the best thing that ever happened to me. He's so sweet and funny, and we go hiking together, and he *really* gets my music—"

"And you get baseball?"

"Sure I do. My dad's in baseball, remember? I've been going to games since I was a baby. When Gordy was choking up early this season, I sat in with him and Nelly sometimes, and Nelly even said I have a good eye for rotational mechanics."

"Rotational . . . ?"

"Mechanics. Here, I'll show you."

She stood up to demonstrate, drawing some stares from passersby, but I interrupted.

"So you'll be watching the World Series game with Gordo tonight?"

Rose stared at me, startled. "Of *course*. Why wouldn't I?"

"No reason. Forget it."

"Whatever." She took her stance again. "OK, the circular path of your hands transfers your body's momentum into bat-head acceleration . . ."

I could see I had a lot to learn—about connecting with the ball, if nothing else—but the wedding gown was waiting, and I had satisfied my conscience. Despite her dubious manners when she drank, when she was sober this bride clearly knew what she was doing. So I interrupted again.

"Some other time, Rose. Let's go on up."

I didn't mean to sound dismissive, but her enthusiasm

vanished. She turned away and marched up the stairs like a teenager trying to pretend her mother isn't really there.

I can't be more than ten years older than her, I thought in annoyance. *OK, maybe twelve. Oh, the hell with it.* And as I followed her, I reminded myself again of just how much Beau was paying me for this assignment.

Le Boutique was unoccupied save for its proprietor. Hazel Cohen, all five foot zero of her, stood beside a delicate reception desk with spindly gilded legs. There was nothing spindly about Hazel, or gilded either. Her rigidly permed hair was resolutely gray above a pugnacious face and rectangular figure.

"I know you," she said in an unmistakable New York accent. "You're the wedding planner with the funny name."

With some people I explain that my father named me for Andrew Carnegie, after educating himself in the small-town libraries that the old robber baron endowed. With other people, like Hazel Cohen, I just smile vaguely and press on.

"I'm helping Rose with her fitting," I said. "Rose McKinney?"

I chuckled as Hazel realized with a start that the tough-looking girl beside me was a paying customer. One of her minions must have handled the original selection of the dress.

"Miss McKinney, of course! I've got your gown all ready in the main dressing room. Just gorgeous. Come on back." As she ushered Rose along, Hazel sent me a quizzical look over her shoulder. "You working for my boy Beau now?"

"Only temporarily."

"Lucky you."

Wondering just how she meant that, I followed her into the gilt and shell-pink salon. It had a round dais in the center and a changing room with a louvered door to one side, and the walls were draped with gauzy curtains. Scattered here and there, more delicate little tables displayed veils and garters and other bridal trimmings. Girl Central.

I took a seat on a plumply brocaded pink and gold settee and looked around me with a happy sigh. I couldn't help picturing myself in this same setting, with Lily and my mother watching from this same seat as I modeled gown after spectacular gown. Not that I could afford anything in Hazel's inventory, but a girl can dream.

Rose, meanwhile, startled Hazel by marching into the changing room where her own gown hung and yanking the door decisively shut behind her.

"You let me know if you need help!" Hazel called through the door, and then turned to me with an inquisitive look.

"She's kind of bashful," I confided. "You know how it is."

Hazel sniffed, unimpressed. "Takes all kinds."

As the minutes passed, I wandered to a display table. *Could I carry off a tiara?* I set a sparkly one on my hair and surveyed the effect in a gilt-framed mirror. *Not bad . . .*

"Getting married yourself?" Hazel asked, with just a touch of sarcasm.

"Actually, I am."

"Really?" I could see her shifting mental gears now that I was a potential customer. "What style of wedding?"

"I'm not really sure yet."

She sniffed again. "Better make it a show-stopper. It'll be one big advertisement for your services, you know. If you screw up, who's going to trust you with their own event?"

I was groping for a reply when the changing room door opened a crack.

"Uh, excuse me?" came Rose's voice. "There's these weird buttons . . ."

Hazel beat me to the door by a step and vanished inside. More minutes went by, while I fingered the filigreed lace of a garter and considered a glittering Cinderella slipper with a stacked heel. *Will people really judge Made in Heaven by my wedding? No pressure, Carnegie.* I put the slipper down.

"Ta da!" Hazel announced as she swung the door wide. "Didn't I tell you? Gorgeous. A vision. Up here on the platform, dear."

The gown was gorgeous all right, a soft creamy silk-satin with silk-chiffon illusion sleeves and a fluted chapel-length skirt. The scoop neckline showed off Rose's pale, clear skin to perfection. Clear and unmarked...

Ah-hah. Something clicked. The anomaly I'd registered last night about Honeysuckle Hell, goddess of Goth, was that she had no tattoos. Also no piercings and no studs. Even the long green fingernails must have been press-on, because her nails were short and unpainted today.

That confirmed my growing sense that the Goth persona was simply a facade, taken on when Honeysuckle Hell picked up her guitar. If it weren't for the dark purple hair, which looked close to black anyway in this soft light, Rose McKinney might have been any blushing bride.

She really was blushing too, though not with demure delight. More like fidgety self-consciousness. Rose stood on the dais like a sacrificial victim, keeping her back to the three-way mirror and staring glumly at the floor.

"Sheila doesn't like it," she muttered.

"And who is this Sheila?" asked Hazel, affronted.

Rose shrugged. "Sort of my maid of honor, I guess. She's in the band, you know? She said she'd be in the ceremony with me, but she doesn't like the dresses. She says they're lame."

"Lame?" Hazel echoed in disbelief. "Listen to me, young lady—"

"Is there a veil?" I cut in. "We need to see the full effect."

There was a veil, a waterfall of silk tulle. It had the weight of an embroidered hem to help it hang properly, but the fabric itself was so sheer that it enveloped the girl like a softening but transparent mist. I settled the headband securely on her hair and fluffed out the tulle into symmetrical waves. Then I took Rose gently by the shoulders and turned her toward the mirror. By the look in her widening eyes, my hunch was right.

"I guess it is kind of pretty," she said shyly. "My dad saw it in a magazine and said he liked it."

"Your dad has a good eye," I said. Then I leaned in to murmur, "And if you ask me, your friend Sheila is full of shit."

That got another smile, a big one, and I winked at Hazel.

"Now, let's get fitting," I went on. "Hazel, do you think the hem is just a touch long in back? We don't want her heel catching..."

We were almost finished with the tucking and pinning, and had backed away from Rose to survey our handiwork, when Hazel's assistant Amber returned from her lunch break. Amber was a big breathless girl who towered over her boss, though right now she hunched her shoulders timidly as she edged into the salon.

I'd always wondered why Hazel employed someone as déclassé as Amber, but after Hazel's crack about my screwing up, I quit wondering. *Will there really be that kind of scrutiny of my wedding?* I asked myself. *How am I supposed to enjoy it if it's one big test? Eloping wouldn't be so bad...*

"Sorry to be late again, Mrs. C.," Amber was saying. "There was such a line at the deli. Oh, that dress is super!"

She took in the gown first, then the wearer. "Oh, it's Rose! Wow, I just heard on the radio what happened at your party. That was your party at the stadium, wasn't it? You're the one marrying the baseball player? Gosh, I would have just freaked out, seeing a dead body like that. Did you just freak out when you saw it, or did you even see it? I can't stand that kind of thing, I would have just . . . are you all right?"

Rose was pale to begin with, but now she went paler than her gown, and the veil quivered with her trembling.

"What happened?" she said woodenly. "What body?"

"That sportswriter guy, Digger something?" Amber was looking doubtfully at my furious scowl. "Somebody took him out with a baseball bat. It's kind of ironic, isn't it, him being a sportswriter and somebody using a baseball bat to—"

She broke off and took a startled step backward, just as Hazel and I darted toward the dais. But we were too late. Rose crumpled to the floor in a dead faint, encircled by a snowdrift of satin and tulle.

Chapter Eight

"Feeling better?"

Rose swallowed another mouthful of her Wholey Grail whole grain special.

"Much."

I'd thought at first that the news of Digger Duvall's murder had caused her to faint, but she had insisted that it was nothing more than hunger and a hangover. As her plate emptied and her color returned, I began to believe her. Hearing about a corpse at a party is shocking, naturally, but not that shocking.

We were seated at a sunny window table in By Bread Alone—BBA to those in the know—a counterculture bakery and café that served fabulous sandwiches. But that wasn't why I chose it for our late lunch. BBA was home base for Juice Nugent, wedding cake baker extraordinaire, who still waited tables here when she wasn't working her magic with almond fondant or hazelnut ganache back in the kitchen.

She was just coming off a shift now, and she laid a clipboard on our table with a gusty sigh.

"Friggin' tourists, they go all year now. I been run off my feet. How ya doing, Kincaid?"

"Doing good, Juice."

Juice Nugent was short and busty, like a pigeon with an

attitude, and her spiky hair was sometimes chartreuse, sometimes magenta, and sometimes, like today, a blinding shade
of crossing-guard-vest orange. Her standard short-shorts
were hidden by a BBA apron, but as usual she wore high-
heeled cowboy boots from her sizable private collection.

Today's pair was appliquéd with pink leather roses, a
sweetly feminine touch for someone sporting a button that
read QUEER AND PROUD, ANY QUESTIONS? Between the baker's
boots and the bride's dog collar, I felt like somebody's maid-
enly great-aunt as I introduced the two of them.

"Nice to meet you," said Rose. "Those boots are totally
cho."

"Thanks, um, Honeysuckle." Juice was gazing at Rose
with shy admiration, an expression I'd never seen or even
imagined on her. "Or do you use Rose off stage? That's your
real name, right? I looked it up."

"Rose is fine," said the bride, surveying her empty plate
with satisfaction.

"Cool. Um, congratulations on getting married and everything." Fascinated by this change in demeanor, I watched
Juice groping for a conversational gambit. "Where you going
on your honeymoon?"

"Santo Domingo." Rose smiled at the thought. "So I can
see where Gordo grew up and meet all the rest of his family
that isn't coming to the wedding."

"Cool." Juice hesitated again, then took the plunge. "I'm,
like, a major fan of yours, Rose. I heard you at NocNoc when
the Fiends were just taking off, and I've downloaded everything from your Web site."

"That's great. You know, I could comp you some tickets
for our next show if you want."

"Hell, yeah! Thanks. You need anything else? We got wicked good tomato polenta soup today."

Rose shook her head, so Juice doffed the apron and took a seat. Her black tank top revealed a winged dragon taking tattooed flight from her cleavage.

I nodded at it. "That's new."

"Yeah," she said, preoccupied with the clipboard. "I always wanted one, only Rita didn't like 'em. When we broke up, the first thing I did was head to Black Cat Tat and get myself inked. So, here's the home run cake that the suits asked for."

She laid a colored drawing before us, of an enormous spherical cheesecake decorated to look like a baseball. The "suits" were the Navigator management, and this was just the kind of photo-op cake they'd had in mind. "Stitched" with red licorice and scribbled with chocolate icing autographs, it was cleverly dusted here and there with cocoa powder to simulate the smudges on a ball that's been smacked into the bleachers.

Very clever, and very much about Gordo, not Gordo-and-Rose. Juice obviously had the same thought, because she overlaid the page with another drawing: a big chocolate guitar with a heart-shaped sound hole and pulled-sugar strings. Rose looked at it thoughtfully but didn't speak, so I jumped in.

"That's fabulous, Juice! I love it. How many would it serve?"

"Only two hundred," she said, flushing with pleasure at the praise, "but anything we do will need cupcakes to go with, 'cause this deal is open to the fans, right?"

"Right, but we won't need a whole lot because of the

chocolate fountain. It's going right in the center of the rotunda, and—"

"Chocolate fountain?" Juice pulled a face. "Kinda corny, isn't—?"

"Gordo's a huge chocoholic," I added, with a quick kick at her shins, "so he's really excited about it."

"Well, who wouldn't be?" said Juice dutifully. "Anyway, the baseball cupcakes are supposed to be frosted white with red stitching, but I thought for the guitar cake we could do white with marzipan musical notes. Whaddya think, um, Rose?"

"It's great, only…" Rose hesitated, choosing her words with care. She hadn't seemed to notice the crack about the fountain—or maybe, judging by her next words, she didn't care. "You see, this whole wedding is for Gordo, really. It's a big celebration for the team and for his home run record."

"But you're the *bride.* You should get what you want. Right, Kincaid?"

I opened my mouth to agree, but Rose preempted me.

"I know," she said. "But all I really want is Gordo."

Who could argue with that?

"And now that I like my dress," she went on, "I'm cool with everything else. I mean, it's just one day out of my whole life. It's not the wedding that's important, it's the marriage. Right?"

She said this with a sly little smile at me, and I laughed aloud. *If only more of my brides felt this way. Of course then I'd be out of a job…*

Juice shrugged, and the dragon flapped its wings. "OK then, we go with the baseball. I got the estimates here, Kincaid, but I dunno if Rose needs to bother with 'em."

"I've got things to do," said Rose. "See you, Juice. 'Bye, Carnegie."

She began to walk away, then hurried back and touched me on the shoulder.

"Thanks for today. Thanks a lot."

"My pleasure," I told her. And somehow it really was.

Juice watched her idol leave the café and disappear into the stream of pedestrians outside.

"Did you hear that? She liked my boots, and she's comping me tickets! You'd think she'd be a freakin' drama queen or something. But she's so down to earth, like a regular person."

"She is a regular person," I said, amused.

"*Not.* Have you ever heard her sing? She's phenomenal." Juice passed me the cost sheet for the cake and cupcakes. "I just hope that Duvall bozo getting offed didn't upset her too much."

"You heard about that?"

"Yeah, on the radio in the kitchen. Did you see it happen?"

"I saw the corpse."

She scowled. "Serves him right, the fascist."

"Juice!"

"OK, OK, maybe not getting killed. But you should see what he said about Honeysuckle, I mean Rose, back when they announced the engagement. He's all gaga about this Gutierrez guy, Gordo is da man, blah blah blah, and then he calls Rose a baseball groupie. A freakin' genius like her, a groupie! Dude said she was 'a bar singer of little talent and less class.' How's that for suck?"

"I didn't know about that." I frowned, remembering the look on Walter McKinney's face last night. *No wonder he*

hated Digger. And what about Gordo—how would he take some-
one insulting his fiancée?

I grew increasingly preoccupied with these thoughts as we
finished our business with the cake, and as I walked back up
Seneca to Vanna White, my white van. I was sure that Boris
hadn't killed Digger, but there remained the question of who
actually did. Gentle, amiable Gordo Gutierrez? Or the mild
and stammering Walter McKinney? Surely not. And yet they
both cherished Rose . . .

My steps had slowed to the point where someone
bumped into me, so I moved aside into the recessed space
between a couple of angled shop windows. The shop was a
jeweler's, and I found myself staring into a window full of diamonds—which distracted me from Walter in a big way.

I wasn't getting a diamond. Once I'd accepted Aaron's
spur-of-the-moment proposal, and we had both calmed
down enough to speak in entire sentences, he'd raised the
question of an engagement ring.

"Is the diamond thing a big deal to you, Stretch? Because
I was thinking we could use the money to start saving for a
down payment on a house."

A house. A home of my own, with Aaron. The prospect
had been so unexpected, and so sweet, that I'd rushed to say
no, the diamond thing wasn't a big deal at all. Only now,
looking into this dazzling window, I wondered if I'd spoken
too soon.

The slender pointed oval of that marquise stone, for instance, would look so elegant on my hand. Or the cushion-
cut diamond that seemed to float in its rose-gold tension
setting like a tiny work of art. Oh, or that baguette diamond
with the pink sapphire side-stones on the engraved platinum
band.

I'd never even liked pink sapphires, but I pulled out my cell phone to take a picture of the ring display. *Just for fun,* I told myself. *Just to show Lily later on.* Then somehow my feet went wandering right through the door of the shop. A wisp of a white-haired lady drifted delicately over to ask if she might assist me.

"I just wondered," I said, pointing, "about the price of that ring?"

"Oh, yes," she cooed. "One of my very favorites."

Then she named a sum that sent me retreating back to the sidewalk. *Holy moley.* Never mind saving for a down payment, that *was* a down payment, and maybe a couple months' mortgage checks to boot. I'd have to tell Aaron about it tonight . . .

The thought of tonight slowed me down all over again. Should I give in and offer to watch the game with him, or stand my ground? *No question what Lily would say,* I thought as I climbed into Vanna and pulled into traffic.

But I wasn't Lily, and Aaron had been so damn cold last night. At least while we were out on the concourse. Once the police showed up at the party, he'd tried to stay by my side, but Starkey had hustled me into an office and kept me there with his endless questions. And when I finally emerged, Aaron was gone. So shouldn't he be the one offering me an olive branch? He practically owed me the whole tree.

I vacillated about it all the way through my grocery shopping, then back to my houseboat, without reaching a decision. Then as I came along the dock, I was sidetracked yet again, this time by the sight of an elderly gentleman waiting at my front door.

The gentleman wore an impeccably tailored black overcoat and an equally impeccable black fedora atop his silver hair. As I approached him, he swept off the hat with a courtly little bow and handed me a business card.

"Miss Kincaid?" he inquired in a rasping but somehow agreeable voice. "Trofim Denisovich, attorney at law, representing Mr. Boris Nevsky."

"Oh, thank goodness." I grasped the card gratefully. *How could I even think about jewelry at a time like this?* "I'm so glad to meet you, Mr. Denisovich."

"Trofim."

"Trofim, then. Please come in." I led the way into the kitchen and set my grocery bags on the table. "How's Boris holding up? If there's anything at all I can do to prove his innocence, just tell me."

"Innocence," said the lawyer thoughtfully, as if the word intrigued him. He had just the faintest trace of an accent, but his English was fluent and precise. "You believe young Boris is innocent?"

"Don't you?" I asked, suddenly uneasy.

"Ah, well. May I sit down?"

"Of course. Here, let's go in the living room."

I hung up his coat, and we settled ourselves on the couch, Denisovich with his back to the glass doors. The sunlight shimmering and sparking off the lake turned him into a shadowy silhouette, like those television interviews meant to mask the identity of the person speaking.

"You were saying?" I prompted.

"Yes," said the shadow. "Certainly Borya is innocent of murder. There is no question of that, no question at all."

"Of course not!" I was so relieved to hear him say it that I almost missed the unfamiliar term. "Borya?"

"A diminutive of Boris. A nickname."

"I see. You know him well, then."

"He employs my sister Irina. He has been very good to her."

Irina was the silent, wizened little woman who sold flowers from the front of the Nevsky floral studio. But I could hardly spare a thought for her now.

"So how do we get Boris released? What do we do?"

"Such loyalty." Denisovich reached forward, I thought to pat my hand, but instead he lifted my fingers to his lips in a ceremonial kiss. "And such beauty. No wonder Borya struck down the man who insulted you."

"*What?* You said he was innocent!"

"Of premeditated murder, yes. That is why I tried to negotiate a plea bargain for manslaughter."

Chapter Nine

"Manslaughter? But he didn't do it! He came back to apologize to me for disrupting the party and found Digger lying there dead."

Denisovich sighed. "That is what Borya kept repeating."

"Of course he did, because it's true! Why don't you believe him?"

"It's not a matter of my belief," said the lawyer, releasing my hand. "What would the jury believe? A moment of madness during a violent argument—perhaps they would have believed that. And I would have raised the possibility of self-defense. But such a coincidence as you describe? Hardly."

"But they'll have to believe it!"

"No. Unfortunately, they will not have to."

"Look, I know Boris. He would never attack someone with a baseball bat. It's just not possible."

"And yet he had already attacked the deceased with his fists." Denisovich turned up his palms and shrugged in a big-shouldered gesture I'd seen Boris make, times without number. "You see? It would be far better to accept a short prison term than to risk a verdict of murder. I told Borya that before the arraignment, but he would not listen."

"Prison, for being in the wrong hallway at the wrong time?"

I rose from the couch, away from this man and his false comfort, and began to pace. "Boris would curl up and die in prison. I'm glad he didn't listen to—wait a minute. The arraignment already happened, even though it's Saturday? Boris pleaded innocent?"

"Indeed he did. And I must follow his direction, however unwise." Denisovich reached into his briefcase and drew out a sheaf of photocopies. "Now, you told the police you heard nothing in the corridor. No voices raised in anger, no sounds of a struggle, nothing?"

"Nothing. The killer must have been long gone. The *real* killer."

I pronounced the word with total conviction. Boris had refused to plead guilty, and I refused to give up on him. So, first things first. The thought of the Mad Russian entombed in a cell was more than I could bear.

"Mr. Denisovich—"

"Trofim."

"Whatever. Can Boris be released on bail?"

He sighed again. "Listen to me, my dear—"

"I'm not your dear! Can he?"

"Bail in a case of violent crime is very high," he said stiffly, affronted. "In this case, three quarters of a million dollars. A bail bondsman typically requires a posting of ten percent."

I did the math. "So I could get him out for seventy-five thousand dollars?"

Even as I said the words, they sounded crazy to me. Crazy, but not impossible. I paced faster. This wasn't just a question of Boris's freedom. What would his prolonged absence do to Nevsky Brothers Flowers?

His brothers couldn't pick up the slack, because he didn't have any brothers; he just thought the name sounded good.

The floral studio was actually a one-man show with a crew of assistants, most of them named Sergei, who jumped to Boris's commands. As a sole proprietor myself, I knew that without him at the helm, the business might never recover.

But where am I going to get that kind of money? The bank, that's where. I'll borrow it. Denisovich stirred impatiently, and I said, "Thanks, that's all I need to know."

"But I need to know more. Your relationship with Borya, for example. It was . . . intimate?"

"What?" I quit pacing. "What business is that of yours?"

"Of mine, none. But if I present you as a character witness, you can be sure that the prosecutor will make it his business. Were you and Borya lovers?"

"I . . . we . . ."

At this interesting juncture a knock sounded at my front door. More of a crashing thump, really—and by the way the walls shuddered with the impact, I knew exactly whose fist was doing the thumping. Excusing myself to Denisovich, I went through the kitchen to answer and found the doorway overflowing with Buckmeisters.

"There she is, girls!" Buck surged inside like a force of nature. He wore a hot pink bandanna and an XXL sweatshirt that said SEATTLE RAIN FESTIVAL, APRIL THROUGH MARCH. The "girls," his wife Betty and his daughter Bonnie, flowed into the room in his wake. "Told ya I saw her van there in the parking lot. Poor little gal."

Buck clapped me sympathetically on the shoulder, and I staggered sideways into Bonnie.

"Daddy told me what happened last night," she said, enfolding me in a sisterly embrace. "What a dreadful experience for you! You must be just as upset as you can be."

Bonnie was almost as big as her father but far more pillowy, and disentangling myself from her was like unrolling
from a goose down comforter.

"Thanks," I managed to get out, "but I'm all right, really."

"All right, my aunt Fanny!" said Betty, taking her turn at
hugging. She was about two feet shorter than me, so it was a
low-altitude hug. "Look at you, you're pale as porridge."

"We tried to talk to ya last night," Buck told me over his
wife's head. "But the policemen told us to go on home. And
then our car wouldn't start! That nice fella of yours, Alan, he
helped us out."

"Aaron," I said automatically. We'd been through this
before.

"I brought you a tin of my favorite herb tea," Betty bur-
bled from the vicinity of my ribcage. "It's called Chamomile
Comfort, doesn't that sound nice? I could make us all a cup
right now."

"I appreciate this, folks, only I'm a little bit busy—" I
glanced toward the living room, but Denisovich was on his
feet and coming into the kitchen with an inquisitive look at
all the commotion.

"Howdy!" Buck boomed. Buck had no volume control and
no mute button. "Didn't mean to interrupt you, friend. I'm
Bruce Buckmeister, call me Buck. My wife here is Betty, and
that's my daughter Bonnie. Pleased to meetcha!"

Denisovich didn't reply, no doubt because his teeth were
rattling from Buck's arm-pumping handshake.

"This is Boris Nevsky's lawyer," I filled in. "Trofim
Denisovich. He's going to prove Boris innocent."

"Really?" Betty blinked her shiny round doll's eyes at me.
"You mean he didn't kill that Digger person?"

"Absolutely not. Boris is an old friend of mine, and I'm certain that he didn't do it."

"Well, if you say so, that's good enough for us," said Buck. "Isn't it, girls?"

"It surely is," chirped Betty. She and Bonnie nodded resolutely, like a pair of bobble-head dolls. "And I'm sure Mr. Dennovich will do a good job. Would you like a nice cup of tea, Mr. Dennovich?"

And so, inevitably, we all ended up in the living room sipping Chamomile Comfort. This was a testament to my fondness for the Killer B's—and gratitude for their vote of confidence in Boris—because for my money herb tea tastes just like hot cologne.

"I don't mean to upset the ladies, Mr. Dennovich," Buck rumbled, slurping down his cup and smacking his lips, "but who do you think really did the murder?"

"It is difficult to know," said Denisovich, with a baleful glance at me. "I can only do my best for my client. I cannot solve the case."

But I can, I thought, setting down my own cup. *Or at least I can try.*

"You haven't finished your tea, dear," said Betty, hopping up. "I bet you'd like it sweeter. Shall I get you some sugar?"

"That's all right, really—"

"You stay there, dear, I can find it. Oh, is that the doorbell? We didn't notice that you had one . . ." A moment later she was back in the living room. "Look, everyone, it's Alan! We were just telling Carnegie how you helped us with our car last night. What did you call it, hot-wiring?"

"That's right!" Buck thundered happily. "You should tell Mr. D. here about hot-wiring. He'd be real interested."

Aaron looked a little dazed—not an uncommon response

to the Buckmeisters—and just pecked me on the cheek when I went to greet him.

"Did they come?" he asked me quietly.

"Who?"

"Never mind."

Betty drew him away to meet Denisovich, and then the lawyer explained that he had to be going.

"We'll walk you out," said Buck, dropping his womenfolk a huge wink. "I bet these lovebirds would like to be alone. You take care of yourself there, Carnegie. A nice girl like you shouldn't be lookin' at dead bodies, should she, Mother? You drink up the rest of that tea and you'll feel better..."

At last, like a receding tidal wave, the Buckmeisters were gone and Denisovich with them. I shut the door and turned eagerly to Aaron.

"How long would it take us to borrow seventy-five thousand dollars?"

"What?"

"I've got my van, and you've got the Volkswagen..." Muttering to myself, I dug around in the kitchen junk drawer for a pad and pen but came up empty. "There's always Made in Heaven too. Can you get a loan against a business, I wonder?"

"Carnegie, what the hell are you talking about?"

"You don't have to yell at me."

"I'm not yelling! I'm trying to keep up. What do you need seventy-five grand for?"

"Oh, sorry. It's to post bail for Boris." I realized that my groceries were still sitting out, so I rescued the carton of milk and opened the fridge. "Denisovich thinks he's guilty, can you imagine that? But of course he's not, so we've got to get him out on bail. It seems to me—"

"Are you nuts?" Aaron shot out a hand and slammed the refrigerator door. "Do you even know what it means to post bail? If Nevsky missed even one court appearance, you'd be responsible for the full amount. You'd lose everything."

I yanked the fridge open again. "But I can't leave him there in jail, Aaron. He's my friend."

"Is that all he is?"

I gasped, but Aaron was poker-faced. I set down the milk.

"I can't believe you said that," I sputtered. "Of all the juvenile—"

"Juvenile? This guy mauls you whenever he sees you, and defends your damn honor like you were his wife or something. For all I know he did whack Duvall last night."

"He did not! I'm sure of it."

"How can you be?" Aaron threw up his hands. "He was drunk and angry, and you saw him yourself with the bat."

"That doesn't mean—"

"And now you're ready to bankrupt yourself for him, and me too. What am I supposed to think?"

"You're supposed to trust me!" I cried. "I'm your fiancée, remember?"

"I wish you'd act like it."

"Me? You're the one who'd rather watch a baseball game than—"

"Are we back to that? Jesus, I want one lousy evening—"

"Dozens of evenings. Hundreds of hours! I'm so sick of baseball I could scream."

"Well, don't let me stop you."

With that Aaron walked out and slammed the door behind him, leaving me hyperventilating with anger. And a little regret too. Maybe more than a little. As my breathing slowed and rational thought returned—I put the milk away—regret was number one with a bullet.

Then the doorbell rang again, and I rushed to answer it with an apology on my lips. Only the ringer wasn't Aaron. It was a bored-looking youth bearing a bouquet of roses and lilies in a cone of cellophane tied with ribbon.

"Kincaid?" he said. "Sign here."

I took the bouquet out to the deck, feeling a little queasy. *Did they come?* Aaron had asked, and I thought he meant people. Could he have been asking about these flowers? I opened the little white florist's envelope and read the note inside.

Sorry, Stretch, it said. *Forget the Cubs. It's just you and me tonight.*

"Oh, hell. Hell and *damnation.*"

In a spasm of frustration and anger, aimed squarely at myself this time, I flung the flowers onto the planks of the deck—from which they bounced right into the water. I dropped to my knees and tried to snatch them back. Too late. The bouquet wobbled on the surface, a flowery little toy boat, and drifted off trailing its ribbons like mooring lines.

"Lose something, Carnegie?" called a beach-ball-shaped fellow from the next houseboat down. Larry Halloway, my ever-present neighborly neighbor, waved a jolly hand. "I could come over and help."

I waved back and gave Larry a big fat fake smile. "That's OK, thanks, it's fine. I'm fine."

Then I went back inside, closed the sliding glass door, and burst into tears.

Chapter Ten

The bedside phone went off like a fire alarm.

I jerked upright in the darkness with my heart slamming, half-convinced that the clamor was my alarm clock and I was late for some critical meeting. But I never got up early on Sunday—or any other day if I could help it—and when I grabbed at the clock, I realized that it wasn't the source of the racket.

As I stared at the spiky red numerals, I came fully awake. Five twenty-three A.M. Why was my telephone ringing? I reached fearfully toward the table again.

"Hello?"

"I'm sorry to wake you, Stretch. I should have waited, but you can't use your cell on the plane—"

"What plane?" I'd gone to bed late and slept badly, but Aaron sounded even worse off than I felt. "Slow down, please, and tell me what's happening."

"It's Izzy. He's had a heart attack."

"Oh, *Aaron*." Izzy was Isaac Gold, Aaron's grandfather, who lived in a Miami retirement home. Both Aaron's parents had died young, so Izzy meant a lot to him. "I'm so sorry. How bad is it?"

"Pretty bad. I can't think straight." He hesitated, and I could hear a babble of airport noises in the distance. "I shouldn't have called so early. I guess . . . I guess I just wanted to hear your voice."

"Of course you should have called." I groped for something to fill the painful silence. "I know your grandfather will be glad to have you there. I wish I could go with you, but—"

"You've got a wedding to run, Stretch. But thanks for the thought."

"Well, I'll be thinking about you the whole time you're there."

"I know that."

Another silence, and I said, "When do you get in?"

Silly question, really, but Aaron jumped on it, just to be talking. "A few minutes past noon. It's a direct flight. Usually I have to go through Atlanta or the Twin Cities."

"That's good, then."

"Yeah. It's a lot better this way."

He sounded so miserable, I wished I could reach through the phone and hold him. Instead I asked, "Did you watch the game?"

"What? Oh, the Cubs won, six–four."

"Chicago fans must have been happy."

"Orgasmic. It all seems kind of pointless now." I heard him sigh. "I'm sorry about last night, Carnegie. I was being stupid."

"Forget it, please. I'm sorry too, but don't even think about it, not now."

"All right. Promise me one thing, though."

"Anything."

"Stay out of this murder case. I know Boris is important to you, but just back off and let the police do their job. Promise?"

I hesitated only for a moment. After all, it wasn't a police job to get Boris out on bail, was it? So technically I was being quite sincere.

"I promise, Aaron. Give my love to Izzy, OK?"

"OK."

"And to you too, you dope."

That made him laugh a little, and we said goodbye. I fell back on my pillow and stared at the invisible ceiling, forgetting Boris for the moment in my concern for Aaron's grandfather. Izzy was a marvelous old man, funny and wise, and he looked exactly like Aaron was going to in about fifty years. The thought of Aaron growing old, and me along with him, made our recent squabbling seem woefully petty.

Why was I fussing at him about something so trivial? One evening of baseball isn't much in the grand scheme of things. And what does it mean that I've been so bitchy with Aaron lately? Maybe nothing. Lots of brides get bitchy. But I never thought I'd be like them.

Uncomfortable thoughts to face in the darkness, so after a while I deliberately turned my thoughts in a happier direction: pondering all the delightful options for my wedding dress, and flowers, and cake.

But somehow this wasn't the panacea I needed. Little whispers of anxiety kept creeping in—*Do I really want a big formal wedding? What if something goes wrong and Made in Heaven looks bad?*—and try as I might, I couldn't banish them. But I was tired, and the houseboat rocked, almost imperceptibly, and after a while it rocked me back to sleep.

On my second groggy awakening I really was late. Joe Solveto had invited me for Sunday morning coffee at his catering office in the Fremont neighborhood, to hear his preliminary thoughts about my wedding supper. He was almost more excited about the prospect than I was.

I dressed quickly and skipped breakfast—Joe was always good for a delectable pastry or two—and hurried down the dock still zipping up my jacket. A dense pale fog had settled in during the night, and though the air wasn't all that cold, it clung damply to my face and hair.

The fog swallowed my footsteps and veiled the other houseboats as they fell behind me. I thought I heard movement, a muffled footfall and then silence, but when I turned to look, I could see only shifting mist.

"Larry? Is that you?"

No answer, and I shivered a little. The hemmed-in visibility felt spooky, menacing almost. I told myself I was being paranoid—but I made sure no one followed me across the parking lot, and when I climbed into Vanna, I locked the doors.

The fog was shredding into tatters as I skirted the south end of Lake Union and headed north again on Westlake Avenue. By the time I passed beneath the blue and orange girders of the Fremont drawbridge, the air had grown brighter and so had my spirits.

I was still worried about Boris, of course, but the sun was shining and I was getting married. Me, the bride! I loved planning other women's weddings, but the prospect of arranging my own was intoxicating—if a little overwhelming. And besides, maybe Joe could pitch in on the bail bond.

Shaking my head at this weird mixture of ideas, I grabbed the first parking space I saw on 36th and walked down to Solveto's Catering. Even on a Sunday morning the so-called Artists' Republic of Fremont was bustling with shoppers and brunchers, and the faces I passed held a glow of surprised contentment that's peculiar to Seattle. You could practically read the thought balloons over all their heads: *Look, more sunshine! It's October, and it hasn't started raining yet!*

Still time to get in one last hike, I thought as I strode along. *Maybe by the time Aaron gets back, the real killer will be in jail and we can forget all this and hike to Snow Lake.* That was a favorite trail of mine, up in the Cascades just off Interstate 90. It led through a wide valley of forest and meadow, up over a ridge, and then down again to an aquamarine gem of an alpine lake. *I bet the fall colors are beautiful up there, and the wet weather's going to start any day now. We could use some quiet time together out of town.*

I turned the corner and dropped down toward the Ship Canal. In the old days Fremont was a funky neighborhood, but funky as in rough-edged, with bars I wasn't comfortable going into. Now development had made it funky as in adorable for tourists, with tempting restaurants and pricey shops I had to struggle to stay out of.

Joe ran his business from a sleek new building right across from the canal near the Fremont Bridge. His offices were upstairs, with a tasting room like a mini-restaurant down at street level.

I entered the tasting room to find him lounging by the tall windows, gazing out at a handsome sailboat as it motored up the canal. The drawbridge bell clanged loud enough to be heard through the glass, then the bridge split in the middle to raise its iron arms to the sky and let the boat pass through.

"I could watch that bridge for hours." Joe sighed. "I must be getting old."

"Ancient," I said. "Can I hit you up for a cappuccino before you expire?"

In truth Joe was only a little older than me and quite a lot more beautiful. He had exquisitely tousled sandy hair above smoky blue eyes, and today his extensive wardrobe had produced a pair of faultless charcoal trousers and a mock turtleneck in wine-colored cashmere.

Along with his good looks and his air of languid sophistication, Joe possessed a killer business instinct. He'd been generous with good counsel for Made in Heaven, and his occasional observations on my personal life were often right on the mark. I crossed the room and we traded air kisses. I know it sounds like that girl-with-gay-friend movie cliché, but we did it ironically. There's a difference.

"For you," he said, "a double cappuccino."

Joe's espresso-making was a minor religious ritual, and there followed a quarter-hour of grinding beans, tamping grounds, steaming milk, and prewarming two cups made of hand-painted Italian ceramic. But finally we were perched at a table with our steaming concoctions, a plate of golden croissants, a little crock of honey—and plenty to talk about.

"I heard about the murder, of course," said Joe, after I'd outlined the events at Yesler Field on Friday night. "The news said a suspect was in custody, but they didn't give a name. Poor old Boris. Are you sure he didn't do it?"

"Of course I am!" I protested, spraying flakes of buttery pastry. "Why does everyone keep saying that?"

"Just think about it, sweetie." Joe reached out with his napkin to dab a flake from my lips. "Take one Mad Russian, add vast amounts of vodka, and stir in a slanderous remark about darling Carnegie from this Duvall character. One could almost script the result. Try the honey, it's got ginger in it."

I pushed the honey pot aside.

"It wasn't like that! All right, Boris threw a punch. But

then he left the party. He says he only came back to apologize, and I believe him. And there's something else." I described how I'd heard a door closing in the side corridor. "I didn't see the person, but I bet it was the killer."

"You told the police that, of course?"

"Of course."

He smeared his own croissant with ginger honey. "Then they'll look into it, won't they? Come on now, you don't think the police and the courts go around convicting people of murder without even investigating?"

"I guess." I made a milky design on the tabletop with the tip of my cappuccino spoon. "But meanwhile it's awfully hard on Boris. And his business."

"True."

I looked up, straight into the smoky blues. "Joe, I want to try and bail Boris out before Nevsky Brothers goes to pieces. I don't suppose you could help me raise the money?"

Joe smiled ruefully. "You know I love you, Carnegie. But I barely know Boris, and money's got such a nasty way of interfering with friendships. Let's not go there, shall we?"

I bit back a hasty answer. He was right. It wasn't fair to get him involved, especially financially.

"I understand," I said. "But Boris is innocent. The police don't believe it and neither does his lawyer, but I'm going to clear him."

"It's quite a hobby with you, isn't it, rushing in where angels fear to tread?" Joe leaned back and crossed his cashmere arms. "I'll tell you what. Once this is resolved, I will personally steer every one of my clients to Nevsky Brothers. How's that?"

"That's wonderful, Joe. Thank you." I hadn't been feeling

weepy, but suddenly the tears were there and I pulled out a handkerchief. "I've been so worried—"

"Now, now," he said briskly. "Happier thoughts. Remember, *you're* my client too, so let's talk about this wedding of yours. I'm afraid we've had a setback about the Olympic Hotel. I know it was your first choice of site, but they absolutely will not let me do the catering. You use their chefs or no one."

"Well, to hell with them," I said, sniffing. "I'd rather have you than the hotel."

It was a near run thing, though. The Olympic had been the grande dame of Seattle hotels for more than eighty years. I loved the vast three-tiered lobby with its gilded columns and barrel vault ceiling, its ornate chandeliers and towering flower arrangements. I'd even directed a few weddings there. How dare they bar my favorite caterer from the premises?

"That's very flattering," Joe was saying as he cleared our dishes.

Then he opened a manila folder marked KINCAID/GOLD. I got a pleasant little kick out of that. How many folders had I labeled with other couple's names?

"I must admit," he went on, "I've come up with some fabulous ideas for you. Everyone around here has been salmoned to death, so I thought, why not trout? I could make it roulade, with a spinach stuffing, and then serve a lobster risotto with saffron—"

"Are you sure we can't get the Olympic?" I broke in. "Don't you have connections there who'd make an exception for you?"

"Alas, no. What about the Chinese Room at the Smith Tower? All that red and black lacquer has a certain exotic charm."

"I don't know. That space feels kind of claustrophobic to me."

"SAM, then?"

That was the Seattle Art Museum. I shrugged. "Too conventional."

"The Petroleum Museum? Very offbeat and funky."

"Too unconventional. I had my heart set on the Olympic."

Joe closed his manila folder. "Oh, dear. It's begun."

"What's begun?"

"Full-blown infection by the Bride Brain Virus. You should see yourself—you're pouting."

"I am not!"

I laughed a little but Joe didn't.

"A word of advice, Carnegie?"

"What?"

"Hire a wedding planner."

"*What?*"

"I'm serious. This way lies madness." He tapped the folder with one manicured fingertip. "Have fun with your gown and your menu, but let someone else work with your vendors and hammer out the logistics. You know too much, and you'll drive yourself crazy."

"Myself, or everyone else?"

He stood up. "I am far too diplomatic to respond to that. Now run along, my dear, and look over these menu suggestions. You might have months to make up your mind and then change it about every little detail, but you may as well start now."

Months, I thought as I drove back home and pulled into the parking lot. *Can I stand to wait months to marry Aaron?* A formal wedding can take a year to plan, and though I'd always thought I would gleefully immerse myself in the process, suddenly now I could imagine myself eloping.

A wedding planner, elope? I frowned as I picked up my tote bag with Joe's folder inside and climbed out of Vanna. That might be a nice respite from my professional tasks, but what would people say? Would my mother be horribly disappointed? Would Aaron? Or maybe he'd feel relieved.

I was so preoccupied with these questions that I actually reached out to unlock the front door—and started in surprise when it swung loose at the touch of the key. The little dead bolt had torn free of the frame when someone kicked or shoved or somehow smashed the door open.

Breaking and entering, I thought stupidly, staring at the lock. *What do you know, somebody broke and entered.*

Chapter Eleven

I'm pretty sure that a solitary woman confronted by a busted-open front door should retreat at once and call the police.

Scratch that. I'm absolutely sure. But I marched right into the houseboat anyway, for two reasons. First, because the air of utter stillness made it seem so unlikely that someone was lurking inside. And second, because I was furious.

"Hey!" I said indignantly. "Hey, what the *hell*—"

The kitchen was a mess. Not a sickening mess, with smashed dishes and food on the floor, as I'd once seen at the home of some unfortunate friends. This was just a ransacked mess of cabinets left open, drawers pulled out, and stacks of dish towels shoved aside, as if the intruders were looking for money or drugs. So, thieves rather than vandals.

And frustrated thieves at that. My drug of choice was chardonnay, and what little cash I carried was safe in my wallet. As for electronics, you could barely sell my TV or CD player at a garage sale, let alone fence them for big bucks. But I did have a few pieces of jewelry...

I dashed into the bedroom, where the dresser drawers were yanked open, the mattress lying askew on the box spring, and my jewelry box upended onto the bedspread. I poked through the sad little heap of treasure and found a couple of pieces gone, but they had no sentimental value. My turquoise earrings from that trip to Santa Fe, and the modest pearl necklace my father gave me for graduation, were still present and accounted for.

"Not good enough for you?" I said aloud. The thought of strangers in my bedroom made me sick. "Bastards."

The living room was the same story. Books dumped off their shelves, personal papers swept from my little desk, even the wastebasket turned upside down. Nothing was missing here that I could see, but the search had been thorough. I didn't touch any surfaces, out of some vague concern for fingerprints, but the sight of my last bank statement lying on the floor made me gasp in dismay.

Paperwork—the office! What if Made in Heaven's office was wrecked?

I headed outside, where a flight of rickety wooden steps led from my living area to the second story of the houseboat. I flew up them two at a time, through a second busted door, and bounded across the "good room" where we meet with brides and into the office. There I stopped, sagging in relief to see that our computers were still intact.

Once again all the office drawers had been rifled through and the shelves disarranged, but not much was missing. Just a camera—the digital one we used to document cakes and flowers and such—and the battered old binoculars that Eddie kept on the windowsill for watching boats on the lake. We'd gotten off lightly. But my heart was anything but light as I dropped into my desk chair and called 911.

We all have our coping mechanisms for life's little unpleasantries, like having a tooth filled or enduring a flu shot. I usually cope by observing the dentist or the nurse going about their technical tasks, noting the tools they use and the techniques they've mastered. Sort of Take Your Wedding Planner to Work Day.

So when two of Seattle's Finest showed up, I tried to bury my dismay at being burgled by watching them prowl around the houseboat. After being scolded, of course.

"Why'd you go inside?" said Officer Rybinski, a fortyish woman who was taking the lead. She was husky, with smooth fair hair skinned back into a disciplined knot, while her partner was a gawky fellow who looked too young to shave. "You took a big risk, you know. Could have been a junkie with a gun in here. Show me the bottom of your shoe?"

I nodded meekly and turned up my foot. She frowned at it, made a scribble in her notebook, then followed her partner into the bedroom, examining the floors as well as the mess. I followed, observing their observation.

"Too bad I cleaned yesterday," I said. "There might have been footprints."

She flicked her eyes at me, looking for sarcasm. "You mind if we dust for fingerprints?"

"Of course not. Why should I mind?"

"Powder's a bitch to clean up." She produced a tin of dark gray particles, dipped a brush in them, and twirled the brush over the lid of my jewelry box. "Be sure and vacuum it off before you use a cleaning product."

But in the end her dusting was fruitless—the intruder had worn gloves, even at the front door.

"Pretty careful for a user," Rybinski commented to her partner, and he nodded importantly. Before they left she handed me a sheet of paper. "Stolen property report. Fill it out later, after you've had time to calm down and look around some more."

I felt like protesting that I *was* calm, but she clearly wasn't interested. I was, though. It was curious that I wasn't more upset about the break-in. But having a good friend arrested for murder put the whole thing into perspective. Aside from wishing that Aaron was around, I was OK. A few stolen items, no real damage, no danger to me. Like they say, No harm, no foul.

As I showed the officers to the door—what remained of it—I saw Mike Graham coming down the dock toward us. Lily's new husband wore a coat and tie, and with his neatly trimmed brown hair and shined shoes, he might have been a middle manager or rising young executive. Until you noticed the dogged set of his jaw and the jaded sadness in his eyes.

The younger officer went right past him, but Rybinski recognized him as a homicide detective and stopped briefly to converse. Then she went her way as I accepted a hug of sympathy from Mike and welcomed him in.

"Can I get you something?" I asked him. "Coffee, tea, fingerprint powder?"

He shook his head. "I'm working today so I've just got a minute, but I heard 'houseboat' on the scanner and realized it was you. I hope you didn't come inside here by yourself?"

I shrugged. "Guilty as charged. But it's not too bad, just a few things missing and nothing damaged except the doors."

"The smart ones know that vandalism is a separate charge from theft, sometimes with bigger penalties." He looked around the kitchen and into the living room. "Must be a nasty feeling, though, having your home violated. Lily's off work today and home with the boys. Maybe you'd like to go over there for a while?"

I thought about it—Marcus and Ethan, who called me

"Aunt Car," were great little spirit-lifters—but then I declined.

"Thanks, Mike, but I'd better stay here and clean up the mess. I'm glad to see you, though. I want to talk to you about Boris Nevsky."

His face changed. "I'm not on that case."

"I know that, but—"

"Carnegie, I cannot and will not interfere with one of my officers' investigations for personal reasons. Lily told me how upset you are, and I understand—"

"It's not a matter of my being upset! It's a matter of justice. Boris is innocent, I *know* he is. Someone else killed Digger Duvall. I just don't know who yet."

"Yet?" He rubbed his forehead as if it hurt. "Tell me you're not getting involved in this."

"I'm already involved. Boris is my dear friend, and I want to help him."

"Then go visit him. Cheer him up. But stay out of—"

"I can visit him in jail?"

"Of course you can. It's not a gulag, you know. In fact, he's being held downtown and not at the regional center out in Kent, so you won't have far to go. Just call first and check on the visiting schedule." Mike patted my shoulder. "I've got to get going. I know all this is distressing for you, but try and have some faith in the system. And get some better locks put on these doors, OK?"

"Sure," I said, already preoccupied. An emergency locksmith shouldn't take long, and I was only minutes from downtown.

The locksmith was fast. By midafternoon there were big heavy deadbolts on my doors, and I was standing on the corner of Fifth and James gazing up at the King County Jail. I'd never paid it much attention before. It looked so ordinary, just a twelve-story gray building with the usual street trees and parking spaces. Just a building full of people, the innocent and the guilty. I shuddered and went inside.

Soon, having been politely but efficiently searched, I was being ushered into an area that looked like an ordinary rec room, where denim-clad men sat in murmured conversation with their wives and friends and even children. It might have been a dormitory lounge, except for the varying ages of the residents—and the armed guards at the door.

Boris rose from a chair in the corner and stood watching me approach, his lips clamped tight and his body rigid with self-consciousness. I wasn't feeling too relaxed myself. I went over and took both his hands, afraid that an embrace would draw the guards' attention.

"Are you all right, Boris? I've been so worried about you. Your lawyer came to see me—"

"Trofim, bah!" he rumbled, as we sat down. "He does not believe me, my Kharnegie. But you believe me, no?"

"Of course I do. I told him that. I was hoping to raise your bail, but I'd have to borrow—"

"*Nyet!*" Boris shook his head and his black beard quivered. "It is too much, and I will not permit. I say this to Sergei also."

Most of Boris's assistants seemed to be named Sergei, so I didn't ask which one.

"We just want to help. How are they managing without you at the studio?"

"Is bad, I think." His broad shoulders dropped. "I give Sergei instructions when he comes to see me, but is not the same." Then his brow creased in sudden alarm. "You will not fire Nevsky Brothers from baseball wedding?"

Boris had had a little trouble pronouncing McKinney/Gutierrez, so this was our unofficial designation.

"Absolutely not! Beau and I wouldn't do that to you." Actually, Beau would have done it in a hot minute, but all the flowers were ordered already and we couldn't possibly find a substitute florist so late in the game. But there was no point in saying that. "You know we're all behind you, Boris."

"Even your man Aaron Gold?"

I smiled a little and fibbed a little. "Even Aaron."

"Good." Boris breathed deeply and rested his chin on his fist, like an especially thoughtful Kodiak bear. "I must consider this Aaron Gold. He is honorable man?"

"Y-yes. Yes, he is."

"You are sure you wish to marry him?"

There was no fibbing about this one. "Absolutely."

Boris lifted his right hand, held it suspended for a moment, then dropped it heavily onto my shoulder.

"Then I am sure also, my Kharnegie. I give you my blessing."

"Oh, Boris!" I was caught between laughter and tears. "That's very—very honorable of you. It means a lot to me."

The Mad Russian nodded solemnly. "Of course it does. Now, tell me more. When do you marry? I will make flowers for you, the finest I have ever made! Waterfall style, I think. You are long woman, you can carry long bouquet. Perhaps lilies, but not stargazer lilies, they are too common."

And so, with no further mention of murder or prison or any other dark realities, Boris Nevsky and I discussed my wedding flowers until visiting hours were through.

Chapter Twelve

I devoted the rest of Sunday to chores and fretting. My topsy-turvy rooms were easy enough to put to rights—though finger-print powder really is a bitch to clean—but my fears for Izzy and Boris and my unease about the break-in just got worse the more I brooded on them. Finally, as evening closed in, I double-checked my deadbolts and resorted to extreme mea-sures: coffee ice cream, chocolate chips, and channel surfing.

Ironically enough, after all the fuss I'd made, I ended up watching game two of the World Series. I figured that Aaron would miss it and I could fill him in, only the Twins pounded the Cubs 16–3 and nobody needs details about a tragedy like that. But I stuck with the Cubbies to the bitter end anyway, then went to bed in a sugar coma.

Aaron called again Monday morning, at a far more reason-able hour this time, and the word from Miami was far better than the news from Chicago.

As I poured a second cup of coffee and set my breakfast dishes in the sink, he told me that Izzy had rallied and that his great-aunt Frances, Izzy's sister, was on her way to Florida to tend the patient. He sounded so relieved and happy that I decided to save my burglary news for later.

I admit, I had an ulterior motive on that point: I was start-ing to wonder if the burglary might be related to Digger's death. I couldn't see how, really. I just had this funny feeling about it—and Aaron might interpret that feeling as getting involved in the murder case.

So I skipped the burglary and focused on Frances. "Can she really take care of him? She must be elderly herself."

"Nah, Aunt Frankie's the baby of the family," Aaron said. "She's only seventy-three. Plays tennis every day! She'll boss Izzy around, and he'll love it."

"That's wonderful. So how long will you be down there?" I almost reminded him about Friday's dinner with Mom and Owen, but I'd done enough nagging about that. So instead I just added, "I miss you."

"Not for long, you won't. I'll be back late on Wednesday night."

"Really? That's great!" I was tired of sleeping alone. "I mean, if Izzy can spare you."

"He's just glad I could come in the first place. And Frankie gets in tomorrow, so I can visit with her too before I leave." A different note came into his voice. "Stretch, could you take Thursday off?"

"Well, I've wrapped up just about everything for Beau, so yes, I think so. Why?"

"Let's take a day together just for us. You're right, we do need to talk about the wedding, and we need some time alone. Besides, I've got a surprise for you."

"I'll just bet you do," I said, imagining his leer. "My place or yours?"

"Seriously, can you take the day?"

"Gee, I don't know," I said, smiling all over my face and bouncing up and down on the balls of my feet. "My calendar is pretty full, but I might be able to fit you in."

"As long as you fit me into your bed," said Aaron, and the

conversation degenerated along those lines for a while. I missed him a *lot*.

"So what else shall we do Thursday?" he said at last. "Your choice, Stretch. Lunch and a matinee, or a drive in the country? I'll even look at china with you, if that's what you want."

"Whoa, what's all this? What have you done with Aaron Gold?"

"Well, spending time with Izzy has got me thinking—I mean, about what's really important, and . . ." He was sounding more sheepish by the minute. I loved it. "Well anyway, what would you like to do?"

"Snow Lake!" I said. "The weather is fabulous this week, and we could do the whole hike and still be back in time for game five."

"Did I hear you say game five? What have you done with Carnegie Kincaid?"

"Izzy must be using ESP. So is a day hike all right with you?"

"Are you kidding? It sounds great, and I promise I'll spend every single minute talking about the wedding. Besides, if it gets me out of shopping for china, I'll climb Mount Rainier. I hate china."

"I'm not that fond of the stuff myself."

"I thought all women wanted formal china and silver and shit."

"I am not all women," I said loftily. "And the sooner you get back here, the sooner I'll prove it."

"You already have. Game five is going to be the pitching duel of all time, and I really want to see it. You're a sweetheart, Stretch."

"You bet I am. Now tell me more about this surprise."

"Hey, gotta run," he said mischievously. "Busy, busy. I'll call you tomorrow night. Love you, Stretch."

"Love you," I said. "Tomorrow night."

Aaron's call left me curious but more cheerful, and I headed upstairs to the office whistling "Take Me Out to the Ballgame." Burglaries happen, after all, and I was unharmed and had lost nothing of serious value. In fact I was surprised not to feel more distressed than I did.

The weather continued to boost my spirits. It was another misty morning, with another fine autumn day to come. Once again the sun was burning off the fog, and through the picture window of the office I could catch glimpses of the lake and even a peek at the Olympic Mountains on the western horizon. They say Seattle with its rain is like a beautiful woman with a bad cold, but this week there was only beauty.

A fine day, and I'd come up with a fine plan to help Boris. Or rather, I thought, mindful of my promise to Aaron, to find out who had burgled my houseboat. I couldn't help getting involved in that, could I? And if the burglar and the murderer turned out to be the same person, that wasn't my fault.

My plan was to call all the engagement party guests, on the pretext of making sure everyone was all right after the shocking finale to our evening. But I'd really be trying to figure out who had been absent from the party at ten o'clock on the night of the murder.

I'd heard that hallway door closing at ten precisely, so every person who was in sight of someone else at that time was in the clear. The rest would go on a short list of possible suspects. What I'd do with the short list was another question, but I had to get going right away.

Sifting all those names by myself could take hours, if

not days. I might have to postpone this afternoon's dress-shopping with Lily, but it was just our first scouting expedition and she would understand. Maybe I'd even ask her to help me work through the guest list, if she promised not to tell Mike what I was doing.

Eddie wasn't at work yet—just as well for him, since I'm a terrible whistler—so I settled in at my desk to review my calendar. As I blocked out Thursday for the hike with Aaron, I noticed something scribbled in for today: "HH NN?"

I was perplexed for a moment, then I remembered with a frown and a groan. HH was for Honeysuckle Hell, and NN was NocNoc, the downtown dance club that Juice had mentioned.

Some local bands were throwing a party there tonight for Rose and Gordo. Not exactly a bridal shower, but the Navigators were sending a photographer to get some shots of their star player socializing. Beau Paliere had requested—as in demanded—my presence at the event, to keep an eye on our volatile bride.

NocNoc didn't sound like my kind of place, and I'd only agreed to attend because I could take Aaron with me for company. I didn't want to go alone, but with my date in Miami and Lily allergic to loud music in small spaces, who else was there?

My frown eased. Who indeed but Juice herself? I called By Bread Alone, got the voice mail for her cake-baking business, and left a message explaining the situation. I was just hanging up when the outside door banged open and Eddie Breen blustered in.

"What the hell is this about a murder?" he demanded, brandishing a copy of the *Seattle Times* like a cavalry saber above his white-haired head. "Are you getting yourself in trouble again?"

"Of course not. I'm completely uninvolved here."

He snorted. "Fat chance. It's that Frenchman, isn't it? Every time he shows up, something goes nuts!"

I should explain about Eddie, my not-so-silent partner. He and my late father were cadets in the merchant marine together, back in the day. But while Dad stayed at sea, Eddie came ashore for a long career in public accounting. He ended up retiring in Seattle just about the time I arrived, and when I started my business, Eddie was more than ready to offer advice.

Somehow Eddie's advice evolved into a job as part-time business manager for Made in Heaven—and full-time commentator on my personal life.

"This has got nothing to do with Beau," I said mildly. "He can't help it if—"

"Don't give me that hooey. The man's a menace."

My partner stomped over to his desk and shed his jacket. Eddie dressed the same every day: an immaculate white shirt with the cuffs folded back like origami, and khakis with creases that could slice bread. He opened the paper with a ferocious snap.

"And what kind of moron claimed to see Boris Nevsky with the murder weapon? Says here 'an unnamed witness.' Must have been a blind man."

"Huh?"

I stared at him, astounded. Eddie had never been fond of the Mad Russian, but now he was defending him? Boris was warm and effusive and sentimental, everything Eddie wasn't. He'd once kissed Eddie on both cheeks in a fit of enthusiasm about something or other, and the old salt had never gotten over it.

I gathered my wits. "*I'm* the witness, Eddie: I don't believe Boris killed Digger, but I did see him holding the bat."

He scowled at me fiercely. "Well, what does that tell you right there? A big hulking fellow like Nevsky, going after a man with a baseball bat? Listen, sister, big men don't use bats. They use their fists!"

"I guess that makes sense."

"Damn right it makes sense."

"In that case , . ." I gazed in speculation at this unlikely ally. "Eddie, I've got an idea about how to clear Boris, or at least how to start. Would you be willing to run through the guest list of that party with me and figure out who has an alibi?"

Eddie harrumphed. "Is this what you call uninvolved? It sounds like something the police ought to be doing."

"They're convinced that Boris is guilty. Even his lawyer thinks so."

I told him briefly about Trofim Denisovich—and about the break-in yesterday. The reaction was classic Eddie: he went immediately to the outside door, yanked it open, and assessed the quality of the new lock I'd had installed. Only after it passed inspection did he rejoin me in the office.

"Probably some goddamn kids looking for drugs. Oughta start drafting them—that'd keep 'em busy."

I spread the guest list on my desk. "Will you help me?"

"Aren't you busy working for the Frenchman today?"

"I can take some time. For Boris. He's in *jail*, Eddie. He could go to prison for life."

I'd always insisted on a nonsmoking office, so when my partner needed to think, he chewed on an unlit cigar. He produced one now and gave it a decisive chomp.

"Two hours. Then I'm going back to work and so should you. You got that?"

"I got it. Thanks, Eddie."

It only took an hour for us to realize that my fine plan was utterly futile. We called the first two dozen guests on the list, and even some bartenders and waiters, but the result was clear: people had been moving in and out of the party all evening, and no one had paid particular attention to the time.

Besides, proving a negative is notoriously tricky. A few guests remembered a few others who were *probably* on the scene at ten o'clock, but no one could say *definitely* who wasn't there. The roster of possible absentees included everyone from Gordo Gutierrez to Nelly Tibbett to Aaron Gold— and almost anyone else could have slipped out just long enough to kill Digger.

"This is hopeless," I said wearily, shutting off my cell. "Anyone could have done it."

" 'Fraid so." Eddie hung up his desk phone. "I can make some more calls while you're out with Lily, but—"

"Maybe I should cancel with her," I said doubtfully. "I'm not much in the mood."

"Nonsense. You girls are always in the mood for dresses. Go on, do you good."

"OK. Listen, if Juice calls—"

But my phone chirped then, and it was Juice. "Are you freakin' kidding, Kincaid? A private party at NocNoc? I am so there!"

"Terrific. I'll pick you up around nine." Then I asked a question I had never imagined myself directing at Juice Nugent. "Um, what do you think I should wear?"

She chortled. "Kinda short on spikes, huh? Got any fish-net stockings?"

"Afraid not."

"Platform boots?"

"You're joking."

"Bondage gear?"

"Juice!"

She sighed. "Just wear black, you'll be fine."

Chapter Thirteen

"Have you got a black T-shirt I could borrow?"

"For yourself?" Lily looked down at her own ample chest, then across the table at my meager one.

I took her point. "Maybe an old T-shirt that shrank in the dryer? Never mind, I'll buy one today. I've already got black jeans."

"What's this for, a dress-down funeral?"

"Even stranger. I'm going to a Goth party." I sighed and cut into one of my almond-crusted sea scallops. "Or maybe it's punk. Or maybe both."

Lily and I had decided to treat ourselves to a fancy lunch at Palomino, a bustling bistro that seems to hang suspended from the mezzanine above the lobby of the City Center building. It was one of my favorite downtown spaces, airy and open with big bright paintings and gorgeous art glass light fixtures.

Today Palomino was filled with sunshine and voices and the savory smells of roasting. We had even ordered wine, but still I was having trouble getting into lighthearted bride mode. Lily had commiserated with me about the burglary and with Aaron in absentia about Izzy. Now I was trying to lighten up, but without much success.

"How did I get so behind-the-times all of a sudden?" I

complained. "I'm usually cooler than my clients, but this makes me feel like a dinosaur."

"A party for Honeysuckle Hell, I assume?" Lily smiled encouragingly. "Maybe it'll be fun."

"Maybe. I'm just so worried about Boris." As we ate, I explained how Eddie and I had tried to narrow down the list of party guests to possible suspects. "I can see now that we should have started with motives, not alibis. But Digger Duvall was so unpopular, that's probably a wide field too. Has Mike said whether Detective Starkey is even looking at anyone besides Boris? I've actually been wondering about Rose's father—"

"Hold on, Carnegie." Lily set down her fork and the garlic-roasted prawn she had just speared with it. "I'd better say this right now. Mike and I are still working out how much he can share with me about his cases. But one thing we're sure about is that he has to be able to rely on my discretion. You understand?"

"Well sure, you can't go blabbing stuff to the newspapers. But just talking with me isn't going to hurt anything."

"It could hurt my marriage."

That stopped me cold. I opened my mouth to protest, then shut it again. Clearly this was important to Lily, and Lily was very important to me. But so was Boris.

The silence was growing awkward, and my best friend was looking anxious. *When in doubt,* I told myself, *do the right thing. And do it with flair.* I raised the last of my excellent sauvignon blanc.

"Of course I understand. And here's to your marriage, my dear. One whole month now, isn't it? Cheers!"

Lily clinked my glass, looking relieved. We drained our glasses, ordered dessert, and shifted to the safer ground of wedding dresses. Even a scouting expedition needs a plan, and so far I didn't have one.

"Where do you want to begin?" Lily asked. "High end or low, or somewhere in the middle? God, this crème brûlée is heavenly. Nordstrom's did a nice job with my gown, but you must know all kinds of specialty shops."

"I know the highest of the high," I said, suddenly decisive. "We are beginning with Le Boutique."

Hazel Cohen wasn't in her shop on Mondays, which was in our favor. Hazel saw brides by appointment only, and her attitude toward casual browsers was frosty. But her assistant Amber was alone this afternoon, doing paperwork in the back office with talk radio for company. As we walked in, she snapped off the radio and snapped to attention, then relaxed when she saw me.

"Hi, Carnegie!" She put on her salesgirl persona and turned to Lily. "Are you looking for a gown? I'd be happy to help you—"

"Not me," said Lily, her eyes wandering to the mannequins in the front windows. "Carnegie's the bride this time."

"Really?" Amber's amazement was less than flattering. "That's just—that's so great! When's your wedding?"

"We don't have a date yet. But could I just look at some styles, maybe try on a few? You could go on with your work."

I was breaking my own cardinal rule for clients here, which was to choose the bridal gown only after determining the site, season, and level of formality of the wedding itself. But everything about my wedding seemed out of order somehow, including my own feelings about it. *If only Aaron was more enthusiastic . . .*

"Oh, that's OK," Amber was saying. "I'm just doing invoices. *Bor*-ing." She giggled. "Don't tell Hazel I said so."

"My lips are sealed. So, show me something wonderful in off-white."

Amber showed me dozens of gowns in dozens of subtle shadings, from eggshell to cream to ivory and on into hues called oyster and mushroom and parchment. But I was somehow dissatisfied with each one. I felt like Goldilocks, only without the "just right." Finally I chose three, as different as possible from each other, and we took them into the shell-pink dressing room.

The first gown was a truly spectacular creation, with a strapless lace-on-lace bodice atop a huge bell of a skirt in gleaming satin. The whole was tied together at the waist with a broad burgundy ribbon.

"I look like a Christmas present," I said, turning slowly on the dais. "Let's try the one with the slimmer silhouette."

Amber helped me into a long-sleeved Grecian column of silk. It had hundreds of narrow pleats that ran, severely vertical, from shoulder to hemline.

"That one's really nice on you. Kind of...dignified, you know?"

I made a face at Lily, who mouthed the word, "*Bor*-ing."

The third gown was the charm. The sweetheart neckline was wonderfully flattering, and a subtle peach tint in the creamy satin warmed and brightened my complexion. As I turned, the bias-cut skirt flowed and swirled and softened my own sticklike lines.

"I don't want to take it off," I said, pirouetting happily.

"Take your time," Amber told me. "Say, is that Rose girl OK? She scared me half to death fainting like that! I almost fainted myself, I honestly almost did."

"She's fine," I said. "Shouldn't have skipped breakfast, that's all."

"I *never* skip meals. But I guess you can tell that. Oops, there's the phone. 'Scuse me."

"Rose fainted?" asked Lily, as Amber left us.

"M-hm," I said absently, studying my reflection in the mirror as I stepped down from the dais. "She heard about the murder and passed out cold. Though she claimed it was blood sugar. You know, there's something familiar about this dress."

Lily laughed out loud. "Of course there is, you idiot. It's almost exactly like the one you wore as my maid of honor! Just a little paler, and probably twice as expensive."

"Twice, nothing."

As she helped me change clothes, I told her the price range of Le Boutique's gowns, and her eyes widened.

"Carnegie, that's more than my *car*. I didn't realize Beau Paliere was paying you that well."

"He's not," I sighed, deflated. Not Goldilocks, more like Cinderella at midnight. "I'm just daydreaming, that's all. Want to go get some coffee? I shouldn't drink at lunch—it gives me a headache."

We waved at Amber on our way out and were soon sitting at a Starbucks. It was around the corner from a Starbucks, and across the street from a Tully's. When an ambulance comes to fetch you in Seattle, they bring an IV drip of caffeine.

Lily frowned into her grande latte, two pumps of hazelnut, extra foam. "So, why do *you* think Rose fainted?"

I tried not to smile. Lily's streak of curiosity is just as wide as mine.

"Well, I did wonder if Rose has a notion about who the killer is. Like maybe her father."

"Her *father*? Why would he want to kill a sportswriter? Did Duvall say something bad about the team?"

"Worse than that. He insulted Walter's daughter in print." Our heads came together over the table, and I related Digger's crack about Rose having "little talent and less class."

"Nasty," Lily agreed. "Really nasty."

"There's something else, too. Eddie says that a big strong man like Boris wouldn't use a baseball bat. So we're looking for someone smaller or weaker than Duvall, like—"

"Wait a minute, we who?" Lily leaned back and frowned. "I was just making conversation."

"But—"

"No buts, Carnegie. Please. Let's get back to wedding business, OK? Let's talk dresses."

"Oh, all right." I was surprised at my own lack of enthusiasm. If I did have Bride Brain Virus, maybe it was wearing off. "So, what did you think of those gowns?"

"That third one was gorgeous, but . . ." She hesitated, then plunged ahead. Lily doesn't pull her punches. "Do you really want to spend that much? What's your budget for this wedding, anyway?"

"I'm not sure. With all the contacts I've got in the business, it's almost a shame *not* to have a big formal affair."

"But?"

I heaved a sigh. "But Aaron's pretty well tapped out because of his medical bills, and I'm not sure how I feel about starting our marriage deep in debt. Maybe a small simple wedding would be better."

"Is that what Aaron wants?"

"Who knows! I can't get him to sit down and talk about it."

"Of course not, with his grandfather in the hospital."

"No, even before that." I drained my cup and set it down. "And even when the World Series is over, I bet he won't care much about the details."

"Aren't all bridegrooms like that?"

"Mike wasn't."

She smiled fondly. "Mike is a detective, he is all about the details. Now come on, let's go find you a black T-shirt."

Chapter Fourteen

I found a black shirt, but as it turned out there was quite a bit of white on display at the party that night. White polyester lace, as a matter of fact.

Juice and I came in separate cars, and she was waiting for me at Club NocNoc's unimposing entrance on Second Avenue. I continued past, looking for a parking space long enough to maneuver Vanna into, and found one just a couple of blocks away.

I could hear the music as I got out of the van. When I joined Juice, NocNoc's doorway was almost visibly bulging from the intensity of the sound inside. We couldn't see in because the windows were plastered over with flyers that said ALL HAIL HONEYSUCKLE HELL.

Juice wasn't looking at them, though. She was looking at me, head to toe.

"Not bad, Kincaid. Not bad at all. You should loosen up more often."

With no real sense of the NocNoc fashion scene, I'd put on lots of eye makeup and fluffed my hair out to give it as much volume as possible—which was quite a bit. I don't usually do the midriff thing, but the T-shirt was on the short side and my jeans were fairly low slung, so what the hell.

"Thanks," I said drily. "I was trying to live up to your standard."

Juice cut a striking figure, of course. She had topped her usual short-shorts and cowboy boots with a heavy denim jacket stitched along the seams with dangling earrings, fishing lures, plastic doll parts, and other trinkets that quivered and swung at her every move.

"You pass," she said, grinning, and pulled open the door of the club.

Inside, NocNoc was a series of narrow high-ceilinged industrial-looking rooms, luridly lit by chandeliers with red bulbs. And each room was jammed to the walls with people far more stare-worthy than one slightly self-conscious wedding planner—or even her date.

Juice might be striking, but as she elbowed a lane for us past the bar and the pool table, toward the source of the tidal wave of cacophonous music, even Juice was overshadowed by the white-clad bodies all around us.

Brides! Dozens and dozens of brides.

In a punk salute to Honeysuckle Hell's impending union, many of her friends and colleagues in the music scene had plundered costume shops, Salvation Army stores, and maybe even their mother's attics for wedding gowns of all shapes and styles to wear to her party.

But not her *female* friends and colleagues, not in this crowd. The musicians doing violence to their instruments up on stage were all in black, and so were most of the women dancing, but almost half the drinkers and dancers at Rose's party were men wearing white dresses.

Juice and I halted at the edge of the dance floor, amazed.

"This is wild!" I shouted to her over the throbbing music, as I was jostled by a swaggering gent in Captain Hook hair, a waxed black mustache, and an off-the-shoulder satin number with ruffles down to the floor. "Pat Robertson's worst nightmare!"

"Coolio!" Juice shouted back. "Check him out."

She pointed at one muscular guy, shiningly bald and ornately tattooed, who'd assembled his fashion statement from a white crinoline half-slip, a puffy-sleeved blouse, and a pair of black high-tops with plastic carnations woven into the laces. He'd also come up with some elbow-length lace gloves that encased his hands like sausage skins.

And even he was outshone by a chubby fellow dancing near him in a peakaboo veil and a white vinyl bustier that dipped below his nipples. As I watched, Chubby, Baldy, and Captain Hook shouted with glee at one another's outfits, clinked their beer bottles in a toast, and danced on.

I was so busy taking in NocNoc's denizens, it took me a while to notice the details of the decor. The occasional framed paintings, for instance, that looked like family portraits from another dimension. And the ceiling, intermittently visible in the strobing red light, that was crisscrossed with barbed wire and adorned with scores of naked Barbie dolls.

NocNoc was weird weird, no doubt about it—and yet somehow I wasn't nearly as uncomfortable as I'd expected. In some ways, in fact, the atmosphere tonight was simpler and more good-natured than the competitive preening I'd seen at the more conventional engagement party Friday night. These people were bizarre-looking, but they were having a hell of a good time.

"Want a drink?" Juice bellowed over the music, and I nodded and groped in my purse. She stopped me with a hand on my arm. "My treat, Kincaid, since you got me in here. You do white wine, right? Watch for Rose for me."

I watched, from a marginally quieter corner of the room, but it wasn't hard to spot Honeysuckle Hell. She was the hub of noise and animation as she moved through the crowd. With every step, well-wishers clustered around her in a flurry of embraces and kisses and lively cries of congratulations.

In any other club in Seattle tonight, all this acclaim would be for the man beside her: Gordo Gutierrez, the Home Run King. But this wasn't a baseball crowd, and tonight was all about Honeysuckle Hell.

Gordo took the role reversal in stride, smiling his usual placid smile, unfazed by all the men in skirts. As for Rose, she was incandescent with happiness. She wore a micromini dress in flaming red patent leather, a pair of teeteringly tall platform shoes, and most flattering of all, a great big girlish grin.

"You came!"

She squealed the words and threw her arms around me in a beer-scented embrace. My bride was tipsy tonight, I could tell, but this wasn't the demolition drinking she'd been doing Friday night. This was straightforward high spirits, and since I found myself oddly fond of this particular bride, I was happy to hug her back.

"Look, Gordy, Carnegie came! She actually came!"

"Of course I did. How are you, Gordo?"

"Fine." The big *Dominicano* had no trouble pitching his voice loud enough to be heard. "Great music, huh?"

"Terrific." I didn't think I was bleeding from the ears yet, but it was just a matter of time. "Has the photographer arrived?"

"Oh, he came and went already." Gordo grinned broadly. "I don't think he liked the scene."

Damn. I tried to think of a diplomatic way to ask him if

Rose had behaved herself for the pictures. But Gordo read my mind.

"No worries," he said, while Rose was distracted by another wave of well-wishers. "He got some nice shots of me and Rosie and Rob."

"Rob is here?" I suddenly wished my T-shirt were more flattering.

"Yeah, he and some of the other Navs." He looked around and then waved one brawny arm over his head. "Yo, Charmin'! Over here!"

Suddenly Rob was beside us—and in men's clothing, thank heaven. Again, in another crowd the baseball fans would have been all over him, but the attention he was getting at NocNoc was strictly due to his looks. He wore a long-sleeved black knit shirt that fit beautifully against his muscles, snug black jeans, and black suede shoes.

Not that I was looking all that closely, you understand.

"Hey there, Carnegie," he said. "How are y'all doing after the other night? Nasty business."

He leaned in close so I could hear him, which didn't bother me one bit. I suppose a woman who's newly engaged should be oblivious to the male sex except for her one true love. But give me a break, I'd had a crush on Rob Harmon at a very impressionable age. Why shouldn't I appreciate both his looks and his personality now that I had the chance? My feelings weren't personal, they were . . . aesthetic.

"I'm fine," I told him. "Thanks for doing the photographs. Are you enjoying the party?"

"Wouldn't have missed it." He smiled that fabulous smile. "Gordo's got himself a wonderful girl."

Rose heard the comment and wrinkled her nose playfully at Rob. He wrinkled back, and Gordo beamed at them both.

Then we were joined by the two band members who had chased after Rose on the baseball diamond, and she made the introductions.

"Hi, JD. Hi, Nick. You know Rob, don't you? And have you met Carnegie? She's helping with the wedding."

Nick, the one with the outlandish haircut, looked me straight in the eye and shook my hand as if he were wearing a suit and running for office. What Eddie would call "a real operator." JD, of the unformed features and the wispy beard, nodded vaguely, but his dark yearning gaze was all for Rose.

I noticed, though, that she wouldn't meet his eyes. Was there trouble among the Fiends? We all kept up some small talk, or rather small shouting, but JD's focus on his lead singer was hard to ignore.

Finally Rose muttered something about the ladies' room and left us. Gordo followed her, looking concerned, while JD stared dolefully after them. Rob excused himself as well, and then JD drifted away, still without speaking a word.

"Cheerful, isn't he?" I commented.

"Don't mind JD," said Nick. "His old man just croaked."

"Oh, I'm so sorry. Was it . . . unexpected?"

"Totally!" Nick laughed, and then rearranged his face in a more decorous expression. "He was that ESPN dude who got whacked at the baseball party."

Chapter Fifteen

"JD is Digger Duvall's son?" The screaming guitars and throbbing drums made a background to my blank astonishment.

"Yeah. James Duvall, JD."

"Oh." I remembered the blond goddess on Digger's arm at the party. Way too young to be JD's mother, and, by the look of her, nobody's wife. "I didn't even know Digger was married."

"Oh, yeah. Treated his old lady like shit, though, from what JD says. Hey, look at Rose. She told us the Fiends weren't playing tonight, but I guess she can't resist."

Rose, having eluded JD, was now being coaxed up onstage. It didn't take much coaxing, though, after her initial hesitation. The crowd began chanting "Honey—suckle—HELL!" over and over, and by the third or fourth repetition she squealed again—I could hear it over the clamor—and threw herself into Gordo's arms.

He must have been expecting it, because he picked her up bodily and passed her over his head and onto the outstretched hands of her admirers. By this point people had packed the dance floor tight enough to give the guest of honor safe passage all the way onto the stage. Flushed and laughing, she reached her destination with a final scramble and a flash of hot-pink underpants. No business like show business.

Once on stage Rose stopped laughing and turned her back to the crowd. People began to quiet down. She struck a straddle-legged stance, plucked a microphone from its holder, and pointed one finger at the ceiling, keeping that pose until the silence was complete but for the muted buzz of voices from the barroom. The three musicians already on stage watched her, their instruments stilled.

We waited.

Rose McKinney was gone now. Honeysuckle Hell's arm swung down like a hammer, she snapped her head to one side to give us her profile, and then she lifted the mike to her curling lips and *sang*.

It was a song I didn't recognize, here at this club where I didn't belong, and I was transfixed. Hot, thick, quivering at the edge of control, Honeysuckle's voice lashed over us like the slash of a cat's claws.

The song was the cry of a woman betrayed, and she poured out phrase after phrase of furious defiance and reluctant lust. Then her voice sank into an anguished purr, a surrender, in words of love and longing.

The tempo picked up, Honeysuckle's left heel marking the time, and as she turned toward us, the drummer followed her lead with an insistent and hypnotic beat. Both guitarists filled in with chords, but only as a backdrop to that black velvet voice. Two more verses, a chorus, then the instruments fell away again as Honeysuckle unleashed a final crescendo, held the closing note impossibly long, and bowed limply from the waist, her passion spent.

The crowd went crazy. I'm pretty sure I did too, because

my throat was sore the next day. I know that when Nick threw his arms around me—everyone in the place was embracing—I gave as good as I got, and when we separated, we were both grinning like two people who've run a race together.

"Amazing," I croaked out. "Just—amazing."

"Yeah, that's the girl. She's too good for us, really, but don't tell her I said so."

Nick and I watched as Honeysuckle descended into Gordo's arms and the band on stage was replaced by another. As the euphoria of her singing ebbed away, my thoughts returned to the bombshell Nick had just dropped on me.

"So you were saying that JD and his father didn't get along?"

Nick shrugged, indifferent. "That's why he won't use a last name. He's just JD. You know, like Bono or whatever. The old man was loaded, but he wouldn't front us a dime when we were starting up the band. Cheap bastard."

"I, um, heard that Digger was pretty rough on Rose in his column. The band must have been unhappy about that too."

Another shrug. "Who cares what some lame sports guy says? Rose and the rest of us, we just laughed about it. Even Gordo shrugged it off. But yeah, JD was pretty pissed. He's had the hots for Rose from day one. Like she'd even look at him. How clueless can you get?"

A rhetorical question, so I didn't reply.

"Speaking of names, Carnegie's a cool name." Nick took a long pull on his beer. "Real unusual, like your hair. You got real pretty hair."

He reached out to touch it, and I stepped away, keeping my distance this time. But this was a young man unused to refusal.

"Can I get you a drink, Carnegie? C'mon, have a drink with me."

"No thanks," I said. "I've got one coming."

As if on cue, Juice arrived and passed me a sloshing tumbler.

"They're out of wine glasses. I drank my whole beer on the way, it took me so long to get through the crowd. Hey, you're lead guitar!" This to Nick, who was looking at her appraisingly—especially her QUEER AND PROUD button. "I love the Fiends, man. You gonna play tonight?"

"I don't think so," said Nick. Then he gave me the same appraising look. "Sorry, Carnegie. I didn't realize."

"Realize what?" I wondered as he moved away.

"He thinks you're with me!" Juice sniggered and poked me roughly in the ribs. "Want me to go tell him you're available? He looks like your type."

"You just leave well enough alone." I sipped doubtfully at my wine. It was warm and sour, and that helped me make up my mind. It would be nice to see more of Rob, but even so . . . "Listen, Juice, I'm off duty after all, and I don't think I can take the noise level in here much longer. Would you mind if I left early?"

"Nah, go ahead." She looked around in satisfaction. "This is the best party I been to in ages. I really owe you one."

"You can give me a break on my wedding cake."

I said it without thinking, but Juice gave me a startled glance. "*You're* getting married?"

"Is that so surprising?"

"No! No way. Who's the lucky hetero?"

"Aaron Gold. He's a reporter. I don't think you've met him."

"Well, good for you!" Juice slapped me on the back hard enough to spill my wine. Not that it was much of a loss. "I'll make you a terrific cake. When's the date?"

"We don't have one yet. Aaron's out of town right now so—"

But Juice was no longer listening. She was gazing past me at a foxy little green-haired girl in a tuxedo, and the girl was returning her gaze with compound interest.

"Whatever. See you later this week, Kincaid?"

"Later," I said to her retreating back. "Have fun."

As I edged my way through the mass of bodies, heading for the door, I thought about the people Digger Duvall had left behind. A wife he neglected and a son he treated with contempt, at least in my brief observation. Colleagues who despised him, and ballplayers who feared the reach of his poisoned pen. Presumably Digger's audience would miss him, but would anyone else?

Gordo was standing near the front door as I approached it, although the tight-packed mass of bodies made my approach a slow one.

"Leaving already?" he asked. "Here, let me help."

With his amiable smile and a hearty "Comin' through!" he plowed a channel through the crowd and held the door open for me.

"Thanks, Gordo. Tell Rose good night for me, would you?"

"Sure thing, Carnegie. It's good that you parked close. This isn't a great neighborhood."

"I'll be fine," I said. "See you later."

It was blissfully cool and uncrowded on Second Avenue, and even the traffic noise seemed muffled after the din inside the club. Or maybe the ringing in my ears drowned it out. I hurried along the sidewalk toward Vanna, eager to get home. At least I wasn't saturated with cigarette smoke, so I wouldn't have to shower and then go to bed with wet hair.

Washington State had made the national news when it banned smoking in *all* public places, even bars. The ban was an economic blow for certain businesses, but heaven sent for people like me who—

If I hadn't been so preoccupied with that thought, and so busy fumbling for my keys, I might have noticed right away that the passenger door on my van was slightly ajar. And I might have heard the person coming up behind me.

As it was, a violent shove between my shoulder blades took me completely off guard. As I crashed painfully onto my hands and knees on the pavement, I was barely aware of my purse being torn from my shoulder, and of the pounding footsteps that raced away into the night.

Chapter Sixteen

"It's an unfortunate coincidence, I'll give you that." Detective Kenneth Starkey had lank ginger hair, a long sardonic face, and heavily freckled forearms revealed by his rolled-up shirtsleeves. He folded his arms now and raised his ginger eyebrows at me. "But I don't see what it's got to do with the Duvall homicide."

"Coincidence!"

I slapped a palm on the edge of his desk, then snatched it back with a little hiss of pain. Both my hands were raw from where they'd scraped along the sidewalk last night, and my left knee had a bruise on it the size of a CD. To use my mother's exasperated phrase from my unruly childhood, I was in No Mood. I took a deep breath, counted to ten by tens, and tried to make my point again.

"Look, on Friday night I discovered a murder victim. Sunday my home was ransacked, and last night my van was broken into and my purse was snatched. You can't possibly think those are unrelated incidents."

Starkey took his own sweet time about consulting a paper on his desk. "Says here that your vehicle was unlocked, but nothing was missing or damaged. You sure you didn't just forget to lock it?"

"Of course I'm sure! The killer must have been searching

for something he thought I had, something that wasn't in my houseboat when he broke in there."

"And that would be what, exactly?"

This was the question I'd been asking myself all night—in between phone calls to cancel my credit cards and my cell phone service. I didn't have an answer.

"OK, I'm not sure. But whatever it is must be connected with the murder somehow."

"Uh-huh." He tipped back his desk chair and gazed at the ceiling. "Watch a lot of television, do you, Ms. Kincaid?"

"*Excuse* me?"

"Sometimes people go looking for clues and connections where there aren't any. They work up a theory and get all excited about it, and then they expect us to—"

"This isn't theory, it's fact! Boris and I both came onto the scene of a murder just after it happened. *He's* in jail, but *I'm* still being watched and burgled and mugged in the street. Doesn't that suggest to you that the killer is still on the loose?"

Big sigh from the long-suffering detective, and the chair legs bumped back to the floor.

"What this suggests to me, Ms. Kincaid, is that you've been the victim of two extremely common urban crimes. Like I said, an unfortunate coincidence. Now I know you think your Russian buddy is innocent, but—"

"Boris Nevsky is an American citizen," I said crisply. "And as I understand it, he's innocent until proven guilty."

"Yeah."

I waited but got no further reply.

"So I assume," I went on, "that you're working hard to find out who else might have killed Duvall. Aren't you?"

"Night and day."

Starkey had been humoring me, no doubt because I was a friend of his boss's, but now the sarcasm came through. He stood up and glanced at his watch.

"So if you'll excuse me, I'll get back to it. We've got your statements about the burglary and the assault, and we'll contact you if there are further developments."

Further developments my ass, I thought furiously on my way back to the houseboat. *That's the last time I'll ask him for help. I'll figure this out myself and make Starkey eat crow.* I had an uneasy thought about my promise to Aaron, but I shoved it aside. He was my fiancé, not my father, and this was my decision, dammit.

Tuesday was another remarkably warm Indian summer day, but the sunshine was lost on me. I was still in No Mood as I entered the Made in Heaven office, which made me less tolerant than usual of Eddie Breen's debonair charm.

"Where the hell have you been, sister?" He scowled over from his desk in the work room. "Half the morning's gone. You going to spend all your time playing bride now?"

"I've been busy getting mugged, if you want to know," I snapped. "I spent half the morning at police headquarters."

"You *what*?"

My desk was piled with paperwork. I lifted the uppermost folder from a toppling stack, then flung it down again.

"I don't have time for this, dammit! Boris is rotting in jail, and Rose's wedding is this weekend, and that Starkey was so snotty with me—"

"Don't, Carnegie. Don't cry." Eddie was at my side, offering a huge and spotless handkerchief. "Are you hurt? You need a doctor?"

"I'm not crying." I swabbed the tears from my face and

blew my nose noisily. "And I'm all right, I just got b-banged up a little. He shoved me and I fell."

"Son of a bitch. Well, sit down, for crying out loud. You look like something the cat dragged in. Did you get a look at him?"

I sat. "No, I didn't see him, and neither did anybody else. So I suppose the police can't do much with that. But I can't convince them that Digger's murderer is still out there. They won't even look for him!"

Eddie set his fists on his hips. "Then we'll have to do it ourselves."

"We?" I gave a final sniffle. "You'll help me with this? And not for just two hours?"

"Whaddya talking about, two hours? Of course I'll help you."

"Thank you, Eddie. Boris will really appreciate it."

"Never mind Boris," he grumped. "You think I'm going to let some son of a bitch get away with hurting you?"

"Oh, *Eddie*."

Dismayed by my detour into sentimentality, my partner stared out the window and worked his cigar from one side of his mouth to the other. Then he said to the glass, "Well, what are we waiting for? You want me to make more of those phone calls?"

I shook my head. "That's a dead end. Dozens of people had the opportunity to follow Digger into the hallway that night. So we've got to look at motive instead. I just heard about a new one last night."

As Eddie rolled his chair over to my desk, I told him about Digger's son and his reputedly neglected wife.

"The trouble is, JD left the party long before the murder, and Judy wasn't there at all. Besides, Digger's being a lousy family man would have been going on for years. Why pick that night to kill him?"

"Or that place, either," said Eddie. "Just as easy to do it at home. No, I'm betting the murder had something to do with this guy's work."

"You're probably right." I powered up my computer. "Tell you what, let's go online and look at Digger's columns. Maybe he trashed somebody who was at the party."

"What about this bride of yours? You said he got snide about her, and anybody can swing a bat."

"Rose is out," I said, my fingers clicking over the keyboard. "She left before the murder too. I put her in a cab myself. OK, here's an archive of his articles and radio transcripts."

Sportswriting is a language of its own, with specialized jargon and inside jokes and the assumption that if you didn't know the language yourself, you wouldn't be reading it in the first place. But even as an outsider, as we skimmed through screen after screen, I could tell that Digger Duvall was a talented columnist and a perceptive observer of the sport.

He was certainly opinionated enough, and cocksure about every single one of his opinions—no matter who got hurt. With no room for doubt, let alone compassion, Digger had dissected and then ridiculed the recent performances of a coach for the Yankees, a catcher with the White Sox, and most of the Detroit Tigers' starting lineup. He was an equal opportunity critic, eviscerating careers in the American League and National League alike.

The phone rang as we were reading, and I picked it up absently.

"*Mon dieu,* are you mad?" said a rich, resonant, and unpleasantly familiar voice.

I rolled my chair away from the computer and gestured at Eddie to keep skimming the columns.

"What's the problem, Beau?"

"There is no problem except you! I have planned this wedding perfectly, all goes perfectly, and then you 'arass Monsieur Theroux's guests with your idiotic phone calls!"

I winced. Apparently the alibi-checking Eddie and I did yesterday had filtered back to my temporary boss.

"I was only trying to—"

"To what? To do the work of the police?"

"Beau, you know Boris Nevsky. You don't think he's a murderer, do you?"

The Frenchman's voice rose half an octave. "I have a wedding to conduct. I do not think of him at all! And you must stop thinking also. Do you wish to be terminated?"

This was a serious threat. I gripped the phone. "You owe me money, Beau, and I expect—"

"There will be no money if you do not cease to ask about the murder. Is that understood?"

"All right, all right. It's understood."

I understand, I just don't agree. I hung up the phone and rolled my eyes at Eddie. "Remind me never to work for him again."

"I already told you that!"

"Tell me again next time, only louder. Find anything else?"

"Just these mentions of Honeysuckle Hell." Eddie worked his cigar some more. "What's he got against the girl, anyway? It's one thing if he doesn't like her singing. I bet I wouldn't either. But this sounds like a personal grudge."

"Knowing Digger, I'd guess that he tried to impress her, and she blew him off. He'd hate that."

I leaned back from the screen and ran my pencil around

Digger's name on the pad in front of me. It had a few other names on it, Leroy Theroux and Walter McKinney and a handful of ballplayers from other teams who hadn't even been at the engagement party. Mostly the sheet was covered with doodles. Discouraged, I let the pencil drop.

"We aren't much farther along, are we? We know that the slurs about Rose infuriated her father. Maybe Gordo too, although he didn't seem upset with Digger at the party. And your idea about only a weak person using a bat for a weapon lets Gordo out anyway."

"I dunno," said Eddie doubtfully. "Would insulting the girl really push her father to murder? And why that particular night? The columns about her ran weeks ago."

"Yeah, way in the past. But . . . wait a minute—" I grabbed up the pencil again and drew a big question mark. "But what about the future?"

"Huh?"

"What about the columns that Digger hadn't written yet? What if he was planning a story that would damage someone at the party, and they found out about it?"

"That's your best idea yet," said Eddie. "Somebody killing Duvall to protect themselves, not just to get back at him for something. Trouble is, how do we find out what kind of stories he was working on?"

"By using my next best idea." I reached for the phone book and pulled it open to the D's. "I doubt that Digger discussed his work with his son. So I'm going to pay a sympathy visit to Mrs. Duvall."

Chapter Seventeen

The widow Duvall was not what I expected.

Extrapolating backward from Digger's arm candy at the engagement party, and with his son JD's appearance in mind, I'd pictured a dowdy older lady with darkly graying hair and a mousy personality. So I grabbed myself some lunch and drove to the upscale suburb of Lake Forest Park with that picture in mind.

But when I knocked on the door of the three-car-garage mini-mansion, I found a handsome fiftyish blonde in a cashmere twinset and impressive pearls. She looked me up and down with something like amusement.

"You're not his usual type, are you? More height and less chest. Want a drink?"

Startled but curious, I followed her inside. The interior was big and bland and in the midst of a makeover. The living room furniture was clustered together like sheep being herded by aluminum painters' ladders, and the beige walls were bare and patched with spackle. A row of uncurtained windows looked onto a big swimming pool, covered up for the season, and beyond that to a flat expanse of grass being worked over by a crew of landscapers.

"I'm having roses and a grape arbor put in," said the lady of the house over her shoulder, as she progressed around a curving granite counter and into the beige-walled kitchen. "Donald called it a putting green out there, but that was a joke. He never used it. And he had no sense of color, none at all, so now I'm getting my burgundy living room after all. And maybe a textured sort of terra cotta color in the kitchen, I haven't decided. Do you want ice? It's not very cold."

She held up an open bottle of chardonnay. Her own glass was on the counter, a deep crystal goblet garlanded with lipstick marks.

"Nothing for me, Mrs. Duvall. I just—"

"Judy, for God's sake. Let's not stand on ceremony." She recharged her glass. "So what are you looking for, money or forgiveness? The last one wanted both."

"I don't understand. The last one of what?"

"Donald's whores." She tossed back a healthy slug and gestured us both to a couple of stools at the counter. "You girls have been coming out of the woodwork. Don't tell me you didn't know about each other."

"But I'm not— Look, I barely knew your husband. I just wanted to express my condolences."

"Why, if you didn't know him?"

Good question. "Well, because I found his, um, I found him, and I was thinking about you, so . . ."

She drank again, staring at me over the rim of the glass. Her hazel eyes were shrewd and held no trace of weeping.

"You don't seem too upset," I blurted.

She shrugged. "That's because I'm not. Donald went his way, I went mine. What can I say?"

But I was more concerned with what *I* could say, now that I knew she wasn't grieving.

"Can I be honest with you?" I asked.

"Were you planning on lying?"

Not at all what I expected. "Candid, then."

"Ah." She swirled the wine in her glass. "By all means."

I plunged in. "Judy, a very dear friend of mine was arrested for your husband's murder. His name is—"

"Nevsky, I know. The police say he was blind drunk, so that should lighten his sentence, don't you think?"

"But he didn't do it! And whoever *did* do it has been shadowing me. You see, I'm a wedding planner . . ."

I explained about my role at the engagement party, and my friendship with Boris, and then described the break-in. When I got to the mugging, her eyes widened.

"But that's terrible!" Maybe it was the wine, or my lack of chest, but I could feel her coming over to my side. "And you have no idea who's been doing this?"

"I was hoping you'd help me figure that out. Was your husband working on a story that might have harmed someone in the baseball world? Some kind of scandal?"

Judy laughed scornfully. "Donald was always searching for a scandal. Or creating one, if he could swing it. He was a player himself, did you know that?"

"Really? Who for?"

"Oh, some minor league team in some podunk town." She took another swallow. "He never made it to the majors, even though he kept at it till he was almost thirty-five. The man adored baseball, and baseball spat in his face."

"Surely not," I protested. "He was terrifically successful as a baseball writer."

"I suppose so. But watching all those spoiled young men getting millions of dollars must have been galling to him."

"Did he talk about that?"

"He didn't talk to me about anything. But . . ."

"But?"

Another little laugh, almost flirtatious, and she tossed her head as if to fling aside the long hair that had vanished with her youth. Judy Duvall had once been arm candy herself, I was sure of it.

"I did overhear some of his phone calls," she admitted. "He'd forget I was even in the house."

"And you heard something recently? Something about the Seattle team?"

She hesitated. I held my breath, watching her decide how far to take this. *Come on, Judy, help me out here.* I could hear the kitchen clock ticking, and the scrape and clang of shovels in the backyard. One of the workmen called to another, and she started slightly. Then she spoke.

"Now that you ask, I think he *was* developing a story about the Navigators. A big one too. I could hear it in his voice when he called his editor the other day. He was practically cackling." She blinked at her wine glass, surprised to find it empty already. "Are you sure you won't join me?"

"Well, why not?" *Anything to prime the pump.* I fetched myself a goblet and refilled hers. "What was Digger, I mean Donald, what was he cackling about, do you know? One of the players, or the management? Did he mention names?"

"Oh, no names, not him. Donald never told anyone who his targets were until he turned a story in. He said he was afraid of being scooped, but I think he just liked to hug his little secrets to himself. Would you believe he kept those notebooks of his under lock and key? As if anyone would bother to read them!"

And how would you know, I thought, *unless you tried to yourself?*

"Did you get a sense of what this big story was about?" I

took a modest sip of wine. "The Navs had a pretty good season, so—"

"It wasn't about anyone's playing, I don't think. It sounded like more of an exposé. About someone who was riding high, because Donald said something about 'bringing him down' or 'taking him down.'"

"'Riding high?'" I echoed, thinking hard.

Judy drained her glass and placed it next to mine. Her aim was off and the goblet wobbled, so I reached out to steady it. She didn't seem to notice.

"That could be anybody," she said, starting to slur. "They're all so full of themselves, these athletes. The money they make is obscene. Millions of dollars, for what? Hitting a ball with a stick."

We were veering off course, but I didn't try to steer her back. Judy had already told me all she knew.

Unless . . . "Tell me, do you have your husband's notebooks?"

"I have all of his trash!"

She gestured sloppily toward a hallway that opened off the living room, knocking over both our glasses in the process. They struck the granite surface and shattered like eggs. Judy cried out in alarm, then stared dully at the puddled shards.

"Oh. I shouldn't have done that."

"Not a problem," I said. "No, don't touch it."

I didn't trust her not to cut herself. A pair of matching dish towels hung over the handle of the oven, so I tugged one off, picked up a plastic wastebasket, and cautiously swept the heap of razor-edged fragments into it.

"Judy, where's your garbage can? I'll take this straight out."

She mumbled something about the garage, so I bore the wastebasket out there and dumped it safely into a bag-lined can. The can and a set of recycling crates, just like mine back at the houseboat, stood next to a silver Lexus whose license plate read JUDYD.

When I came back, the kitchen was empty.

"Judy?" I heard movement behind a closed door in the hallway that must be the powder room. "Judy, are you all right?"

"Fine." Her voice sounded woozy. "Won't be long."

That seemed doubtful, but I waited a few minutes, and then a few more. And then I tiptoed down that same hallway to look for Digger's office. His widow was being helpful so far, but drunks are fickle. So just in case she changed her mind...

The office was beige like the rest of the house, but its walls were anything but bare. Framed photographs covered every surface, from the walls to the bookcases to the top of the oversize reproduction roll-top desk. Each picture featured a different celebrity, mostly sports figures but also the occasional actor or politician. And every single celebrity was shaking hands or trading grins with the late, great Digger Duvall.

The photographs had one more thing in common, though. Someone had smashed the glass on every single one.

Chapter Eighteen

"She claimed that JD smashed the pictures, but I don't know, Eddie. That is one bitter woman."

"Bitter enough to kill the guy herself?"

"*What?*" I almost choked on my beer. "Judy wasn't even at the party!"

Eddie and I were out on my deck in the surprising warmth of late afternoon, conferring over a couple of bottles of Moose Drool Ale. He rarely entered my private quarters, but once I got back from Lake Forest Park, he'd insisted on helping me buy a new cell phone. His offer sprang less from generosity than from distrust of my technological know-how, but afterward I'd insisted that he come in for a drink.

"I don't mean Judy Duvall personally," he said now, squinting against the glare off the lake. Eddie's been squinting into the sun his whole life, but he thinks sunglasses are for sissies. "You can always hire some thug for a job like that, though. And it sounds like she's a lot better off without her husband."

I shook my head. "A hired thug couldn't have gotten inside the stadium. The doors were locked."

"You sure of that?"

"Sure I'm sure. I just wish I'd found Digger's notebook. Who knows what it might have told us?"

Judy Duvall, once she emerged from the powder room, had willingly shown me the contents of Digger's desk. One drawer was filled with small reporters' notebooks, rubber-banded together by year—but the most recent one was missing.

"Maybe the cops found it and kept it," Eddie ventured.

"No, Judy said they gave her back his keys and wallet. If they'd found something they wanted to keep as evidence, they would have told her."

Eddie made his hmphing noise, then we sat in silence for a while. A squadron of Canada geese came paddling by, leaving overlapping wakes on the still water, their white chinstraps bright and tidy against their tall black necks. Good-looking birds, but they pooped on my deck.

The goslings sure are cute, though, I thought, letting my mind slip out of gear and coast for a while. *Little yellow fluff balls with tiny beaks that—* I sat bolt upright in my deck chair.

"Oh, no." I'd just remembered something. "Oh, *no.*"

"What?" Eddie looked at me sharply. "Come on, spit it out."

"When Walter and I put Rose in a cab," I said reluctantly, "and then went back inside, I meant to check that the door locked behind me. But I was in a hurry to catch up with Walter, and I didn't. What if the killer came in from the street?"

"Did you tell the cops about this?"

"No! It just came back to me now. I suppose I should tell Starkey, but—"

"But he'd just say that no one else could have known that the door would be unlocked. And he'd be right."

"I suppose." I recalled Starkey's crack about my watching too much television. "But he's not right about Boris, and I'm not telling him a damn thing. Want another beer?"

"No, time for me to shove off. How are the McKinney flowers coming along, with Nevsky locked up?"

"I'll find out tomorrow when I go to the studio. The basic designs weren't too complicated, so the Sergeis should be able to handle it." I smiled at him. "It's Beau's wedding anyway, not ours. How come you care?"

"I don't!" He planted his fists on his hips. "But if this wedding doesn't go right, the Frenchman's going to make sure the blame lands on Made in Heaven. You know that, don't you?"

"I know, Eddie," I said, my shoulders sagging. "I know."

"All right then. You going to be OK tonight?"

Coming from Eddie, this was an outpouring of tender concern.

"I'll be fine. Why shouldn't I be?"

He shrugged. "No reason. Just with Gold out of town—"

"For heaven's sake, I lived without Aaron for years. I think I can manage a few nights here and there."

Brave words, but once Eddie was gone and my microwave lasagna was eaten, I contemplated my evening rather glumly. I washed the dishes and then checked the time. Aaron was supposed to call tonight, but it was already getting late in Miami, so he probably wouldn't. Maybe it was just as well, since I'd have to skate over most of what I'd done since we spoke yesterday morning.

And what had been done to me. Aaron would be home soon enough, and there was no point getting him worried about purse-snatchers before then. I wandered into the living room and closed the drapes against the darkness, then turned on the TV. I should have been reviewing my notes about Rose's wedding—there was something I was supposed to check on, though I couldn't think what it was—but first I wanted to zone out for a while.

Meanwhile there were the good old Chicago Cubs again, trying their hardest to make hell freeze over and win the World Series. Hell was looking pretty warm, though. The Minnesota Twins were playing at home, and with their fans cheering them on, they were shutting down the visitors with a vengeance. Third inning, and the score was already 5–0 against the Cubbies.

I fetched what was left of my coffee ice cream and curled up on the couch to watch. But my conscience kept nagging at me. *Was it something about the flowers? No, those are all set. The limos? They're already scheduled. Oh, to hell with it.*

Whatever it was I needed to do for McKinney/Gutierrez, I'd think of it in the morning. The Twins' pitcher was fearsome in his concentration, staring down each batter with eyes like lasers and showing not a twitch of emotion as he struck them out one after another.

I wondered what it was like to have that kind of focus, to shut out the world and bend events to your will while thousands of people screamed at you. Next to that kind of aggressively relentless control, wedding planning was a walk in the park.

I was scraping the bottom of the carton when I heard voices at the door, and a knocking that made my windows shiver. *Not the Killer B's again,* I thought in dismay. *I could pretend I'm not home, but they'll have heard the TV.* The knocking came again, and the sound of laughter. *Well, maybe I can use a laugh.* I pitched the carton in the trash on my way through the kitchen and pulled open the door, remembering at the last minute that I was supposed to use the peephole. Too late.

"Boris!" I could hardly believe it was him. "Boris, you're out! I mean, come in!"

I couldn't get another word out, smothered as I was in a classic Nevsky bear hug. This involved serious stress on the ribcage, and one's feet leaving the floor. Only when Boris put me down in the kitchen did I realize that all three Buckmeisters had followed him inside. It was like playing host to a herd of buffalo, all of them talking and laughing at once.

Boris's voice rose above the din. "I am free man, my Kharnegie! I am outbailed by these good friends!"

"Out *on* bail," corrected Betty, gazing happily upward at all the oversize figures in the room. "Are you surprised, dear? We wanted to surprise you."

"I'm astonished," I said, laughing with them, "and absolutely delighted."

"We thought you would be." Bonnie's round black eyes, so like her mother's, twinkled merrily. "I said, Father, she is going to be just amazed. Didn't I say that, Father?"

"You surely did, honey."

The three of them went on congratulating one another at top volume, while I shut off the TV and took Boris aside. "Are you hungry? Should we go out and get you some dinner to celebrate?"

"*Nyet,* I do not stay. I must sleep. A man cannot sleep in that terrible place." Boris was indeed haggard-looking, even weaving on his feet a little. "But I had to see you first, my Kharnegie. Tomorrow you come to the studio and approve flowers for baseball wedding?"

"I'll be there with bells on."

"What bells?"

"Never mind, I'll just be there. Buck? Buck!" I had to tug

on the Texan's sleeve to get his attention. "Boris needs to go home now. Can you take him?"

"Course we can, little lady," he boomed. "We just stopped in to—say, is that your telephone? You go right ahead and answer, we'll let ourselves out. C'mon now, Boris. Ladies, out we go!"

I shut the door behind them, happily dazed, and picked up the phone.

"What's happening, Stretch?"

"Aaron!" I said the first thing on my mind. "Guess what, Boris is out on bail."

"Oh?"

At the chill in his voice, I rushed to add, "Buck Buckmeister put up the bail money. Isn't that great? I didn't even know it was happening until he showed up on my doorstep tonight."

"Sorry to interrupt the party."

"He's not here now, idiot. The Killer B's brought him by to surprise me, but they've left. What's happening there? Has Frances come?"

"Yeah, we've been watching the game in Izzy's room. I'm glad she's here—I'm pretty wiped out." Aaron's voice relaxed a bit, and I realized I could hear hospital noises in the background. "I just wanted to catch you before it got too late."

"I'm glad you did. Still coming home tomorrow?"

"Tomorrow night, late. I've got a layover in the Twin Cities. It was the best I could get on short notice, but I'm going to miss game four, so could you record it for me?"

"Sure, no problem." We were being polite with each other, which always made me nervous. "Will I see you, or—?"

"I'd better go straight to my place. But I'll be over bright and early Thursday for our hike."

That was better. "Terrific. I'll make us the best picnic lunch you ever had."

"You mean make as in *buy*, right? I'm not sure I can hike and eat your cooking on the same day."

"Ha, ha." Better yet. My cooking wasn't that bad, but if Aaron could needle me about it, we were on safer ground. "I'll *buy* us a wonderful picnic, wiseguy. Be nice to me, or I'll forget to record your game."

"You could sure forget tonight's game," he said ruefully. "Are you watching?"

"I've been busy with Buckmeisters."

"Understood. Well, the Cubs were down eight–zip when I left. Maybe a miracle will happen and they'll rally. I pity the poor bastards if they finally get into the Series and then blow it. They've got a solid pitcher for tomorrow night, though—"

"Aaron, can you hold on? I think someone's at my door."

I looked through the peephole this time: nobody. Then as I turned away, I heard another little *rat-a-tat*. So I opened up, and there was Betty Buckmeister, too short to show up, holding out something in her hand. Something I stared at in shock.

" 'Scuse me, dear," she said, "but I made Father turn the car right around so I could give you this. He found it on the floor after that party, and we thought maybe there was a central lost and found, but when he called Yesler Field they said that for private functions the person who scheduled the event usually collected these things—"

I tried to stem the tide. "Betty—"

"—and we thought that would be you, so Father meant to give it to you and then he kept forgetting! I always say that man doesn't have a memory, he has a forgettery."

I nodded and smiled as she prattled away, and when she finally left I closed the door mechanically. Just as mechanically, I picked up the phone and finished my conversation with Aaron.

Then I sat down at my kitchen table and began reading the little brown notebook written by the late unlamented Digger Duvall.

Chapter Nineteen

That damn notebook kept me up most of the night.

The handwriting was tiny and cramped, and Digger used a sort of personal shorthand that made very little sense to me. After the first hour or so of scrutinizing the dog-eared pages, my eyes were crossing and my brain was blank.

I got up and wandered from room to empty room, finally turning on the television just for company. The game was still going, and the Cubs were still getting pounded. I knew just how they felt.

I tried calling Eddie, to see if he could come over to help. But when his typically Eddie message came on—"Breen residence, leave your number and don't mumble!"—I hung up and went back to wandering. Should I call Aaron? No, we'd just argue about my getting involved with the investigation. And Lily had put herself firmly out of bounds. I was striking out right along with the Chicago batters.

At last the Cubs went down to defeat, 10–0. That put the Series at two games to one against them, in a best-of-seven contest. They still had a chance to win the Series, of course, but you could see them losing heart as the game went on.

Aaron was right, it would feel like hell to make it to the World Series for the first time in decades and then blow it. The pitiless TV cameras zoomed right into the losers' dugout, lingering on their bleak eyes and tightly clamped lips. Poor bastards. I slumped on the couch in discouragement.

Then I frowned at myself and hit the OFF button on my remote. Why on earth was I identifying so closely with a bunch of highly paid young strangers in Chicago? I had work to do here in Seattle.

I tried Eddie again, with no luck. He was probably downtown playing pool, his most frequent nighttime activity beside going to cheesy blockbuster movies with me. I saw art films and ate sushi with Lily or Aaron, but Eddie and I watched car crashes and aliens while feeding our faces with candy-counter junk.

Smiling at the thought, I opened the notebook again—and soon quit smiling. These squiggles and abbreviations could mean anything at all, there was no way to tell . . . *Wait a minute. Of course there's a way.* I could take the notebook to my computer upstairs and compare Digger's notes to his published columns. *Why didn't I think of that before?*

Outside the houseboat the evening air was cool and still and tasted like salt. I locked the front door carefully behind me, mindful of my possible failure to do so at the stadium the night of the murder. Just the word *murder* forming in my mind sent me tap-dancing fast up the outer steps, to pause on the landing and scan the dock nervously.

The other houseboats were quiet, just a few windows alight. There was no one around except a solitary gray cat perched on Larry Halloway's front windowsill. It made a humped-up silhouette against the flickering blue television glow. Then as I watched, it morphed into a long fluid shape that dropped to his deck and melted into the shadows.

I slipped into the office and turned the deadbolt, annoyed to find myself breathing hard, my heartbeat fast and fluttery. *Calm down.* Whoever the murderer was, he couldn't possibly know that I now had the notebook he'd been searching for.

I thought it over. Clearly the killer must have called the stadium's lost and found number just as Buck had done and gotten my name and address. Then he ransacked my home and followed me to NocNoc to search my van and finally my purse.

But he's given up on me by now, so calm down.

Soon I had something to distract me from my anxiety: synchronizing Digger's scribbles with his finished works was harder than I expected. I wasn't sure how far back to go—the notebook pages weren't dated—but finally I found an article that matched up with the first entries in the notebook.

Eureka! That gave me a kind of translation key, and the scribblings made more and more sense as I riffled the pages, making my own notes as I sorted out Digger's pattern of abbreviations. Nothing was written out in full except the occasional proper name for accurate spelling—not nicknames, but first, last, and even middle—and those became initials after the first mention.

Gordon Jesus Gutierrez, for example, appeared early in the notebook with the "rr" circled, and only as GG after that. I noted that down and kept going. Crouched in the pool of light from my desk lamp, surrounded by the night-blackened windows of my office, I felt like a code breaker in some old war movie. All I needed was a big-shouldered dress and a date with Alec Guinness.

As I flipped faster and faster through the little book, Digger's secretive and malicious personality seemed to seep from the pages like a bad odor. I could feel his glee at documenting one player's pattern of choking up, or uncovering a dirty personal secret about another.

There were less inflammatory pieces as well, about team-hopping general managers and front office strategies. One of these threw me, until I realized that it didn't correlate to the notebook at all. Apparently Digger could write about the voting process for the Baseball Hall of Fame off the top of his head, without notes.

That piece was interesting to me, because I'd never understood who did the Hall of Fame voting. It's professional baseball writers with at least ten years of experience, and a very picky group they are. Of the thousands of men who ever played in the majors, only two hundred or so have been enshrined in the sacred hall. In these times of proliferating awards and cheapened honors, I thought, this particular Hall of Fame was a true elite.

But that didn't get me any further in my search for suspects, so I went back to work. At last I reached the final half-dozen pages of the notebook, followed by the blank sheets that would never be filled. These pages didn't correlate to anything that had yet been published, but I had developed enough of a glossary of Digger's shorthand to try and ferret out their meaning.

And perhaps a clue to the murder.

GG showed up here a couple of times, so at first I wondered if this unwritten story was about Gordo's wedding. But Rose—or Honeysuckle—wasn't mentioned, nor was anything else wedding-related that I could decipher. Mostly there were dates and times and addresses, for interviews perhaps, and the names or initials of various other Navigators.

LT was there without being spelled out, but that would be

Leroy Theroux. "LT knows????" it said, each question mark
bigger than the last. Knows what? I wondered. Theroux was
the Navs general manager, so presumably he'd know just
about everything that went on with the team. But what in
particular?

Another, rather odd name appeared for the first time,
printed out in block letters: DECA DURABOLIN. That sounded
eastern European, but I'd never heard of him. Or her? Deca
might be female, but there weren't many women of note in
baseball. Of course I was hardly a walking baseball encyclo-
pedia, so I ran a Google search on the name, carefully tap-
ping in the odd spelling.

The search results made me sit back in my chair to stare
openmouthed at my own pale reflection in the window glass.
Instead of citations to baseball articles, what appeared was a
column of medical texts, with a sidebar of ads from sleazy-
sounding mail-order pharmacies.

Deca Durabolin wasn't a person. It was a drug.

I knew a little about the steroid scandal that had shaken
major league baseball a few years back, with reverberations
that reached all the way up to hearings in Congress. But I
learned a lot more as I skimmed through one Web page after
another.

It was a sad and sordid tale. Muscle-pumping steroids like
this Deca stuff had been banned from baseball, but not before tainting the record-breaking careers of several marquee
players. Now anyone suspected of "juicing" himself with
drugs was guilty till proven innocent, at least in the mind of
the public.

Violations of the ban carried heavy penalties in terms of
suspension or even expulsion from the league. So if Digger

had turned up evidence that someone on the Navigators was using—

Wait a minute. Record-breaking?

What about Gordo Gutierrez's all-time home run record? That would be tainted, or maybe even disqualified, if it could be shown that he had used steroids. *Not Gordo,* I protested silently. *Surely Digger wasn't going after Gordo.* But then I turned a page and saw it, heavily printed and underlined twice: "GG/DD??"

I turned away from my computer, feeling queasy.

"Something about bringing someone down," Judy Duvall had said. Even the suspicion that Gordo's home run performance was drug-enhanced would bring him down in a big way—and create a public relations catastrophe for the Navigators.

But never mind the Navigators. *What about Rose?* I blew out a breath and raked my hands through my hair. The real catastrophe here would be for Rose. If Gordo was using illicit drugs—if Gordo was a *murderer*—what would that do to her?

I'm usually fond of my brides, except for a few monsters of ego, but Rose McKinney had really gotten to me. The aching sense of loss from her mother's death that she tried so hard to hide. Her discomfort with the badly fitting tough-girl persona that she put on as Honeysuckle Hell. And on top of that her extraordinary voice—Rose was a remarkable girl.

And she trusted me, I could tell, though she wasn't a girl who trusted easily. How would she feel if I destroyed the myth of her gentle and beloved Gordo?

But maybe it isn't a myth?

I went over to the window, confronting my reflection,

arguing with myself. Maybe Digger was just speculating, fishing for scandal, looking for mud to sling at the man who'd reached the pinnacle in a sport that had rejected him.

I had only Digger's suspicions to go on, after all. It wasn't as if I'd seen Gordo searching my houseboat, or checking out my van when it was parked at—

Parked.

Suddenly I remembered something, and the thought of it gave me a cold shiver. Gordo had been standing near the door of NocNoc when I left, and he'd made some comment about parking.

"It's good that you parked close"—that was it. *But how did he know where I'd parked?* Had he been out to the van already, to break in and search for the notebook? Had he followed me out to grab my purse, had he been watching my houseboat— was he watching me now?

"Stop it!" I said aloud. I was getting tied up in paranoid knots inside my own head. "Just stop it."

I sat down again and took some deep slow breaths. Was I getting carried away with all this? Quite a few athletes had been accused of steroid use in the recent past, and none of them had committed murder. Maybe I was blowing the idea way out of proportion.

I thought about what to do next. OK, so Gordo was a possible suspect in Digger's murder. Should I call Detective Starkey? *No way, he'd never listen.* What else, then? Find out more about Gordo and drugs, obviously. Ask someone with expertise, someone discreet who was outside the Navigators organization.

Someone like Holly Crider! With a sigh of relief, I looked up the phone number of the downtown condo that she and her bridegroom had bought.

"Hi, it's Carnegie. Have you got a few minutes?"

Holly sounded harried. "I don't have one single minute, Carnegie. I'm on deadline, and I leave for Minneapolis tomorrow to cover games four and five. The cheap old *Sentinel* actually came up with some travel money, just for these two games. I'll catch you when I get back."

"It's kind of important, Holly. If I could just—"

"Hang on, would you? I've got another call."

I waited.

"That was my editor again, I've got to go." Then she hesitated. "Really important?"

"Really, really."

"All right, I can take a little time after my run in the morning before I head to the airport. Can you make it to the Market around seven?"

"I'll be there," I told her. "Meet you at the pig."

Then I went straight downstairs and got into bed. But I didn't sleep.

Chapter Twenty

Rachel the Pig is a life-size bronze sculpture, a piggybank for charity, and a landmark at the Pike Place Market. Instead of meeting someone "in that spice shop where we went that time," or "by that stall where we got the great raspberries," you just say "Meet you at the pig," and there you are. Rachel stands squat and four-square at the crossroads of the main market buildings, smiling her piggy smile, and she's unmissable.

Holly Crider was already hanging around Rachel when I arrived. She wore running clothes, and despite the morning chill her cropped dark hair was damp with sweat.

"Mind if we walk?" she said, still breathing hard. "I need to cool down some before I head for the airport."

There was no shortage of walking space. The market covers nine acres of sloping land between First Avenue and the waterfront, with a subterranean maze of shops and stairways underneath. We passed Pike Place Fish, where they sling whole salmon through the air to fill your order, and headed down the wide aisle of tables devoted to fresh produce.

Most of the craft and curio shops would be shuttered for a while yet, but the cobblestones of Pike Place were rumbling with trucks and bustling with deliverymen as the farmers and flower vendors began to set out their wares. Their brisk instructions and friendly greetings filled the air, along with the aroma of coffee poured from Thermoses and hot cinnamon rolls from the cafés across the street.

Holly walked quickly, so I matched her long stride with my own. Or tried to—her cool-down was practically a workout for me.

"So what's up?" she said as we strode past gleaming ranks of apples and tumbles of golden squash and sheaves of chrysanthemums and strawflowers. "What's really, really important?"

Now that the moment had come, I wasn't quite sure how to frame my question.

"I, um, need to ask you something. But strictly in confidence."

She glanced at her watch and kept striding. "Shoot."

A squeaky-wheeled dolly stacked with fruit crates came rolling toward us, pushed by a grinning woman in coveralls, and I had to wait as Holly and I dodged to either side of it. Once we reunited, I took the plunge.

"Have you ever heard anything about Gordo Gutierrez using steroids?"

It was as though I'd suddenly caught on fire. Holly stopped and stared at me, her mouth open and her eyes wide.

"Holy heaven, Carnegie, don't say that kind of thing in public!"

She grabbed my elbow and steered me out of the building, across Western Avenue, and onto grassy little Victor Steinbrueck Park, named for the architect who helped save the market from demolition back in the 1960s. There were only a few people around, and the traffic roar from the

Alaskan Way Viaduct below us guaranteed that they couldn't eavesdrop.

"The answer is no," Holly told me, her voice low and urgent. "And the question is, what on earth made you ask?"

"Strictly in confidence?" I said again. "I mean completely strictly, Holly. No notes, no follow-up queries to other people. Not one word to anyone."

She hesitated, her dark brows drawn together and her lower lip caught in her teeth. But the hesitation didn't cause me to doubt her. On the contrary, Holly Crider was taking her time and making a serious decision.

She stared unseeing at the view, which was well worth seeing. The October morning mist had begun to disperse over Elliott Bay, unveiling the snowy Olympics on the western horizon. To the south, beyond the viaduct and the arch of Yesler Field's retractable roof, the grand blue-white pyramid of Mount Rainier was taking shape. I admired it while I waited.

"OK," said Holly at last, with a sharp resolute nod of her head. "For you, not one word to anyone. Now tell me what's going on."

I told her, as briefly as I could, about my search for Digger's killer. I almost brought out the notebook to show her—it was zipped securely into my purse, with the strap securely slung across my chest—but somehow I didn't want to be seen in public with it. You never knew who was watching.

Holly listened to my tale without interruption—and without advising me to let the police handle it.

"So you see," I concluded, "if Digger really did turn up some evidence of steroid use, I can't help wondering if—"

"If Gordo Gutierrez is a murderer?"

Stated out loud like that, it sounded shocking.

"I know," I said miserably. "He's the sweetest guy in the world, and it's crazy even to imagine it. But somebody killed Digger, and it wasn't Boris Nevsky. I'm just wondering how likely it is that Gordo's been using steroids."

She sighed. "It's possible, of course. He showed phenomenal power this last season. But Gordo's always been powerful, and players these days have the benefit of highly scientific training."

"Rotational mechanics," I said, remembering Rose's demonstration.

Holly smiled a little. "You've been doing your homework. Yeah, there's a really technical approach now to hitting the ball. They call it 'bat swing science.' Three-D computer modeling of the ideal hitter, statistical analysis of pitch speed and angles, the whole nine yards. And of course players work with nutritionists and do targeted weight training. Babe Ruth used to spend the off season shooting pool and boozing. It's a different game today."

"So you think Gordo broke the home run record without any chemical help?"

"That's what I think, and what I want to believe. But there's no way to know for sure. Let's move over there."

She led the way to a bench, propped one foot on it, and began doing hamstring stretches with her forehead dropping almost to her kneecap. I sat on the bench, watching her ruefully. Carnegie Kincaid, Couch Potato.

"OK," I said, "supposing that Digger did uncover some evidence, do you think a steroid scandal is enough of a motive for murder?"

Holly grunted, stretching harder. "Could be. Breaking the home run record put Gordo in the stratosphere. He got a huge new contract with the Navigators, and he's booked for commercial endorsements for a couple of years at least. A drug rap would bring all that crashing down."

"And push him off his pedestal."

"You said it. Pro athletes live in the spotlight. They perform in public, and if they make it to the top, they're idolized in a way that you and I can hardly imagine."

She did a final shoulder roll and a back bend, then joined me on the bench to retie her sneakers.

"But their careers are short," she continued. "Imagine being celebrated and applauded for game after game, and then having to retire in your thirties. Where do you go from there? What's going to feed your ego? The home run champion's got that validation for life. He's always going to be somebody in the world."

"I see what you mean. But do you think—"

"Carnegie, I've really got to get going."

"Sure." We rose and walked back toward the market. Traffic was picking up, and we had to wait at the corner before crossing. "I appreciate your time, Holly. And your discretion."

"No problem. Just be discreet yourself while you're asking around about this. Gordo could be clean, and you could start a rumor that would cause him a lot of grief."

"I'll be careful. Have fun at the games."

"Thanks. Too bad Aaron couldn't come."

"Aaron?" Startled, I stumbled a little stepping off the curb.

"Yeah, I've got a second press pass and no one to use it. I called him in Florida about it, 'cause I thought he could fly back via Minneapolis. But he said he has to come straight back here for something important going on tomorrow. See you."

"See you, Holly."

As she disappeared in the crowd, I found myself smiling giddily. *Something important.* Aaron had the chance to attend not one but two World Series games, and he passed it up to spend the day with me. So what if we bickered a little? If that wasn't true love, I'd eat my . . .

Actually, I was feeling eager to eat my breakfast. It was tempting to drop into one of the market's many restaurants, but I decided to go home and grab some toast while reviewing my notes for Rose's wedding. I still had the nagging feeling that there was a detail or two I'd neglected—and the whole role of a wedding planner is to handle every detail.

If there's even going to be a wedding. As I walked back to Vanna, I pondered the consequences of my suspicion. If I was really convinced that Gordo was guilty—even if I couldn't prove it—shouldn't I try to stop the wedding, or at least delay it until Rose learned the truth? I couldn't stand by and let her marry a murderer.

Besides, wasn't there something about wives not testifying against their husbands? That complicated things further, if Gordo planned to use Rose as his alibi somehow. And yet I wasn't fully convinced he was guilty, so how could I possibly convince her? This was the man she loved, the man she trusted—

As I slammed the driver's door, a thought slammed into my brain. Rose McKinney trusted Gordo with her future. With her life. What if she was in danger right now? I fumbled out my cell phone and tapped in her number. Paranoia or not, I wanted to hear her voice and know that she was safe.

It was early in the morning to call a musician, but Rose answered right away. We talked a bit about the party at NocNoc, then I steered the conversation to Gordo.

"So how's the bridegroom doing? Any signs of cold feet?"
Or a guilty conscience?

Rose laughed. "Gordy can't wait for Saturday! He says our wedding's going to be the best party of his life. I just wish he didn't have to be gone so much this week."

"Gone? Where?"

I heard myself sounding the wrong note, sounding urgent. Had Gordo fled the country while I was dithering? But Rose's next remark nixed that idea.

"Yeah, he's in L.A. till Friday taping interviews and a commercial. He left yesterday, so I'm kind of at loose ends. I've got a couple of rehearsals with the Fiends, but mostly I'm just hanging out." Her voice grew carefully nonchalant. "I don't guess you'd like to get together tomorrow, would you? Just to hang out."

"I'm sorry, Rose, I'm busy tomorrow." My relief at having Gordo out of the way made me effusive. "I'd reschedule, but it's really important."

"Oh." She sounded deflated. "It's just...there's something I was going to ask you about."

"About the wedding?"

"Yeah."

After a short pause I said, "Well, what is it?"

"It's, like, kind of personal." The next pause was a long one. "I don't want to talk about it on the phone. I just...oh, never mind."

"I'm heading back to my office now. Why don't you stop by, and we'll talk about it there?"

"I said never mind! No big deal."

I could have pressed her further, but from her sullen tone I knew it wouldn't help. And if the question was really important, she'd bring it up again.

So instead I said, "I'll just see you Saturday, then."

"OK, sure. Is everything on track?"

"Absolutely. Everything's just fine."

As fine as it can be, considering, I thought as I drove back to the houseboat. I just wished I could remember that one particular detail about the wedding arrangements. And that I knew whether this particular bridegroom had blood on his hands.

Chapter Twenty-one

As I neared my front door, I heard voices from out on the deck, so I went around the corner of the houseboat to see who was visiting this early in the day.

"Mom, Owen! I didn't expect you till Friday."

Mom and I hugged, then her fiancé shook my hand warmly. Mom wasn't a big hugger as a rule, but her relationship with Owen Winter had softened her. There were other changes too—she'd bought a snazzy new car, and her perpetually permed and colored hair was now a free and feathery silver—but whether those were pre- or post-Owen I wasn't sure.

Owen himself was a bluff and hearty executive type, retired early from Boeing, who'd met Mom in Sun Valley when she drove up from Boise for an author's reading. He was well read and good-natured, and so smitten with my mother that I had to approve of him.

I even let him call me Carrie, the way she did. I didn't offer the same leeway to Adrienne and Kimmie, Owen's obnoxious daughters, but they did it anyway. The whole family called my mother Lou, for Louise, which took some getting used to. I'd never get used to the daughters, who I thought of privately as the Bitch Sisters.

"Of course I'm happy for you, Mom. I think a ceremony in this Orvieto place will be sweet and romantic and *perfect*. You should do exactly what you want with your wedding. After all, you're the bride."

She blushed and smiled. "A bride, after all these years. I never dreamed. But now what about your wedding? What sort of thing are you planning?"

"I'm not really sure. Something big and fancy, I suppose."

"And when?" She looked at me quizzically. "Have you and Aaron picked a date? I want to make sure we get back in time."

"You mean you'll be out of the country while I'm planning my wedding?"

"I might be," she said, surprised. "Would that be a problem?"

"N-no, of course not. I just thought you'd want to be in-ed, that's all."

re was another odd thing about my upcoming nuptials.
ly was I veering back and forth between Bride Brain
thought of eloping myself, but Mom was acting
detached about the whole affair. I'd always been
amused by hysterical mothers of the bride who
iths obsessing about pink napkins versus coral
whether grilled citrus prawns would be more
han Dungeness crab tartlets. But now that my
as being sensible, I was rather miffed.

iffed, in fact. I actually felt myself swaying on
ull-fledged Bridezilla temper tantrum. What
ng! I considered shrieking. What about *my*
my crab tartlets and me me *me*! And then,
en one for shrieking, I began to laugh at
and then aloud.

"Good to see you, Carrie," Owen was saying now. "Quite a view you've got here. How do you like houseboat living?"

"Love it," I said, thinking, *They haven't heard about the murder yet. Good.* "Come on inside. Can you stay long?"

"Owen can't stay at all," Mom explained, as I unlocked the sliding glass doors that led through the porch and into the living room. "He has a board meeting at his bank for a few hours, and then we're going up to Snoqualmie Falls for two nights at the lodge. Isn't that lovely?"

My mother was a hardworking teacher throughout her marriage to my hardworking dad, then well into her widowhood. It did my heart good to see her relaxed and retired now, squired around to fancy places by her well-to-do beau.

"Sounds wonderful, Mom. Especially with all this sunshine."

"I was hoping you'd have time to visit with me this morning," she went on. "I would have called ahead, but it was a spur-of-the-moment decision, and then your cell phone didn't answer."

"New number," I said.

"But why—"

"Eddie helped me find a better phone plan." I'd learned to edit my reports to my mother, and the purse snatching wasn't something I wanted to discuss. "I do have some things going on today, but why don't you come along to Boris's studio with me? He's expecting me soon, and I know he'd love to see you, especially after—well, I'll tell you in the car."

I couldn't very well edit away the fact that Boris had been accused of murder, but somehow I didn't feel like relating the whole thing in front of my future step-father. "Then we can have an early lunch at By Bread Alone. I need to check in with Juice."

"Juice?" said Owen.

"She makes wedding cakes," Mom, who'd met her once, explained. "Such a . . . colorful girl. I'd be happy to tag along, dear, and you could drop me off at the bank so Owen doesn't have to come back here. But you really shouldn't have gone out without breakfast. You know it's the most—"

"Most important meal of the day," I filled in. I'd been hearing this since I was three. "Yes, Mom, I know."

Owen chuckled and excused himself to go off to his meeting, leaving Mom to gush about him while I inhaled some toast and grapefruit juice. She talked about the sailing trips on Owen's yacht, and the peaceful evenings at Owen's house in Roche Harbor, and even the pleasant times—"pleasant" was Mom's euphemism for tolerable—they'd had with Owen's daughters.

What she didn't talk about was their wedding plans, which made me so curious that I finally brought it up.

"So have you set a date yet, Mom?" I put my dishes in the sink and rinsed my hands. "We should really get moving on reserving a site. The best places book up so far in advance that—"

"Oh, Carrie, I wasn't sure how to tell you."

I turned to see the look of dismay on her face and felt it mirrored on my own. "Don't tell me the wedding is off?"

"Goodness, no! It's just that we've decided—I know you offered to manage the whole thing for me, so good of you, but Owen thought, that is, we thought . . ."

"Thought what, Mom?" For a moment I was sure that Owen had hired some other wedding planner, probably at

his daughters' urging. There was no love lost between me and the Bitch Sisters. "Just tell me."

Mom took a deep breath. "We're getting married in Italy."

"What?!"

"Owen and I have been planning a long trip, to Italy and a lot of other places. I'll tell you more about it later. But, well, we decided to have a simple ceremony in Orvieto. It's a lovely little city that—"

"But I don't do weddings abroad!" I sputtered. "I don't know any vendors, I'll have to research the legal requirements, I'll have to—"

"You don't have to do anything, dear. We're going to do ourselves."

"But—but—Mom, you agreed to have me plan you ding!"

"I know I did, Carrie, and I'm sure you would a fine job. But Owen and I have looked into what we want. We just take our documents and ask our innkeepers or whoever to be

"Wait a minute. You mean I'm not ev

"Well . . ." She stood up and made with her hands. "Well, no. Don't be

"I'm not angry. Who's angry leaned back against the sink. " me that you could have . . . M you're eloping!"

She laughed, as if sh my age! Be happy for

It was the laugh like a girl, like a gia ing at her like such a senses. I threw my arms arou

"If you want to me to stay and help, of course I will," Mom was saying. "I need to know your date, though, so we can make our plane reservations and—what's so funny, dear?"

"Nothing, Mom. Everything. We haven't picked a date yet."

"But—"

"Let's get going, all right? I don't want to be late for Boris."

"Of course. Now what was it you were going to tell me about him?"

"Let's get ourselves downtown first. It's a long story."

Chapter Twenty-two

As we headed downtown I had to concentrate on the traffic, but after we parked I told Mom about Digger's death, and Boris being bailed out by the Buckmeisters. She reacted just as I thought she would. Digger was just a name to her, but she'd always liked Boris.

"Of course he's innocent!" she exclaimed. "The poor man, being arrested like some criminal. Does he have a good lawyer? Owen knows so many people—maybe he could help."

"He has a lawyer," I told her, as we walked up the block to Nevsky Brothers with the sun warm on our faces. "Whether he's any good or not is another story."

Nevsky Brothers was unique, just like its proprietor. Set amongst the restaurants, blues bars, and T-shirt stores of the Pioneer Square district, it didn't have the standard florist showroom up front displaying flower arrangements and hard goods like vases and greeting cards. Instead, Trofim Denisovich's elderly sister Irina tended a tiny bucket shop, shyly selling blossoms by the stem to passersby.

Behind the shop was Boris's domain, a huge skylighted workroom with exposed brick walls. It housed long design tables and supply shelves and humming coolers full of flowers and greenery and completed works of floral art.

Irina waved us through, and Mom and I both paused inside the workroom door to take a deep, delighted breath. Nevsky Brothers smelled like springtime in paradise, a heady mix of freesias and roses and lily of the valley, intertwined with the smoky scent rising from the vast silver samovar over in one corner.

"Khar-rnegie, and the bee-yutiful Louise!" Boris broke off from a conversation with various Sergeis and rushed over to us. "Welcome!"

As he swept us each into a grizzly bear embrace, I was happy to note that Boris handled me far more decorously than he had at Yesler Field. He was grinning broadly, but his eyes still showed sleeplessness and worry.

"Boris, dear," said Mom, catching her breath from the hug and patting his arm, "Carrie told me about this terrible business. I'm sure you'll be found innocent in no time at all."

"Thenk you, Louise," he said, with a little bow. "With such friends as your daughter, and her friend Mr. Buckmeister, I have confidence. Kharnegie, you wish to see drawings for baseball wedding, no? Sergei, bring tea!"

As Mom sipped her tea and wandered the workroom, Boris unrolled his colored sketches for Rose's wedding flowers. Her color theme—if you could call it hers—was the Navigators' navy, green, and white, so he was using a lot of deep-blue irises and white lilies and stephanotis, with his usual imaginative mix of greenery.

His first design for Rose's bouquet had been inspired by her name and her youth: a hundred white tea roses shorn of their stems and wired thickly together in the shape of a heart. Sweet and demure and so very *not* in tune with the butt-kicking bride. So he'd tried again and come up with a striking new design: a crescent of deep blue delphiniums, anemones, and viburnum berries, arched over a handle wrapped in blue and green ribbons. Perfect.

I gave the sketches a perfunctory going-over before initialing my approval, and just for fun I took some snapshots of them with my new phone, thinking to send them to Beau and Rose later on. But Boris and I had more than flowers on our minds. As he rolled up the drawing paper, I told him about Digger's notebook, choosing my words carefully and trying not to exaggerate its possible importance in solving the murder.

After all, Boris needed to hope, but it would be cruel to raise those hopes too high. I didn't get into the steroid issue; he wouldn't know anything about that. But there was something he might know, something the police might not be asking about.

"You spent some time alone with Digger at the party," I said. "How did he seem?"

"Seem?" Boris hoisted broad shoulders in a puzzled shrug. "He seemed like good fellow at beginning, before he makes insult at you. He asked for drink of Stolichnaya, I gave to him, we drank."

Frowning, I sipped at my own tea, winced, and put it down. I kept forgetting that battery acid was smooth compared to what came out of that samovar.

"I don't suppose Digger said anything about a story he was working on?" I asked, but Boris shook his head. "Well, did anyone else come and talk to him at your table?"

The Mad Russian knit his brows. "Pretty blond girl tells him she goes to ladies' room, and sad-looking man asks if we want anything from buffet."

"Digger's date," I confirmed, "and Nelly Tibbett. Anyone else?"

"No—yes! Leetle black man, I think he is official with baseball team."

"Leroy Theroux!" I said eagerly. "I saw them looking daggers at each other earlier on in the party."

Boris looked shocked. "They had *knives*?"

"It's just an expression, Boris. Forget it. What did Leroy say?"

"He said, 'Later, Duvall.' "

"Just that?"

"*Da.* 'Later, Duvall,' and then he goes away. Is important, you think?"

"It could be. Leroy's initials are in the notebook, but I'm not sure why. I'll have to think about it and maybe talk with him myself. I could make up some excuse, a question about the wedding preparations—"

Boris covered my hand with his own massive paw. "You are good to try and help me, my Kharnegie. I should do this for myself, but Trofim says I must not talk to vitnesses."

"He's right about that. The police might think you were trying to influence the case somehow, and revoke your bail."

"Revoke?"

"Put you back in jail."

He shuddered. "This I could not bear. But be careful! If you think leetle man is killer, you should stay away from him."

"Don't worry," I told him, as I signaled Mom that I was ready to leave. "I'll be extra-careful. Nothing's going to happen to me."

Chapter Twenty-three

I couldn't very well chat about murder over lunch with my mother, so instead it was back to weddings. Hers, mine, and Rose's.

We started with Rose's, because Juice spotted us on our way into By Bread Alone and beckoned us back to a far corner of the kitchen. There between the flour bins and the oversize dough mixer, out of the way of the bustling cooks, she had us sample various cheesecake recipes that might be used for the giant baseball.

"I like the Jamaican rum raisin," I said, licking my fork. "But I'm not sure everybody would. What do you call the marbled one again?"

"Three-Chocolate Thriller." Juice pointed at one of the plates from the row of five on the stainless-steel work counter. "Milk, bittersweet, and white. Real crowd-pleaser. But what does Honeysuckle want? Rose, I mean."

"She told me to go ahead and pick, so let's use the chocolate. Don't you think, Mom?"

My mother lifted her mesmerized eyes from the tattooed dragon between Juice's breasts.

"What? Oh, the cinnamon-citrus would be my own choice . . . but everyone likes chocolate, don't they?"

"Good enough," said Juice, making notes on her clipboard. "I gotta tell ya, Louise, your new haircut is totally cho."

"Why, thank you, dear." Mom gazed in wonder at Juice's hair, which was currently a poisonous green—just like the cute girl in the tuxedo at NocNoc. "It's nice to make a change, isn't it?"

"Too friggin' right. You guys having lunch here? Come on, I'll get you set up."

Juice set us up at the same window table where I'd sat with Rose, and soon we were enjoying BBA's chard and lentil soup and the organic greens with roasted garlic vinaigrette. While Mom mused aloud about the vagaries of obtaining a marriage license in Italy, I mused silently about Digger's notebook and Leroy Theroux.

LT knows. If Theroux knew that his home run champion had been on steroids, Digger Duvall would be the last person he'd tell. But maybe Digger was pressuring him somehow, maybe that's why they were glowering at each other at the party . . .

"Carrie? You're miles away."

"Sorry, Mom. What were you saying?"

She gave me a long, considering look—the look that used to ferret out my adolescent secrets. "I was saying that you don't seem terribly excited about your own wedding, some-how. Are you and Aaron having problems, dear?"

"Of course not. What makes you say that?"

"Oh, sometimes he doesn't seem quite as smitten with you as I'd like. But then I'm biased, aren't I?"

"Maybe just a little. But he's smitten all right. He turned down a chance to see some World Series games, just to be with me."

I told her about Holly's extra press pass, and Aaron flying

back to Seattle instead. But was she thrilled with that? She was not.

"That's quite a sacrifice," she said in a carefully neutral tone. "Especially since you could always go hiking another day."

"But this nice weather isn't going to last! And he promised me a whole day for us to talk about the wedding." I heard the defensiveness in my own voice and shifted my ground. "Of course I'm excited about it. I'm not sure about how large and formal to go. I mean, I know big weddings inside and out, but planning one for myself feels like . . ."

"Like what, dear?"

"Like work!" The word just popped out, but the minute I said it, I knew it was true. "I keep thinking I should dive into all the details, but then it starts to feel like just another job. And I'm not sure what Aaron wants."

"I expect he just wants you," she said, and gave me a reassuring pat on the hand. "Men don't care that much about weddings. You'll work it out, Carrie. I'm just glad you've found someone who suits you. Oh, look at the time! I don't want to keep Owen waiting."

We hurried back to Vanna, and I dropped Mom at the bank building across Madison from the huge weirdly faceted chunk of glass and gleaming metal that is the Seattle Public Library. Not that I was thinking about architecture, though. As I left downtown and drove up Eastlake, I was thinking about Aaron, and sacrifices. And my own selfishness.

Aaron wasn't just a baseball fan, he was a baseball fanatic. And this wasn't just the World Series, it was the Chicago Cubs in the World Series. He must have longed to accept Holly Crider's offer. But did he turn it down because he wanted to spend tomorrow with me, or because he knew I'd go ballistic if he didn't?

I knew the answer to that question, and it didn't do much for my self-esteem. The more I thought it over, the more anxious I was to talk to Aaron. I don't like phoning while I drive—too many near-misses on the freeway—so the minute I pulled into the houseboat lot I called him.

"Hello, it's Aaron—"

"Aaron, it's me!"

"—Gold. Leave a message, and don't talk faster than I can write."

Feeling deflated, I waited for the beep. Then I started again.

"Aaron, it's me. Listen, Holly told me about the extra press pass for the game tonight, and if you can get to Minneapolis this afternoon, you should use it! You should definitely go to tomorrow night's game anyway. We can go hiking some other time."

I hesitated, then went on, "Look, I'm sorry I've been such a bitch about baseball lately. I'm just, I don't know, I'm just preoccupied about Rose's wedding and our wedding and"— I caught myself before I mentioned Boris—"and everything. So get yourself to those games, have fun, and we'll rendezvous on Friday. I can't wait for that surprise! I love you."

As I climbed the stairs to the office, dazzled by the sunlight throwing sparks off the water, I began to regret my noble decision about Snow Lake just a little bit. I hadn't been out of town in what seemed like forever, and I was suffering the Seattle syndrome: the conviction that any given sunny day might be the last one for months.

In October that is actually true. Once the rain starts down

here, the snow will start up high, and Snow Lake isn't some-place you can ski into. I could always go by myself, I thought. It was an easy drive and a safe trail. But I'd never been crazy about solo hiking. And even if she wanted to go, Lily could rarely get time off at the last minute. *Oh, well.*

Inside, my partner was already at his desk and gnawing a cigar. Eddie's not big on small talk. He looked over at me and said, "Well?"

"Well, what?"

He hmphed. "Well, how are the McKinney flowers, and have you thought of anything new about the Nevsky business?"

"New..." My mind was still on Aaron, but I shifted gears and dug into my bag for Digger's notebook. "How's this for new?"

"Holy *moley*," said Eddie, flipping the pages. "Where'd this come from? Did you figure out what Duvall was working on before he died?"

I leaned back in my chair and took a deep breath. "Let me start at the beginning. A lot's happened since yesterday."

I told him about Boris being out on bail—which prompted a brief digression about Rose's flowers—then about the mentions of steroids and Gordo in the notebook, and my conversation with Holly Crider.

"So you think Gutierrez might be the killer?"

"I don't want to, but it's a possibility." I propped my chin on my fists. "Poor Rose. Maybe I should try and stop the wedding."

"Are you nuts?" Eddie's cigar waggled furiously. "What if you're wrong? The Navigators would sue you from here till next week, and so would that Frenchman."

"But I can't let her marry a killer! Rose is just a kid, Eddie, and she's had a rough time. If I'm right about this, it's going to break her heart."

He brought the notebook over and laid it on my desk. "You're forgetting something, sister."

"What's that?"

"Maybe she already knows."

"*What*? You think she's covering up a murder for Gordo's sake? Impossible."

"Maybe, maybe not." Eddie stabbed at the notebook with one weathered forefinger. "Even if she doesn't know about the murder, I bet she knows about the steroids. You should talk to her, see what you can find out."

"Just casually ask if her fiancé takes drugs?"

"Course not! Work your way around to it. Girl talk, that kind of thing. Can't you spend some time with her before the wedding?"

"Actually, she did say she had a personal question for me . . ." The light dawned, and I stared at Eddie openmouthed. "That must be what it was! Rose is suspicious of Gordo, and she wanted to ask to me about it. Why didn't I realize that?"

"More likely she wants to fuss about her dress or her flowers," said Eddie, who had a low opinion of brides in general. "Why don't you take her out for a beer and ask her?"

"Forget beer. I've got a better idea."

While Eddie watched, I called my bride and proposed a little day hike. She accepted immediately.

"That would be awesome, Carnegie! You sure you're not too busy?"

"Not at all," I said, flinching with guilt at her girlish enthusiasm. Her trust in me. "Something else fell through, so I've got all day free. We can talk about that question of yours. If you still want to?"

"Y-yeah." She sounded doubtful at first, then more decided. "Yeah, I do. But will we be back in time for the World Series?"

"Sure. The drive's only an hour or so, and it's not that long a hike."

"Cool. A bunch of Navs got a private room at the Batter's Box to watch the game."

The Batter's Box was a big new sports bar and microbrewery near Yesler Field, where Beau and I had met with the Navs management a couple of times.

"Sounds like fun," I told her. "We'll make sure to get you back for it."

We settled the details—Rose driving, me bringing lunch, and directions to the houseboat—and after I hung up, I turned to Eddie.

"Satisfied?"

He hmphed again. "Just be careful up there in the mountains with nobody around."

"Oh please, Eddie. You think she's going to stab me with a Swiss Army knife? It's Gordo I'm worried about, not Rose. And I'm going to steer clear of him until we know for certain who killed Digger."

"Yeah, but he's the groom," Eddie grumbled. "You're bound to be together some, and if Gutierrez thinks you're on to him—"

"Don't worry! He's safely out of town for now, and when he gets back, I'll make sure I'm always with Beau or someone." The thought of that bloody bat—and the idea of Gordo wielding it—lent conviction to my words. I zipped the little notebook back into my bag, determined not to let it out of my reach for a minute. "Now I'm going out for picnic supplies. See you later."

After my grocery run, the rest of the day went along quietly enough. I placed that call to Leroy Theroux, leaving a message that I needed to talk with him about the wedding. But every time my phone sounded, it was only Beau, harassing me with little assignments about McKinney/Gutierrez. I would *never* work for him again.

Finally Eddie left for the day, and after trying Leroy again I did too. Might as well watch game four and see if the Cubs had any fight left in them.

They did, but barely enough: after lagging behind 2–0 for the entire game, Chicago managed to scratch out a single and a double in the eighth inning. Then a fielding error by Minnesota turned a fly ball into an inside-the-park home run, and the Cubs won 3–2 in the bottom of the ninth.

A squeaker of a win, but it tied the Series two games to two, which made the squeaker a major victory. The Twins fans were filing glumly out of their seats when my phone chirped one last time.

"Hey, Stretch. Guess where I am?"

"Minneapolis?"

"Right up here in the press box! You sure it's all right about tomorrow?"

"Of course it is. I really need to be with Rose anyway." I didn't tell him why. "Did you enjoy the game?"

"Oh, did I ever. I'll never forget this. You are *such* a sweetheart. How 'bout lunch at Luigi's on Friday?"

Luigi's Grotto was a favorite of ours, an old-time Pioneer Square bistro with a twenty-five-cent perfume dispenser in the ladies' room and *penne alla grappa* to die for.

"You're on."

I hung up the phone in a glow of virtue and went to get out my daypack and hiking boots for the morning.

Chapter Twenty-four

Morning came early, but I was ready. The gourmet picnic I'd planned for Aaron had scaled down to simpler but still appealing fare: crusty sourdough rolls, a chunk of sharp cheddar, a couple of crisp apples, and my hiking standby, a bar of Cadbury's milk chocolate. Extra-large.

All this I'd stowed in my pack along with water bottles, my little first aid kit, basic safety stuff like matches and a flashlight—but no topo map since the Snow Lake trail was so familiar—and a rolled-up rain shell in case the weather turned. Not that it seemed likely to. Once again in this remarkable October, the day began in a bright white mist that promised sunshine to come.

I stood out in the parking lot as I'd promised Rose. Despite the damp chill in the air, I could see my shadow taking shape on the asphalt as the sun grew stronger. Suddenly the thought of all that sunshine and scenery sent me scampering back to the houseboat to fetch a camera.

It was just a little disposable, one of several made especially for weddings that I was trying out. The stolen camera had probably been fenced by now. I tucked the disposable into the inner pocket where I'd put Digger's notebook.

The notebook was coming with me for security, and I did

plan to question Rose, quite casually, about the recent behavior of her fiancé. But mostly I wanted to counsel her on whatever the personal question was and enjoy my day in the mountains. The prospect of getting back on a trail had me feeling more carefree than I'd been in weeks.

I hummed to myself as I relocked the door, excited about making an escape from the city, taking a break from wedding work, and best of all relaxing a bit from the strain of the last several days. Then a car horn double-beeped from the parking lot, and I hurried back down the dock toward the silver SUV that waited there with a light heart and a wide smile.

But my smile died when I saw the man at the wheel. Gordo Gutierrez, looking large and formidable and almost sinister behind his mirror shades.

"He came back early!" Rose called from the passenger side. In a Fiends T-shirt and no cosmetics at all, she looked very young. She sent me a private shrug and a little grimace. "Isn't this great?"

"Great," I said weakly, and climbed into the backseat.

What else could I do, feign sudden illness with my gear all packed? Anyway, if Gordo was guilty, I shouldn't leave Rose alone with him. But there went our heart-to-heart talk about her personal question—and my chance to question her.

"So," I went on, "what happened to the trip to L.A.?"

"The commercial fell through," said Gordo, rotating the wheel with one muscular hand as he reversed out of the lot. "My lawyers started fighting with their lawyers, so I said *adiós,* I'm outta here. You navigate, OK?"

He gunned the engine and had us roaring south on I-5 in a matter of minutes. I was glad of my shoulder belt. Gordo was an uncomfortable driver, all sudden speeding and swerving, but Rose just giggled. Young people think they're immortal.

"We're stopping in Issaquah to pick up Rob Harmon," she told me, hanging over her seat back like a kid. "He's staying with friends there. I hope it's OK with you that he's coming?"

"That's *fine* with me. What a terrific idea!" I was nearly babbling with relief. "It'll be more fun with four of us, and I'd love to spend some time with Rob."

"I bet!" Rose crowed with laughter, mistaking the source of my enthusiasm. She nudged her fiancé playfully. "He is pretty handsome, for an older guy."

"Charmin' Harmon," said Gordo, chuckling along. "Gets 'em every time. Were you a big fan of his, Carnegie?"

"No," I protested, feeling a blush creeping up my cheeks. "I mean, sure, Rob was a great pitcher, but—"

"Don't worry," teased Rose, "we'll keep your secret. Won't we, Gordy?"

"Oh, yeah," he said, watching me in the rearview mirror. His sunglasses were like a mask. "We'll keep your secret."

Issaquah used to be a quiet hamlet in the foothills, on the road that crossed the Cascades over Snoqualmie Pass. Now Snoqualmie is a popular ski area, the road is the I-90 freeway, and Issaquah is a burgeoning bedroom community for Seattle and Bellevue, with upscale condos and pricey tract houses creeping up into the evergreen slopes.

Rob's friends had a four-car-garage house near the freeway exit. Gordo pulled up and beeped, and Rob emerged from the white-columned entrance and ambled over to us. He wore jeans and a denim jacket and carried a blue knapsack with a gold emblem slung over one shoulder.

"Morning, everybody." Rob's cheeks were stubbly and his eyes were sleepy, but he looked all-American gorgeous. As he climbed into the backseat and buckled up, two feet away from me, I was suddenly sorry that the car was so big. "I had to borrow a pack from one of the kids, so I'm a Boy Scout today."

"Some Boy Scout you are!" cried Gordo, zooming back to the interstate. "Remember that weekend in Vegas at the end of your last season? Rosie, this guy was putting down vodka shooters like they were water..."

The raucous reminiscing between the two men went on for the next half-hour, as the highway shook off towns and malls and gas stations to curve its way into the forest, and the hills rose to mountains around us. But I would have enjoyed the scenery more if Gordo hadn't taken to teasing me about my enthusiasm for Rob's presence.

"You should have seen Carnegie's face when she found out you were coming, Charmin'." Gordo gave me a big grin in the rearview mirror. "She lit up like a Christmas tree."

"All the ladies have a crush on Rob," Rose chimed in. "Don't they, Carnegie?"

I didn't like the sound of "ladies"—it went right along with "older guy"—but as the engaged couple chortled and Rob raised an eyebrow at me, I didn't reply. I could hardly explain the real reason I was glad to have Rob along. And what's a graceful way to say that you're not attracted to a man, especially when you are?

Luckily, the scenery soon took everyone's attention. At first the peaks were clothed in fir trees right to their tops, but as we gained elevation the lofty summits became silvery granite with patches of snow, their skylines sharp-edged against the azure sky of a perfect October day.

The Cascade Range stretches from Canada into California, but the Alpine Lakes Wilderness that lies north of I-90 is its heart and soul—at least in my book. Studded with glaciers and scattered with meadows and dotted with hundreds of high-elevation lakes, the area is sometimes called the American Alps. I've never been to Switzerland, but I love the Alpine Lakes more than any place on the planet.

As we crested the final rise to the vast bench of Snoqualmie Pass, the steeply tilted mountain meadows were tapestries of crimson and burgundy and gold. The others exclaimed at the panorama, and I was eager for the trailhead myself, but there was one vital stop to make first.

"Take the exit for the ski area," I told Gordo. "You might want to slow d—*own*!"

He geared down abruptly, throwing me and Rob against our seatbelts and making Rose squeal. We rolled past the ski lodge and the chairlifts on our right and the Summit Motel on our left. The motel lot held a scatter of cars on this early weekday morning, but also rows of huge long-distance trucks. Interstate 90 runs from Seattle to Boston, so for truckers Snoqualmie Pass is just a stop on the way.

Then, just before the frontage road swung back to the freeway, I spied my objective: a cute little building that, here at three thousand feet, was no doubt the highest espresso stand in Washington State. "That's it, pull over."

There was much kidding about Carnegie's caffeine addiction, but three of us bought lattes and Gordo got a quadruple Americano—making me wonder about his pumped-up metabolism. But I was distracted, as we stood in the chilly sunshine with our drinks, by the pointed attentions of Rob Harmon.

He'd insisted on paying for my coffee and was now sipping at his in unnervingly close proximity. *Damn Gordo and his teasing,* I thought, as a blush rose up my throat and across my cheeks—no doubt adding to Rob's mistaken impression about me.

"Y'all should see your hair in this light," he said quietly. "It's like fire."

I mumbled something or other, but we both could have shouted without being noticed. Gordo was nuzzling the back of Rose's neck, and she was clearly oblivious to us, the mountains, and the rest of the universe.

This is not a girl who thinks her guy is a killer, I thought as we bore our cups into the SUV. Then, as I directed us to the trailhead, *But if he isn't, then who is?* "LT knows," the notebook said. Maybe I should have stayed in town and tracked down Leroy Theroux.

One reason I love hiking is that I lose myself in nature and in the rhythm of moving my body along the earth. But I'd never done a hike before with so much on my mind. The first stretch of the trail, a steep pitch through woods, went by before I knew it. Then as it leveled out into a string of little meadows between groves of Douglas fir, I went on pondering, with no useful result.

Enough! I told myself at last. *You're here now, so you might as well enjoy it.*

I always enjoyed the trip to Snow Lake. It was a hike I'd done many times, with many different friends, in the snowdrifts of June and the skinny-dipping heat of August and the blazing colors of October, just like today. So while the sun rose into the bowl of blue above us, my thoughts slowed and my senses awakened.

The air smelled of evergreens and warm rock, while birdcalls rose thin and sweet from the tree shadows. And everywhere around us, the foliage colors of the dwarf huckleberry and shrub willow and mountain ash were bright enough to break your heart.

My companions were certainly enjoying themselves. Rose and Gordo, in the lead, had eyes mostly for each other, but also for the view up the broad valley up ahead. And Rob, walking behind me, was stopping often to take photographs.

"Can I get one of you?" he asked as we picked our way across a field of tumbled boulders. "Just for scale, you know. Come sit over here . . . Beautiful."

I perched on the sofa-sized stone, shaded my eyes from the sun, and smiled a most self-conscious smile as the camera whirred and clicked. Then he helped me down from my perch and held my hand just a moment longer than necessary. Was this just simple friendliness on Rob's part or the first steps in a dance of casual seduction? Professional athletes, even retired ones, tend to be good at that dance.

Years ago I would have been thrilled at the prospect, but not now. Maybe I was flattering myself, but just in case . . .

"If that comes out," I said, retying the scarf in my hair, "I'll have to get a print for Aaron."

"Aaron?"

"My fiancé. He's with the *Sentinel*. You might have met him the other night."

"Oh, right, Aaron Gold. Nice fellow."

There, I thought, as the four of us reached the switchbacks that zigzag up the final ridge above the lake. *That takes care of that.* We stopped for a breather, gazing back down the valley and marveling at how high we'd climbed already—and when I moved away from Rob, he didn't come closer.

Then we tackled the switchbacks, me huffing and puffing a little, Rose leaping lightly ahead, and the two ballplayers taking the climb with measured, apparently effortless strides. I noticed, with some satisfaction, that none of us had breath to spare for conversation until we reached the top of the ridge and looked down the other side at the lake. Then we all found our voices.

"Wow!" said Gordo, between swigs from his water bottle. "It looks like a calendar or something."

"It sure does." Rob's camera was going nonstop.

With good reason. On a day like this one, the view down to Snow Lake was postcard-perfect. The water was turquoise in the shallows, shading to deepest cobalt in the center and sparkling with the reflected glints of light that my mother calls sun pennies. The shore of the lake winds in and out to form miniature fjords and peninsulas, and in places it juts out in granite ledges high above the water's surface, making perfect picnic spots.

The only other people visible this morning were a trio of fishermen on the farther shore, but they were too distant to show up in a photograph. I'd taken innumerable snapshots of Snow Lake, but I got out my own camera anyway. I left my pack open at my feet while I focused, then moved away to get a better angle.

With my eye at the viewfinder, I didn't see Gordo until after I'd snapped the picture. When I turned around, he was rummaging in my pack—which held Digger Duvall's notebook.

"Hey, what's this?" he said, straightening up.

"Leave that alone!" It came out loud and angry, startling us both as I rushed over to him.

"Sorry," he said, dropping the object in his hand. "Just joking."

"Um . . ." I trailed off sheepishly when I saw what it was that Gordo had reached for: my extra-large Cadbury bar.

Rose and Rob were staring at me curiously. "Um, so was I. Anybody want some chocolate?"

We each ate a sweet creamy bite or two, but first I hung my camera around my neck and zipped up that inner pocket. Then we made our way down to the lake.

Chapter Twenty-five

Had Gordo seen the notebook or not? I couldn't be sure, and I pondered the question all through lunch. I also wondered what Rose's personal question might be, because she had made no effort to take me aside and ask it. *She must be afraid of Gordo overhearing*, I thought. *Though she doesn't seem afraid of Gordo.*

The four of us sat cross-legged on a little promontory of rock, squinting against the glitter of sunlight on the rippling blue-green of the lake. Rose and me with our rolls and cheese, Rob with a roast beef on rye that his friend's wife had made for him, and Gordo with a submarine sandwich the size of both my boots. He devoured it with implausible speed, washing down each mouthful with a slug of dark beer from an outsized bottle that he'd brought wrapped in a jacket.

"You guys sure you don't want any?" he asked, extending the bottle.

No takers, but sadly enough everyone accepted more of my chocolate when I offered it around. I tried to hide my disappointment, but Rob chuckled at my rueful expression.

"Don't worry, Carnegie." He rummaged in his own pack and produced a double handful of baby Mars Bars. "Boy Scouts come prepared. Here everybody, dig in."

Lolling back against our plateau's single fir tree, alternating bites of apple and candy, I alternated between worrying about Gordo and absorbing the serenity of the lake. It was hard to suspect anyone in a benign and exquisite setting like this, and as our conversation died away, my worries dissolved into the stillness and the sunshine. I drifted into a reverie, only half awake.

"Carnegie?" came a whisper, followed by a light touch on my shoulder.

I sat up. Rob smiled at me, then glanced over at Rose and Gordo. The groom was sprawled flat on his back on the warm stone, snoring placidly, while his bride lay curled into his shoulder, also in dreamland.

"I'm setting off exploring," whispered Rob. "Want to come?"

There's something mischievous about being awake while others are sleeping, and the one thing I did feel sure about now was Gordo's affection for Rose. Whatever the truth about Digger, I was no longer concerned about leaving her alone with him. In fact, the notion that this good-natured teddy bear of a fellow was a cold-blooded killer was seeming more and more absurd.

But then what was her personal question about? If not the murder, then maybe just the steroids? Gordo could be a drug user without being a murderer. But whatever the question, Rose wasn't going to ask it until she woke up. So I nodded, and Rob helped me to my feet. Once again he retained my hand for an extra moment, and once again I pretended not to notice.

We didn't talk much as the main trail took us up over another promontory and on around to a small half-moon bay with a pebbly beach. Here the trail dipped right down to the water's glistening edge, and we paused to admire the bay. Then Rob plucked up a flat stone and, with a deft sideways flick of his arm, skimmed it far out on the silvery surface. The stone made a long shallow curve of tiny splashes before it disappeared.

"Oh, do it again," I said. "I want to get a picture."

Rob complied, and I backed up along the crunching pebbles to photograph the legendary Navigator pitcher skipping stones. *If only Aaron was here, he'd love this*. It was funny, but I didn't feel a bit guilty about letting Rob appreciate my company. Now that he knew I was engaged, what was the harm?

Done with the pebbles, Rob looked around and pointed at a rocky crag that rose beyond the next bend of the trail.

"Think we can get up there? I bet the view is great."

I was feeling adventurous. "Let's try."

We weren't the first to try. A faint side trail led around the crag and sketched a route up the farther, less-precipitous side. We stepped from rocks to tree-roots to rocks again, sometimes grabbing at a trunk for a handhold but mostly just stair-climbing. They were nearly vertical stairs, and several times Rob reached back a hand to help me up a steep bit. He was remarkably strong.

"This'll be harder going down," I said, panting happily. I took the last giant step up to stand on the summit, a tilted platform of rock barely five feet square. "But it's worth it!"

The view was glorious, with the half-moon bay opening before us like an arc of green glass. At our feet the face of the crag dropped a hundred yards straight down to a perfect still life of tumbled rock and bright-hued foliage. I lifted my camera, but a stray breeze set the leaves quivering, so I stepped back—and right into Rob.

"Carnegie." His arms went around me.

"Rob, this isn't—"

"Just a kiss." His face was close to mine. "C'mon..."

It really isn't fair on a girl, to be offered the kiss she used to daydream about and then have to refuse it. And I was about to refuse Rob—I'm pretty sure I was—when a man's voice came from the trail below.

"How'd they get up there?"

"Shut up, idiot, can't you see they're makin' out?"

We broke apart, me blushing and Rob scowling, and I peered over the edge of our little mountain. The trio of fishermen stood gazing up at us, their faces tipped skyward like curious cows. I waved and tried to find my voice.

"There's a trail up the back," I called. "It's steep but not too bad. Wait, though, we're coming down."

Rob was silent on our way back to the picnic site, until we reached a spot on the trail overlooking the picnic site. Rose and Gordo were wide awake now, packing up for the hike out, but they hadn't seen us yet.

"Carnegie, I am truly sorry." Rob was frowning into the distance. "That was out of line."

"It's all right," I said. "I was flattered, actually. It's just that I'm—"

"Engaged, I know. You made good and sure to drop Aaron's name back there, didn't you?"

"Well, yes."

He shook his head. "I should be better than that at picking up signals. I guess what Gordo was saying on the drive up here just went to my head. Friends?"

He looked straight at me and held out a hand. I shook it and smiled.

"Friends."

"Hey, guys, over there!"

Rose waved an arm, and I waved back. We rejoined them, and the four of us fell into line on the trail, taking the climb over the ridge at a rapid clip. As we began to descend the switchbacks on the other side, I gestured the men ahead.

"You guys go on," I said, sinking onto a convenient log. "I need a breather. Rose, could you help me fix this scarf?"

Rob and Gordo kept going, no doubt to talk baseball, and Rose returned. She gave me a quizzical look as I pulled the scarf off altogether and tucked it into my pack.

"What's up?"

"What's up with you?" I patted the log beside me in invitation. "What's this personal matter you wanted to talk about?"

Rose took a seat without speaking. I waited. She picked up a stick and poked at the dirt with it. A preoccupied chipmunk came hip-hopping down the path until it noticed us, then squeaked in alarm and hightailed it—literally—out of sight.

"Rose," I said, "you can trust me. If it's something about Gordo's . . . well, his career—"

"What do mean, his career?"

I tried again. "Look, if there's something about Gordo that you're uneasy about, you can tell me."

She poked harder, and the stick snapped. "It's not Gordo I'm worried about, it's me!"

"You? What's worrying you?"

Her face reddened, and her lips clenched tight, as if to guard some secret. Then she blurted, "Sex!"

"Sex." A flurry of possibilities arose in my mind. Infidelity? Incompatibility? Disease? Every guess but the right one. "What exactly is the—"

"I've never done it!" Rose muttered hoarsely. "I'm a god-damn virgin, all right?"

I almost did the unforgivable and laughed aloud. But I swallowed the laugh and kept my voice steady. "Well, that's ... perfectly reasonable."

She snorted. "Yeah, try telling my friends that. They do it all the time, and they figure I do too. So of course I can't say anything to them."

Remembering the overconfident Nick and his advances at the club, I had to agree. And I didn't bother to suggest that Rose talk to her father. I put a tentative arm around her shoulder, and she leaned into me, this lonely and rebellious girl whose musical talent had suddenly thrust her into the spotlight. It wasn't easy being Honeysuckle Hell.

"Is Gordo pressuring you about this?" I asked gently.

"No way! He wants to wait till we're married." She tilted her head to look up at me. "It's just that I don't want to mess up, you know?"

"You're not going to mess up, Rose. You're going to be fine. Honestly, it'll just be the two of you together, loving each other the way you do now, and things will take their course naturally. Sex is—well, it's fun. It's not a test, it's just a private way to love each other. Take it easy on yourself, and you'll be fine."

That was my very best shot at wisdom, and I heard Gordo shouting for us with a distinct sense of relief.

"We'd better get going," said Rose. "Thanks, Carnegie."

"You're welcome," I said, thinking, *You're not going to thank me if I have to put a stop to your wedding. You're going to hate me.*

We caught up to the fellows at a meadow down below, where they were indeed talking about the World Series.

Maybe Gordo didn't see the notebook. Or if he did, maybe he didn't recognize it. I desperately wanted Rose's new husband to be an innocent man.

"Game five tonight," Gordo announced with relish as the four of us set off again. "Pitchers' duel, and Rob's going to do the play-by-play for us. You want to come along, Carnegie? The Box brewed a new beer just for the Series, and their food is *muy bueno*."

"Are you sure I'd be welcome? I'm sort of an outsider."

"No, you're not," said Rob. He stepped off the trail to let Gordo precede him, then fell in beside me to urge softly, "Y'all should come. Please?"

"All right, I will," I said, pleased. "I'll just go home and clean up first. We've got plenty of time if we beat rush hour."

Trying to beat rush hour traffic is the official outdoor sport of Seattle these days, but it's getting tougher and tougher to win. Even coming off the trail by midafternoon, we found plenty of other cars on the freeway back into the city. We dropped Rob at his friends' place, then spent a tedious time idling on the I-90 floating bridge with the spires of downtown ahead of us and the westering sun in our eyes.

Oddly enough, that was when I began to feel guilty, because I'd had more fun today than I'd been having with Aaron lately.

Once we get the wedding plans settled, I thought, *we can go back to being ourselves.* And I resolved to be extra-agreeable when he arrived tomorrow. But I still planned to have a good time tonight. I was practically Rob Harmon's date!

"I'll be there by the first pitch," I promised as Gordo dropped me off. "Don't drink all the beer."

One of the many satisfactions of hiking is scrubbing away the dust of the trail, and I did that first before checking my messages. Just as well, because the series of recorded rants from Beau would have spoiled it for me. First he requested that I call him to confirm the limos for Saturday, then he demanded that I report on Boris's flowers, and then he commanded me to fax him the contract for the musicians.

Which was all very annoying, because these were tasks I'd already handled. By his fourth and equally unnecessary call, Monsieur Paliere was sounding like a French monarch with the guillotine at the ready for unruly serfs like me.

"Oh, to hell with you," I said to the phone. "If you're going to treat me like that, you can wait till tomorrow."

But the final message got my instant attention. Leroy Theroux had finally returned my calls—but not willingly.

"What the blue blazes are you pestering me for?" said his wheezy, irascible voice. "If you want to fuss around about the blasted wedding, talk to the Yesler facilities people. I'm sorry we ever got into this."

I flinched as I heard him slam down his phone. Not much of an opening there to question Theroux about his star slugger. I'd taken the wrong tack with him altogether. *Maybe he'll be at the party,* I thought. *I could make amends and then lead the conversation around to Digger's story somehow. But how?*

Then Aaron called, and I set the issue on the back burner of my brain. He was already in the press box at the Minnesota stadium, which I pictured as being like the one at Yesler Field. And of course I was picturing Aaron, who in his own way was just as handsome as Rob Harmon. If not more so, really.

"Hey, Stretch, how was your day?" His New England voice seemed a little harsh after listening to Rob's drawl and Gordo's soft inflections all day. "Sorry about the hike, but I'm getting some great material here."

"Actually, I made it to Snow Lake anyway." I told him

about the plan with Rose that turned into a foursome, without mentioning my suspicions of Gordo. Not outright lying, exactly, but I still felt uneasy about it. "It was such a beautiful day, I can't wait to show you the photos that—"

"Whoa!" cried Aaron. "You spent the day with Charmin' Harmon? Was your girlish heart throbbing? Did you get his autograph and draw little stars around it? Did you—"

"Enough, enough! He's a perfectly nice guy, but I'm not a teenager, all right?"

Aaron chuckled. He could always get a rise out of me. "Seriously, though, was he decent company?"

"Better than decent. But the main thing is that I got into the mountains before the weather turns." I changed the subject, not too subtly. "So, who's got the advantage tonight, the Twins or the Cubs?"

"I've got to admit it's the Twins, but it's going to be a wicked good game no matter what."

"I'll be watching on a big screen, so wave at the cameras for me."

Aaron's voice sank to an insinuating murmur. "I'm going to do a lot more than wave at you when I get home."

We continued in that vein for a few minutes, then said good night. As I got ready for the Batter's Box, I told myself that the hike really had been the main thing. That and questioning Rose about Gordo's use of steroids, which unfortunately hadn't panned out. But it might still be possible to jolt Leroy Theroux into shedding some light on the subject.

I had an idea about how to jolt him, and the more I thought it over, the cleverer it seemed. Though I had to admit, as I slipped into some slim-fitting slacks and pulled on my most flattering sweater, it wasn't the Navigators' general manager that I was dressing for.

Chapter Twenty-six

The private party at the Batter's Box was Testosterone Central. I did see Rose, all in black but minus the spiked collar, sitting atop the bar with her feet dangling and Gordo by her side. She lit up when she saw me and waved me over. There were some other women too, the wives or girlfriends of players, along with a battery of bustling waitresses uniformed like major league umpires—if umpires wore short skirts and high heels.

But other than that the place was wall-to-wall guys, almost all of them Navigator players, executives, and staff. I didn't see Leroy Theroux, but Walter McKinney sat at a far table, nursing a beer and gazing across at his daughter with a quiet smile. And Nelly Tibbett, the sad-faced batting coach, was slumped against a pillar with an empty glass hugged to his Navigators jacket. To judge by the slump, it wasn't his first drink, or even his third.

Neither man was watching the huge video screen above the bar, but neither was anyone else. There were smaller televisions scattered around this wide, low-ceilinged, pine-paneled space, all of them tuned to the same sports channel, but the volume was off and no one was watching.

This professional baseball crowd didn't care about the

pregame analysis, much less the commercials. So as the talking heads on screen mouthed their silent pontifications, the partygoers drank and laughed and argued and ate the Box's famous onion rings.

The aroma of onions set my mouth watering, and the picnic seemed a long time ago. I was working my way through the crowd toward Rose—and that platter of rings on the bar—when I heard a soft drawl at my elbow.

"Here you are. I'm glad you came." Rob looked at me almost shyly. "No hard feelings?"

"None."

The famous smile appeared. "In that case, light beer or dark?"

"Light, thanks."

He was handsome from the back too. But as I watched him snag a waiter for me, I had one of those moments of self-scrutiny that so often spoil a girl's fun. How could I be trading words of love with Aaron and so soon afterward feel gratified to catch Rob Harmon's eye? What's wrong with this picture? *Maybe I'm not mature enough to get married*, I thought glumly. *But thirty-three isn't any too young.*

But that was just the low blood sugar talking. Half an hour later, with a beer and some onion rings inside me, I was heckling the batters on the screen with the rest of the gang. Several people recognized me from the engagement party, and the rest just accepted me as a friend of Gordo's—or of Rob's.

But as the innings progressed, Rob paid more and more attention to the game and his buddies and less and less to me. Meanwhile Rose, though happy to see me, was taken up with Gordo. No more heart-to-hearts tonight, and not much conversation with my not-quite-date. I began to wonder why

I'd been so eager to come to this party. Then the waitresses unveiled a buffet of fried chicken with all the fixings, to the loud approval of the crowd, and Rob soothed my ego by offering to fetch some for both of us.

I saw a couple of the other women follow him across the room with their eyes. They turned to look me over appraisingly, then gave each other knowing glances. *Eat your hearts out,* I thought. *If you only knew.*

Then Leroy Theroux came in, and my focus shifted with a snap. The general manager stopped by a screen near the doorway to watch the last pitch of the inning, a look of furious concentration on his dark wizened face. The Cubs were pitching, and the Twins batter hit a pop-up to center field.

It looked like an easy out, but in the World Series every play can be the pivot that the game turns on. As the ball climbed high and then dropped slowly toward the outstretched glove of the Cubs fielder, to maintain the 0–0 score, everyone in Minneapolis, in Chicago, and here in the Batter's Box was tracking it intently.

Everyone but me. I was hastily buying a bottle of the imported ale that I'd seen Theroux order at the engagement party. Once the inning ended and the buzz of conversation arose, I carried it over to him. Time to try out my clever idea.

"Hi, Leroy. Sorry about those phone calls. Will this do for a peace offering?"

He looked at me suspiciously, then took the bottle and allowed himself a grudging nod. "Guess so. Did you get whatever it was straightened out with the facilities folks? I can't be bothered with every little—"

"Of course not," I said soothingly. "Everything about the wedding is taken care of. You must have enough on your mind with Digger Duvall's murder."

He took a pull on his ale. "That's up to the police now. None of my business any longer."

"Sure. I just meant that this rumor going around must be worrisome for you."

"What's that? What rumor?"

I glanced to either side, making sure we weren't over-heard. I didn't want to launch a scandal, just provoke a reaction.

"Well, that Digger was working on a piece about steroids"—at the word, the general manager's eyes bulged wide—"and the possibility that Gordo Gutierrez used them to break the home run record."

I was watching Theroux carefully, hoping to see some sign of guilt or wariness. But after that first look of shock his face went blank, and what happened next took me completely by surprise: he laughed in my face.

"Gordy, a juicer?" Theroux took a long pull on his ale, vastly amused and entirely at ease. "He don't even take aspirin! Who've you been talking to, anyway? They could cause a lot of trouble saying things like that." He frowned a little, then laughed again. "Not that anybody'd believe it."

"I certainly didn't," I said quickly. "I don't even remember where I heard it. Just one of those silly comments people make without thinking."

"You can say that again. Dumbest thing I ever heard. Evening, Rob."

The pitcher had appeared with two loaded plates and a couple of big cloth napkins draped over his shoulder. "Evening, Leroy. Want some?"

"Don't mind if I do." Theroux reached for a drumstick, gnawed for a moment, then said, "I heard the first half of the inning on the way down here. What the hell was Laventhol thinking, throwing Pataki a slider like that?"

"Well, it wasn't so much a slider as a—"

As the conversation sank into technicalities, I felt myself becoming invisible to Rob again—and found myself missing Aaron. He enjoyed talking baseball, but he talked it *with* me, explaining the finer points and turning insider anecdotes into funny stories. Why had Rob urged me to come tonight if he was going to ignore me?

I sighed in resignation and addressed myself to my chicken. As I ate, I pondered Leroy's reaction to the bait I'd dangled. The notebook—which was now safely zipped inside my well-worn but favorite shoulder bag—said *"LT knows."* But he didn't seem to know anything about Gordo and steroids. Or was he just a good actor who'd practiced his response in case anyone came too near the truth?

Finally I excused myself for the ladies' room, though the two men barely noticed. As the restroom door swung open on silent hinges, I caught a comment that wasn't meant for my ears.

"I think she's working on Gordo's wedding. But what Rob sees in a stick-figure type like that I—oh!"

It was the glamorous-looking blonde I'd last seen on the arm of Digger Duvall, now looking quite disconcerted. She'd been talking to another woman, also generously endowed, who gave me a bright, blank smile and made her exit. As the blonde began to follow her out, Rose emerged from a stall.

"Carnegie, Rob's been looking for you everywhere!" She winked at me. "Poor bastard, you're breaking his heart."

Then the blonde and her friend were gone, and Rose broke into wicked laughter.

"What do you think you're doing?" I demanded, though I couldn't suppress a snicker myself.

"Just cranking up a little gossip." She grinned into the mirror as she washed her hands and reapplied her lipstick. It was the color of dried blood, and her eye shadow was black with purple sparkles. "I hate groupies. It's pathetic the way they're drooling after Rob. Hey, can I ask you something about the wedding, or are you off duty tonight?"

"No, of course you can."

"It's about the chocolate fountain. Could we have dried apricots to dip in it along with the other stuff? I was just thinking, I really like dried—"

"Oh, no. Oh, hell!"

"What?" Rose looked alarmed. "Are you OK?"

"Fine." I rummaged in the shoulder bag for my cell, noticing absently that the bag really was getting shabby. "I just remembered something I forgot. Um, sure, apricots are no problem. Excuse me, I need to call someone right away . . ."

We parted outside the restroom, and I found myself a semiquiet corner of the party to use my phone. Beau picked up on the first ring, and he was not a happy Frenchman.

"At last! I am generous, I allow you a day off, but then you do not return my calls. Your contract is most clear about—"

"Beau, I'm calling now, OK? Listen, I just realized—" I paused while a couple of Navs came by, raucously arguing about Peterson and Laventhol.

"I cannot hear you!" Beau complained. "Where are you, at a riot?"

"At the Batter's Box with the bride and groom," I told him, just to make it most clear that I was on the job tonight. "But listen, about the chocolate fountain—"

"*Exactement!* This is what I call you about! I am looking at the floor plan for the rotunda, and I see no power outlet where the fountain is to go!"

"All right, calm down." I closed my eyes, visualizing the reception site. "We could put it against the north wall, next to the staircase. In fact it might look better there."

"But is there an outlet at that place? It does not show on the plan."

"Y-yes, I'm pretty sure there is."

"Pretty sure is not sufficient! You must go and see."

"All right, tomorrow morning I'll—"

"Now! This Battered Box is merely across the street, *c'est vrai*? You will find out at once and then call me back. Go!"

And with that he hung up, no doubt pleased to be ordering me around once more. I muttered a few choice curses and considered defying my temporary lord and master. But I needed that contract, so I went to tell Rob and the others that I'd be back shortly.

"Whatever," said Rose over her shoulder. Gordo just grunted, and Rob's eyes barely left the television screen.

I wasn't all that sorry to leave them, or the game, which was scoreless. Pitchers' duels are fine for baseball fanatics who can analyze every pitch and every swing. But casual fans like me want to see somebody hit the damn ball once in a while.

Call me crude, I thought as I jaywalked First Avenue to the stadium, *but give me a slugfest every time.*

It was cool and breezy out tonight, with a clear taste of autumn in the air. Traffic was minimal and the sidewalk almost vacant as I used my passkey to enter Yesler Field through a side door. The low-level safety lights were on inside, as I knew they would be, so I had no trouble making my way to the rotunda.

There the vast vaulted space threw back my footsteps as I crisscrossed the main floor, verifying the lack of outlets at our chosen spot for the chocolate fountain, then examining the new location I'd suggested. *Aha.* I found a double outlet, properly grounded, in the center of the north wall.

Even better, the wall looked long enough. We had to accommodate not just the fountain itself but also the attendant who would keep it flowing, the table of goodies to dip into it, and the hordes of guests who always converge when there's chocolate in the air. I took measurements just to make sure—I carry a little tape measure for just these occasions—and jotted down some figures along with a note about Rose's apricots.

Then my pencil jumped and slithered as I was startled by the sound of footsteps in the gallery above my head.

"Hello?" I peered up, past the darkened chandelier of bats, but saw nothing. "Who's there?"

The footsteps halted. A moment of breathless silence, then a rapid clatter as someone strode rapidly along the gallery and through the double doors at the far end, heading toward the owners' suite.

I shouldn't have followed, of course. I should have left the building and called stadium security from the safety of the Batter's Box. I should have minded my own business.

As Eddie would say, Fat chance.

Chapter Twenty-seven

I am not entirely dim. As I took the stairs to the gallery two at a time, I speed-dialed stadium security.

"This is Carnegie Kincaid," I gasped out. "Is that Eugene?"

"Nope, George. You're the one works for Monsoor Paliere, right?"

"Right," I said, and grimaced. Eugene was the smart one. "Listen, I need you. I was in the rotunda—"

"Okey-doke, I'll head over there."

"No, wait, I'm up in the gallery now, but I'm taking the main corridor toward the owners' suite. I heard someone running—"

"Who was it?"

"That's just *it*," I said through gritted teeth. *And they give these people guns*. "I don't know who it was, but they didn't answer when I called, so it seemed suspicious. Can you meet me there?"

"Uh, where?"

"The owners' suite. Hurry, would you? It might be someone who belongs here, but it might not."

"Well, all right." He sounded doubtful. "I'm way over here by the Third Avenue exit, so it'll take me a while to—"

"Just hurry."

I snapped off my phone and shoved it in my pocket as I pushed through the double doors and rushed along the corridor, my shoulder bag flapping wildly against my side. But now I could hear no one's footsteps but my own, and when I reached the owners' suite, the door was closed. I eased it open a crack to listen but heard nothing at all, so I stepped inside. My breathing—and my thinking—slowed to normal as I looked around the suite, which was unoccupied and undisturbed.

Party spaces, when they're empty, always remind me of stage sets after the play has ended and the audience gone home. There were no safety lights in here, just a twilight dimness spreading softly through the windows. Chairs were neatly upended on their tables, and bar glasses gleamed in orderly ranks on their shelves. The buffets, which I'd last seen cloaked in linen and graced with flowers, were stripped bare and pushed back against the walls.

All very normal, and what else had I expected? The person I'd heard was probably a janitor, or one of the office staff working late. It was curious that they hadn't answered me, but then people do curious things. I left the suite shaking my head at myself and preparing to apologize to George.

But George hadn't arrived yet, so I waited for him in the hallway outside the suite. With my eyes adjusted to the lowered light, I could just make out the memorabilia on the walls. Not well enough to read the texts, but enough to recognize the faces in the photographs. There was Gordo shaking hands with the mayor of Seattle, and there was Leroy Theroux grinning through a cascade of champagne after last year's playoff victory, and there . . .

Half a dozen photos later, I pressed the button on my light-up watch face. *Come on, George, I haven't got all night*. At last I gave up on him and returned down the corridor toward the double doors. *Probably went to the rotunda after all, the idiot. I'd better make sure Eugene's on duty for the ceremony Sunday, or else—*

Suddenly I heard a sound that lifted the hair on the back of my neck like a frightened cat's. Suddenly it was the night of the murder again, just moments before I encountered Digger's corpse. Walking down this same corridor, I had heard this same little sound.

A door clicking shut, in a side passage not far from where I stood. Only this time the sound was followed by a man's voice fading into the distance. I couldn't make out the words, but after a moment the voice rose to a muffled shouting. Someone was in trouble.

I found the door in seconds and raced down one hallway, around a corner and down another, to stumble at last into a large and rather peculiar room. Rows of folding chairs faced a podium complete with microphone, and a video camera stood on a tripod in the center aisle. The wall behind the podium was covered by a repeating pattern of Navigator logos like some kind of baseball-mad wallpaper.

The logos were there, I realized later, to make a backdrop for TV cameras. This was the team's media interview room. But I didn't take that in at first because my gaze was riveted on the room's only occupant: Nelly Tibbett.

Nelly was standing at the podium, or rather clutching it to hold himself upright. The Navigators jacket was gone, and his light gray polo shirt, hanging loose over his paunch, was stained with sweat under the arms and down the chest. He didn't react to my presence, and no wonder. With his slackened mouth and disheveled hair, his face a grayish yellow in

the harsh fluorescent light, he looked drunk almost to un-
consciousness.

"Years!" he was saying plaintively, his sorrowful hound's
eyes glinting with tears. "Worked my guts out for years, and
now I get thrown out like some nobody. You don't understand what it's been like . . . Everybody remembers the he-
roes, nobody's going to remember *me*."

His eyes wandered across the empty chairs, and I had the
eerie feeling that for Nelly they weren't empty. He was making his case to an imaginary audience. Of reporters, or fellow
ballplayers? Or maybe everyone in his life who had ever dis-
missed his talents or condemned his failings. Or who now,
in his fevered mind, rose up to accuse him of something
dreadful.

"No!" The word tore itself from Nelly's throat, as he
shouted at some ghost in the back of the room. "I couldn't
help it, don't you see? He made me do it, I couldn't help it!"

I had to ask. "What couldn't you help doing, Nelly? Who
made you do it?"

He looked blearily in my direction, unfazed by the appearance of a real person in the midst of his phantoms.

"Duvall," he said, as if the single word explained everything.

And maybe it did. Maybe Digger's dysfunctional family,
and his ferreting around about Gordo, were both red her-
rings here. Take an arrogant power-monger who can't keep
his mouth shut, add a drunken loser about to lose the job
that provides his only shred of dignity, and what do you get?
Maybe Digger told Nelly the bad news, and Nelly killed the
messenger. His next words seemed to confirm it.

"Duvall kept *laughing* at me," said Nelly, as if pleading for
my understanding. Or my forgiveness? "He said he could get

me my job back, but he wasn't going to . . . What else could I do?"

Nelly left the podium and moved closer to me. I backed away toward the door and slid a hand into my pocket, wishing that my phone wasn't a flip-up. I could probably outrun the man, drunk as he was, but there was no guarantee. And half the world carried a gun these days. I needed that speed-dial ASAP, but I'd have to pull the phone out first.

"Nothing," I said gently, my fingers curling around the smooth metal shell. "There was nothing else you could do. I understand completely."

"You do?"

"Absolutely. Let's sit down and talk about it, all right? Go on, take a seat in that chair right behind you."

Everything happened at once. As Nelly looked vaguely around, I dragged out the phone, flipped it open, and stabbed the speed-dial button. But he took alarm at my sudden movement and lunged toward me with a yell. I leaped away from him—and right into a folding chair.

I've never been physically nimble—Lily comes right out and calls me clumsy—and somehow the chair turned into a leg-hold trap that snared both my ankles and brought me crashing face-down to the floor. I brought my hands up to shield myself, the phone skittered away, and as I grabbed for it in vain, I saw Nelly's shoes just feet from my face.

I've never been all that brave, either. Cringing, I cried out, "Don't!"

But the shoes stopped, and Nelly's raving resumed as if I were no longer there.

"Nobody's going to remember me," he croaked out. "I'm glad Duvall's dead! He was such a bastard, he deserved it! He laughed at me, and I hated him, I hated the son of a bitch."

He went on like that for a couple of minutes, but I wasn't listening. Slowly, painstakingly, I was trying to extricate myself from the chair without drawing Nelly's attention away from his own hysteria. If I could get to my feet I'd make a run for it.

But by the time I stood up, Nelly had turned away from me, sobbing, and somehow I no longer feared him. His shoulders were bowed and heaving, his voice an unintelligible jumble of impotent anger and abject misery. I kept a clear line of escape between me and the door, but somehow all I felt now was pity.

"It's OK," I said soothingly, as if to a child. "Nelly, don't. Try to—"

"I should be dead too!" He swung toward me, his eyes wild. "After what I did, I should be dead!"

With that he fled from the room by a different door, to leave me frantically scanning the floor for my phone. I was afraid he'd stepped on it, but in fact I couldn't see it at all. So after a few minutes of searching, and another few of indecision, I followed Nelly Tibbett. Fools rush in and all that, but what else can you do when someone threatens suicide?

Nelly wasn't hard to follow as he lumbered through the maze of service hallways. I caught up with him just as he emerged from the building onto the outdoor concourse where we first met. It was dim, as it had been that night, illuminated only by the bright doorway that sent my shadow stretching out ahead of me.

I called after Nelly to stop, but he made a rapid if wavering line for the railing where I'd watched him throwing bread to the gulls. The breeze was a fitful wind now, and a gust of it seemed to snatch away my words.

"Wait, please, let's talk about this. You don't have to—"

"Stop right there!" he shouted.

I stopped.

Awkward and unsteady, Nelly wobbled on one leg as he swung the other over the railing. His foot must have found an edge on the outer surface, because he stood astride the rail before he looked back at me. His face turned toward me, round and pale, hollow-eyed. Remembering the gulls wheeling down and down toward First Avenue far below, I froze in place and kept silent.

"Tell them I'm sorry," said Nelly, his raised voice breaking on the word. "Tell Rob that I— *No!*"

A long shadow, a man's, materialized from behind me, and I turned to see George, the security guard, rushing onto the concourse with a gun in his hand. He shouted something, but I couldn't make sense of it. I couldn't make sense of anything, as I stood there in the gusty darkness staring at the concourse rail.

Nelly Tibbett was gone.

Chapter Twenty-eight

"The police found a bloodstained shirt in Nelly's apartment," I told Aaron as I prodded bleakly at my *penne alla grappa*. It was lunchtime on Friday, but our romantic rendezvous at Luigi's Grotto had begun with a post-mortem on Nelly Tibbett. "They're pretty sure it's Digger's blood."

Aaron nodded, somber and attentive. His plane had been late, so he'd come straight to the restaurant from the airport, and he had to report in at the *Sentinel* once we were finished. Just as well, since I was asleep on my feet. I'd been up late with the police, then gotten up early to fill Eddie in on the situation. I was hoping for a nap before the engagement dinner with Mom and Owen tonight.

"I'm surprised the cops got a search warrant based on a hearsay confession," Aaron said. "Especially hearsay from someone like you, with a vested interest in springing the prime suspect. But they took your word for it, even Starkey?"

"He didn't want to." I set down my fork and sighed. I didn't have much appetite. "But the weirdest thing happened."

I explained how I'd dropped my cell phone there in the interview room, then failed to find it after Nelly fled. Later, as I was being questioned and the dead man's remains were being collected from the surface of First Avenue, one of the crime scene officers spotted a tiny blinking light in the darkness under the podium.

"The phone was still on," I said. "I was trying to speed-dial security, but I hit Beau's number instead. *His* phone was on voice mail, so everything Nelly shouted at me was recorded. After they heard that, they had to believe me. Beau was furious when they confiscated his phone for evidence."

I smiled a little at the thought, but Aaron went on staring into the candle flame between us. Luigi's is wonderfully dim even in daytime, with dark red walls and shadowy alcoves and murky little oil paintings of Rome.

"I wonder," he said, sipping at his Barolo. He'd already polished off his *rigatoni verde*. "I wonder how it played out that night. Tibbett must have followed Duvall out of the party, although I didn't notice him."

"No one ever noticed Nelly. It's like he was invisible. When Eddie and I were trying to establish alibis on Monday, hardly anyone remembered that Nelly was even at the party in the first place."

Aaron's left eyebrow went up. It was always just the left one, and I loved how that looked.

"Alibis? You promised me you'd let the police do their job on this."

"But they weren't doing it! And besides—"

"Besides," he said with a resigned smile, "it's all over now, so there's no point arguing. Though I bet Starkey will be glad to get you out of his hair."

I chuckled, but inside I was wincing with guilt. At my interview with Detective Starkey last night, I had been wracked with indecision. Hand over Digger's notebook, or continue to keep it secret? I'd left my shoulder bag in the interview room when I ran after Nelly, then quietly retrieved it while the scene-of-crime people were fooling with my cell phone. And all during Starkey's questioning I clutched it tightly in my lap—and of course it didn't occur to Starkey to examine a witness's purse.

In the end I kept the notebook secret. Why start rumors about Gordo, now that Digger's killer was dead? The coded scribblings were just speculation anyway. Of course, I had a selfish motive too—protecting myself from the charge of withholding evidence. My conscience was so uneasy, I hadn't even looked at the notebook since. I was sick of the damn thing, and sick of this whole sordid affair.

Aaron, meanwhile, was still puzzling things out. "Duvall must have thrown it in Tibbett's face that he'd be getting fired soon, and Tibbett just snapped."

"The poor man," I said, half to myself. "I've never seen anyone so miserable."

Aaron's hand felt warm and reassuring as he placed it over mine.

"Tibbett was a murderer, Carnegie. And he took his own way out. I'm just sorry you had to be there."

"But if I *hadn't* been there, maybe he wouldn't have—"

"Hey now, none of that." He squeezed my fingers. "If Tibbett were still alive, other people might be in danger. Including you, Nancy Drew. And Boris would be standing trial. You cleared him, just like you wanted. Congratulations."

"But—"

"But nothing. Quit beating yourself up." He lifted the last of his wine in a toast. "Here's to Boris Nevsky, long may he wave. And here's to you, Stretch."

The rims of our glasses kissed with a tiny chime, and I suddenly remembered something.

"The surprise! I'm sorry, Aaron. I've been so caught up in all this that I forgot to ask. What's your surprise?"

He shook his head. "Don't worry about it. This isn't the time, with you so upset and—"

"Believe me, this is exactly the time. I'm happy about Boris, of course, but last night was so ghastly." I took a deep breath and blew it out, trying to move on from Nelly's tragedy to my own love story. "Please, if you've got good news, I want to hear it."

"All right, but it isn't news." Aaron reached into his breast pocket and drew out a small envelope, brittle with age. "It's this."

He tipped the envelope onto his palm, and I caught a flash of crimson in the candlelight. In his hand lay a slender gold ring with a single ruby, Burmese by the depth of its color, circled by a delicate halo of bead-set diamonds.

"It was my grandmother's, so it's kind of old-fashioned, but I was hoping you'd like it. Um, do you like it?"

"Aaron, it's exquisite. I *love* it."

"Oh, good." He grinned with relief and tried to slip the jewel onto my ring finger—but it jammed at the knuckle.

"It doesn't fit!" he said, stricken. "God, I'm such an idiot, I didn't even think about size. Rings come in sizes, don't they?"

Now I did the reassuring. "Yes, they do. Mine would be a seven and a half, and this is tiny, a five or even less. But rings can be resized. It's done all the time."

I transferred the ring to my pinky, where it barely fit above the knuckle, and extended my arm in admiration. Our waiter, a barrel-shaped fellow with a piratical mustache, caught the gesture and bustled over.

"The lady would like something else?" Then he saw the

ring—and the looks on our faces—and flung his hands above his balding head. "The lady said yes! Bravo! Eh, Tonio, a song for the lady!"

So Aaron and I, under almost-false pretenses, had to sit there while the waiters did violence to "That's Amore" and the other diners looked on and sighed. Aaron was trying so hard not to laugh he had tears in his eyes, and if I had tears in mine, well, maybe I wanted a ring after all.

After the finale and the applause, we sipped cappuccino and he told me the story.

"You were such a good sport about not buying a diamond, Stretch. And I really do think we've got better uses for that kind of money. Only then I remembered Bella's ring."

"Bella was Izzy's wife?"

"Right. I used to play with the ring on her finger when I was a kid." He touched the ring on my pinky now, tracing the circle of diamonds with his fingertip. "I knew Izzy kept it after she died, but not if he still had it after all these years. And his memory's so bad, I didn't want to mention it to you until I actually had it in my hand."

"So you asked him about it when you went down there."

"I didn't have to! The minute I told him we were engaged, he couldn't wait to get home from the hospital so he could give it to me. I honestly think it helped his recovery."

"Bless his heart." I'd met Izzy once, the previous winter, and fallen for him on sight. But I'd never met Great-Aunt Frances. "Tell me, Aaron, does he mind that I'm not Jewish? Or does—anyone else?"

"You mean Frankie?" He hesitated a moment, then shrugged. "Izzy's crazy about you, but Frankie's pretty traditional. You know how it is."

"Actually I don't, but I can imagine."

Aaron's first wife, Barbara, was Jewish. It was one of the few things I knew about her. Jewish, ambitious, disappointed in Aaron's lack of ambition. And toward the end, unfaithful to him. *Your loss,* I thought, and slipped the ring back into its envelope.

"I'll have this resized next week. There's one particular jeweler I want to use, and he's in the middle of moving his store." I yawned so wide that my jaws cracked. "Right now I'm going to go home and crash."

"So you're too sleepy for the rest of your surprise?" Aaron's eyes were sparkling. "That's too bad, because it was really—"

"What? You've got something else up your sleeve? Of course I'm not too sleepy."

"In that case we're out of here." He paid our bill, then held my chair for me. "Let's take a little walk."

"Where to?"

"You'll see."

Part two of the surprise wasn't quite the triumph of part one, though Aaron was quite proud of it and I played along. He led me up James Street, through the lunch hour crowds, and into the stolid gray King County administration building on Fourth Avenue. I guessed our destination right away, and I *almost* protested that it was going to be a wasted trip. But then I figured, why rain on the man's parade?

"I know I've been a typical guy," Aaron said as we crossed the lobby and he waved me into an elevator. "I mean, leaving all the planning to you. So I researched this part myself. Ta da!"

The elevator doors whooshed open on the Records, Elections and Licensing Services Division—the place where you apply for a marriage license. Aaron was so pleased with himself as we joined the line of waiting couples, I didn't have the heart to tell him what every wedding planner in Seattle knows by heart: a King County marriage license is only valid for sixty days after it's issued.

Aaron and I hadn't even picked a date yet, so the odds of our tying the knot in the next sixty days were zip to nil. A large formal wedding takes at least a year to plan, and if I wanted one of the primo sites in Seattle, ours would take even longer.

But you can always reapply for a license, and we could stand to wait a year. It was fun anyway—and just a little scary—to fill out the "Affidavit of Female" section of the application and watch Aaron complete "Affidavit of Male." Typically for him, he didn't read the fine print about the time limit. He just signed the form with a flourish and handed it to the smiling clerk, along with a check for the fee that he'd written out in advance.

"So tell me," he said triumphantly as we left the counter, "now that you've got a ring and a license, are you feeling thoroughly engaged?"

"I'll do more than tell you. I'll show you."

We had the down elevator all to ourselves and made good use of it. By the time we reached the ground floor, Aaron had decided that the *Sentinel* could wait, and I'd decided that I wasn't all that sleepy after all.

Chapter Twenty-nine

I woke up hours later that afternoon, stretching luxuriously in my own bed. Aaron had slipped away to go to work, but I'd mumbled my goodbye and plunged straight back to sleep. Self-employment has its privileges.

I rolled over and glanced at the clock. Plenty of time to get ready and make a few phone calls as well. As I got up, I saw the ring in its envelope lying on my dresser. On one corner of the faded old paper, Aaron had scribbled a little heart pierced by an arrow.

Humming dreamily to myself, I lifted a thin gold chain from my jewelry box and threaded it through the ruby ring. Then I slid the chain over my head and dropped my robe to the floor, admiring the effect of the jewel on my naked skin. Too bad we had this dinner tonight. I didn't feel like sharing Aaron with anyone. Of course there was always afterward . . .

But for now I pulled on jeans and an old sweatshirt. I had wedding work to do, and I wanted to check in with the bride. Last night after the police were done with me I'd returned to the Batter's Box, only to find that Rose had gone home along with almost everyone else. The news of Nelly's death had arrived before me, just as the Cubs lost in a humiliating 13–2 rout, and the party had broken up.

So now I climbed the outside stairs to the office, still

stretching and yawning, with Rose's wedding on my mind. Eddie had already left for the day, and the sunset over Queen Anne Hill suffused the empty workroom with a golden glow. I admired it for a few moments, and then as the glow faded, I flipped on the lights and got down to business.

First, to get it over with, a call to Beautiful Beau. He was still fuming about his phone.

"Who was this Tibbett?" he complained. "I do not know the name."

Briefly, I explained Nelly's role with the team.

"So, not an important person? His death does not affect the wedding?"

"No," I said sadly. "I don't suppose it does."

"*Bon*. Now, the outlet for the chocolate fountain, what did you find?"

And with this outpouring of compassion, Beau and I ran through the final details for McKinney/Gutierrez. There wasn't much, but this late in the game it was important not to let anything slip. Game, as in baseball, was the operative word here. In addition to the baseball cake and the chocolate fountain, we'd have waiters with old-fashioned vendor trays strolling through the crowd to offer little bags of peanuts and, what else, Cracker Jack.

Which meant that someone had to check that the bags were filled and stapled, and the trays had proper carrying straps, and the waiters remembered to wear their Navigator logo ties. Somebody meaning me. I scribbled notes as Beau and I talked, and when we finally finished, I went through the notes Eddie had left me, including the latest weather forecast.

Continued unseasonably warm and sunny through the weekend, it said, and I recalled the old proverb, "Happy is the bride the sun shines upon." As I worked, I was feeling like a busy but fairly sunny bride-to-be myself—if I could just keep the dark picture of Nelly Tibbett out of my thoughts. I held it at bay by concentrating on the tasks before me, like the bride's request for apricots.

You can dip anything in a chocolate fountain. I'd even heard about a southern-fried celebration that offered—oh, the horror—pork rinds. Fortunately, we were sticking with a conventional array of fresh fruits, macaroons, almond biscotti, and honey wheat pretzel rods for that sweet-salt taste that so many people, including me, find irresistible.

And now an additional item. I reached the Navigators' caterer, and after a token protest at this last-minute change, he promised me a platter of the finest apricots to be had. Then, duty done, I called Rose.

"How are you doing? Nervous?"

"Nah. Gordo's a little edgy, but I'm cool."

Of course, I thought. *This bride is used to the spotlight.*

"What about you?" she was saying. "Must have been gross, seeing somebody off himself like that."

"It was—disturbing. Did you hear much about it?"

"Just that Nelly did a face plant from the concourse." The words were crude, but Rose's voice wobbled a bit as she kept up her tough-girl front. "We heard he was the one who killed Duvall. Is that for real?"

I found myself strangely reluctant to confirm it. "It seems that way, yes."

"Gordo says he had a hunch it was him all along."

"Did he really?"

"Yeah, he's telling everyone that Duvall was always nasty to poor old Nelly, and he must have pushed him over the edge. He says Nelly was drunk enough to do anything that night. What a loser."

"Rose, the man is *dead*. ● I felt a spurt of anger at her and Gordo both, taking their youth and success for granted while they belittled Nelly Tibbett. Stupid nickname, anyway. None of us even knew his real name. "Show a little respect, for God's sake. You were drunk yourself, as I remember."

"Hey, don't yell at me. I was just—"

"I'm not yelling!" I realized that I was, though, in some kind of delayed reaction to last night. I made myself take a deep breath. "Sorry, Rose. I'm still shaken up, that's all."

"Yeah, that figures." She added in a subdued voice, "I guess I'll see you in the morning? You don't have to help me get dressed if you don't want."

"Oh, I wouldn't miss it! That's one of my favorite parts of a wedding, and the gown is so lovely on you. Come on, let's go over the schedule one last time . . ."

By the time we finished, both of us were in better spirits— though I still had a nagging question about Gordo. Where had this hunch of his come from? He hadn't mentioned it earlier, at least not in my hearing. But then there was no reason he should. As I locked the office door and went downstairs to dress for dinner, I told myself I was just being paranoid.

But still, if someone other than Nelly was the killer, wouldn't that person do everything possible to promote the idea of the dead man's guilt? The thought niggled at me as I pawed through my closet. Owen was taking us to Canlis, one of Seattle's oldest and most expensive fine-dining establishments. They no longer required formal dress, but Aaron had offered to suit up for the occasion. The trouble was, with everything else going on, I hadn't selected an outfit for my-self.

My jade silk? Getting shabby after way too many wearings. That red dress I'd bought last summer? I hardly ever wore it—because I'd bought it for a date with Mr. Extremely Wrong and it carried bad memories. The long-sleeved black velvet? A little warm for tonight. The off-white silk suit? Not festive enough.

"Enough, already," I said aloud. "Get a grip!"

I fled the bedroom for the cool salt air of the deck, deter-mined to clear my mind and conjure up a better mood. Tonight was a celebration of my mother's engagement and my own, and I refused to be tense and distracted. After all, I'd just been given a beautiful engagement ring...

Breathing slowly, listening to the wavelets lap against the floats beneath my feet, I made two decisions. First, to wear the black velvet after all, as a splendid backdrop for the ruby. And second, to call Aaron's grandfather and thank him for his remarkable gift.

It was getting late in Florida, but I knew from Aaron that Izzy was a night owl. Besides, he always turned off the phone in his assisted living apartment when he wanted to sleep. So I got dressed and did my makeup, to be all ready when the others arrived, before I sat down in the kitchen and placed the call.

The phone barely rang once before someone picked up—a woman. I was so prepared for the old man's voice that this threw me off balance.

"Gold residence."

"Oh. Oh, is that Frances? I mean . . ." What the hell was the aunt's last name, Gold or something else? "This is Carnegie Kincaid, Aaron's fiancée? I was hoping to speak to Izzy."

"He's indisposed."

"Is he all right? It's not his heart?"

"What are you talking about, his heart?" Frances had a New York accent and a voice that could etch glass. "I said indisposed, not sick. He's in the bathroom! I'll tell him you called."

"Wait, I wanted to—to introduce myself, if that's all right. Should I call you Frances or—"

"Frankie is fine. Even strangers call me that."

"Frankie, then. It's, um, good to talk with you."

An uncomfortable pause, and then she said, "So. You're Aaron's new girlfriend. Izzy says you're very nice."

She made it sound like a dubious claim on his part.

"He's a wonderful person," I said, trying to warm things up. "I was sorry I couldn't come down there with Aaron, but—"

"It's fine. It's good Aaron was here. He and Barbara had a few laughs, that was nice."

"Barbara?"

"Aaron's ex. Izzy's very fond of our Barbara. Didn't Aaron tell you she was here?"

"Of course." I was gripping the phone so hard it hurt. "Of course he did. Well, I'm going out in a few minutes, so I'll try calling tomorrow."

"You do that," she said, and hung up.

I stared at the phone in my hand, my thoughts spinning and colliding and spinning away again like a rack of pool balls after a violent break.

Barbara? He's spending time with goddamn Barbara and not telling about it? . . . No, it's all right, she was just visiting the old man . . . So what? He was with her and he lied to me about it and that's nowhere near all right . . . The son of a bitch didn't even tell

me about her in the first place, and now he's lying to me again...
I didn't know whether to weep or smash dishes or both.

But I didn't have the chance to do either, because just
then a jaunty rapping sounded at the door. I wrenched it
open and saw Aaron—with my mom and her man right behind him.

"Look who we found in the parking lot!" Owen said in his
hearty, self-confident way. As the three of them trooped inside, the men in dark suits and Mom in dark blue silk, he
added, "Look at you, Carrie. You must have had lots of sun
on that hike of yours. You're all red!"

"Hush, Owen," said my mother. "You look lovely, dear,
just a pretty glow. And there's the ring Aaron was telling us
about. You must be thrilled to have it."

"Oh, yes," I said, not looking at my treasonous fiancé.
"Thrilled to bits."

Chapter Thirty

To say that the mother-daughter engagement dinner did not go well is to say that the *Titanic* had a fender-bender.

Not that it was the restaurant's fault. When Peter Canlis founded the place on a hilltop above Lake Union back in 1950, he envisioned a bastion of elegance, sophistication, and the very finest food. He succeeded admirably, and since then his sons and now his grandsons have only enlarged on the tradition.

The Canlis building alone is a work of art, with natural stone columns, old-growth cedar beams, and a wall of windows cantilevered over a breathtaking view of the lake, the Seattle valley, and the Cascades in the distance. The mountains were barely visible tonight, of course, but as the four of us emerged from Owen's car, the stars were out and the nighttime glitter of the city was spectacular.

For all the good it did me. While the others oohed and aahed and pointed out landmarks like Gas Works Park, whose rusting machinery looked like spot-lit metal sculptures in the darkness, I just stood there silently, trying to control my temper.

Not to mention my disappointment. I'd arranged parties at Canlis for my clients but never dined here myself, and I'd been looking forward to this dinner for weeks. But now I barely noticed the famous valet parking, where instead of is-suing numbered receipts the attendants simply remember each guest's vehicle. And as Mark Canlis himself escorted us to our window table, all I could think about was how royally pissed off I was at Aaron Gold.

Aaron knew something was amiss. He was seated across from me at the round table, and as Mom admired the hand-crafted wall hangings and the heavy damask table linens, he nudged me with his foot and raised an eyebrow inquiringly.

But what was I supposed to do, open an interrogation about his ex-wife in front of my mother? I just gave him a flash-frozen smile, ignored the frown I got in reply, and lis-tened to Owen expounding on the wine list.

"Fifteen thousand bottles," he announced, as proudly as if he'd stocked the cellar himself. "They have eight somme-liers here, *and* their own whiskey consultant in Scotland. Supposed to be one of the best collections of single malts in the country. We'll have to test that out, won't we, Aaron?"

"What? Oh, sure. Absolutely. Carnegie, are you—?"

"I've read that they use only Riedel crystal stemware," I chimed in, speaking solely to Owen. "It makes the wine taste even better."

"Oh, come on," said Aaron with a good-natured smile. "Glass is glass."

"It's twenty-four percent lead crystal," I said icily, "not glass. There's a big difference."

"No kidding," he said, growing testy. "So now you're an expert in—"

"Aren't these candleholders lovely?" said my mother the diplomat. "Honestly, Owen, every single detail here is just perfect. This bud vase, Carrie, isn't it pretty?"

"It's beautiful, Mom. Look, here's our champagne."

Owen had preordered a premium bottle, which fizzed merrily as the waiter poured and we raised our flutes to offer toasts all around. Owen said some charming things about the Kincaid girls, Mom offered Aaron and me her love and best wishes, and Aaron congratulated Owen on his lovely bride. That left me. I lifted my champagne and stared deliberately at Aaron.

"To truth," I said. Then, as Mom looked puzzled, "To truth and beauty and romance, now and in the future. Cheers."

"Cheers!" they chorused in varying tones, and we directed our attention to the menu.

We were still debating appetizers—prawns with vermouth and garlic, or the Maine lobster claw with foie gras demi-glace?—when a familiar, and to me most unwelcome, voice came trilling across the dining room.

"There they are, over there!"

We looked up to see a buxom blonde sailing toward us, with a dour-faced brunette and an attentive waiter in her wake.

"Kimmie!" said Owen, rising to embrace his daughter. "And Adrienne, what a wonderful surprise. Remember, Lou, how I invited the girls but they couldn't make it? Just wonderful. Waiter, if we could get some chairs . . ."

With the deft service that was a trademark of Canlis, the newcomers were seated and more champagne flutes appeared. Shoulder to shoulder to shoulder with the Bitch Sisters, I knocked back my first glass and held it out for another.

"We knew you'd miss us, Carrie," said Adrienne in her gravelly voice, turning her trademark red eyeglasses toward me. Dree, as the family called her, wore a chopped bob hair-style and a sardonic smirk. "Especially on this historic occasion. So you finally popped the question, Aaron. Took you long enough, didn't it?"

There wasn't a good answer to that, and Aaron didn't answer. In any case he was distracted by Kimmie and her so-called dress, a strapless scarlet number that barely contained her charms. Picture two scoops of vanilla ice cream in an undersize red dish, and you've got the general idea.

"It's just *too* thrilling," she breathed, leaning forward to give him the full effect. "Just think, Aaron, you and I will be related. Won't it be fun? We'll see each other all the time!"

Over his dead body, I thought. *And yours too, sweetheart.*

"Show the girls your ring, Carrie," said Owen, oblivious. "It's really something special."

I complied, and Adrienne gave my impromptu necklace a dismissive glance.

"How odd." Owen cleared his throat, and she amended, "Unique, I mean. Very—unique. So, what's for dinner?"

Dinner began reasonably enough, since the wine was flowing freely and the menu made a safe topic of conversation. And once we were done discussing the scallops with coriander butter, and the lamb chops with couscous and chard, and of course the Kobe-style wagyu tenderloin, the men resorted to baseball and the women to travel.

Specifically, last night's World Series game, and Dree and Kimmie's upcoming jaunt to a destination spa in Belize. As our plates emptied and our glasses were refilled—the Riedel crystal was a revelation, the merest film between one's mouth and one's wine—the talk grew loud and lively.

". . . this detoxifying seaweed wrap and then a body polish . . ."

". . . should have pulled Laventhol in the fifth inning . . ."

". . . sort of French-Caribbean cuisine, organic of course . . ."

". . . Cubs don't have a snowball's chance in hell after that fiasco . . ."

I didn't contribute much, but Aaron tried to coax me into responding to Owen's jab at his favorite underdogs.

"Don't write the Cubs off yet," he said. "Carnegie and I are still betting on them. Aren't we, Stretch?"

"Are we?" I snapped. Mom was gazing at me with concern, so I tried to muster up some manners. But my reply still came out with a sharp edge. "I guess so. You never know, do you? You never know about anyone."

An uneasy silence followed. Even Owen sensed the tension now, but his attempt to defuse it led to further trouble.

"So tell us about your wedding, you two. Lou and I are running off to Italy like a couple of crazy college kids, but what are your plans?"

"We're still working on them," said Aaron smoothly. "But we got our license today, so we're official. I have to tell you, Louise, my grandfather was so delighted to give Carnegie that ring . . ."

He went on to recount a warm and amusing story about Izzy and Bella, which led to reminiscences about Owen's grandparents, and I realized with a pang of conscience what Aaron was doing. Unable to figure out my sulky mood, he was pouring on the charm, trying to make peace with me by playing up to my mother and soon-to-be-stepfather. He even included the Bitch Sisters, calmly answering Dree's brusque questions about his family and inviting them both to be wedding guests.

My conscience was panging like crazy by now, pointing out that Aaron was acting the gracious grown-up here, and me the sullen child. *But he lied to me,* I told myself over and over. *How can I trust him if he keeps lying to me?*

Then Aaron went a step too far and complimented Kimmie on her dress. She immediately ramped up her flirting, and grew more girlishly animated the more I retreated into resentful silence. We had reached dessert by then, and Kimmie insisted that Aaron taste her chocolate lava cake.

"Just one bite," she giggled, reaching across the table with her fork. "Honestly, you should serve this at your wedding!"

Aaron leaned forward to accept the dark morsel, licked his lips in appreciation, and said, "Wow, good suggestion."

"I'm full of good suggestions," said Kimmie, with a wicked little glance at me. "And I'd just love to help with your wedding, you know. Why, Dree and I could be bridesmaids!"

My eyes bulged with horror at the thought, but Aaron was still determined to be charming, the moron.

"What a terrific idea," he said, and beamed at me like a dog who's dragged in something slimy from the backyard and expects to be praised for it.

Meanwhile Owen, the other moron, chimed in, "Now wouldn't that be nice? A real family affair. What do you say, Carrie?"

My mother, perhaps noting the smoke issuing from my ears, offered me a graceful way out. "It's still so early in your planning, isn't it, dear? You'll be making all those decisions later."

But Dree, ever the willing co-conspirator in her sister's nasty schemes, said quickly, "Oh, it's never too early to pick your bridesmaids. We'd be happy to do it, Aaron, thanks for asking. So now that we've got that settled, Carrie, what are your thoughts about our dresses?"

I opened my mouth to share my thoughts, no doubt in terms that I'd regret later on. But I was saved from embarrassing my mother and alienating my step-family by an eruption of male voices from the lounge behind us.

"To freedom!"

"*Da,* to freedom!"

"To Borya!"

Borya? I craned around to look, and there indeed was the Mad Russian, standing in the lounge with half a dozen Sergeis. They were all in black turtleneck sweaters, raising their vodka glasses and looking cheerfully inebriated—especially Boris. But if I'd just been cleared of a murder charge, I'd be drinking too. In fact, vodka sounded awfully good just now . . .

"Excuse me," I said, rising. "I see a friend of mine."

"Kharrnegie!" Boris stepped away from the bar to hug me so hard that my ribs protested. "Such news! They know who was killer, they know it was not me. Come, celebrate!"

The next half-hour made for a considerable improvement in my evening. Boris was joy personified, and I got to kiss each and every Sergei, some of them more than once. And who knew that Stolichnaya Elit would go down so smoothly?

"Stretch?" came a voice through the rumble of Russian hilarity. Aaron sounded irked but patient, and he was holding my coat and shoulder bag like a dutiful date. "Come on, we're leaving. Or are you staying?"

"I might," I said haughtily, snatching my belongings from him. "I just might. I could take a cab home, I've got the cash . . ."

I fumbled in my bag, but things were a bit out of focus, and there seemed to be endless zippers and compartments. At one point my fingers slid right through the torn seam of a

pocket, and I finally located my wallet lurking down beneath
the bag's lining. But as I fished it out through the tear, I
stopped, dumbfounded. Then I searched again, but not for
the wallet this time, and came up empty.

Digger Duvall's notebook was missing.

Chapter Thirty-one

"Why do you keep calling it lying?" Aaron rose abruptly from my couch, shoved his hands in his pockets, and stared out through my living room windows across Lake Union. You could see the lights of Canlis over there, if you knew where to look. "Barbara had a layover at the Miami airport and she came by to see Izzy. No big deal."

"That's not what Frankie said," I retorted, though without much spirit.

It was almost midnight, and we were both weary from arguing. And I was seriously distracted by the thought of Digger's missing notebook—which Aaron knew nothing about. But still I kept on nursing my grievance.

"Frankie," I said stubbornly, "made it sound like a joyful family reunion."

"I told you, she's a big fan of Barbara's, and she doesn't like the idea of my taking up with a shiksa. Frankie's hobby is making trouble."

"There wouldn't *be* any trouble if you'd told me about this in the first place."

"Are you sure?" Aaron returned to the couch and took my hands in his. That lock of hair fell across his eyes, and I wanted to smooth it down. I wanted to hold him and have him hold me. "Honest to God, Stretch, the only reason I didn't mention Barbara is that I thought it might upset you. I thought I was doing the right thing."

"Well, you weren't."

"No kidding."

He grinned, and though I tried to resist, I couldn't help softening a little. But I had a point to make.

"Seriously, Aaron, can you see why this is bothering me?"

He put the grin away. "Yeah, I suppose I can. Better to keep everything out in the open. So, full disclosure from now on. Deal?"

"Deal. But you still owe me an apology."

"Forgive me, fair lady!" Aaron flung himself flat on the couch, his head in my lap, and cried piteously, "Don't throw me in the dungeon again! The rats keep stealing my bread and water!"

"Quit clowning," I said with an unwilling laugh, and pushed him upright. "This is serious."

"No, it isn't. I told you, Barbara just happened to be—"

"I don't mean her. I mean—" I drew in a deep breath, then took the plunge. "Listen, there's a problem about Digger's murder. I don't think Nelly Tibbett did it."

"What?" Aaron went blank, and then his brows drew together and his focus sharpened. "But it's so clear cut. He confessed to you, and—"

"But did he really? Nelly said he was sorry, sure, but he didn't say exactly what for. And he's the one person who *couldn't* have taken Digger's notebook from my bag, so—"

"Wait a minute, what notebook?"

"I wasn't going to tell you about it, but now I suppose I'd better. Actually, I should tell Eddie too." I frowned, trying to think straight. It had been a long day. "I mean, tell him that someone took the notebook. He already knows it exists."

Aaron snapped his fingers in front of my face. "Earth to Carnegie! You're zoning out on me, Stretch. Never mind what Eddie knows—I don't know anything. Start at the beginning, would you?"

So I started, beginning with the morning that my houseboat was burgled, which seemed like the distant past by now. I went over each step I'd taken, from testing out alibis with Eddie, to scoping out Digger's son, to trying to convince Starkey that the purse-snatching outside NocNoc was not some random urban crime.

"You got *mugged* and you didn't tell me?" Aaron pulled me to him, his hands tangled in my hair. It felt very good. "Oh, sweetheart. You weren't hurt, were you?"

"Only my pride. After that I was determined to solve this thing and clear Boris. So I went to see Judy Duvall. She showed me Digger's old notebooks, and I started wondering about the latest one . . ."

I went on to recount my theory that Digger had been working on an incriminating story, and described the way Betty Buckmeister had suddenly produced the notebook.

"And I suppose it never occurred to you," Aaron asked blandly, "that this was crucial evidence that should be turned over to the police?"

I shifted on the couch cushions. "Sure it did. But they were so convinced that Boris was guilty, I thought I'd better take a look through it myself."

"You're incorrigible. Do you understand that you're incorrigible?"

"Whatever. You want to hear this or not?"

"Keep talking, I'm listening."

Aaron listened ever more intently, as I told him about decoding Digger's notes, and getting background on steroids from Holly Crider, and hearing from Boris about Leroy Theroux's cryptic remark to Digger not long before the murder.

"The notebook said 'LT knows,' " I said, "so I figure that Theroux must know something about one of his players taking steroids."

"And you think he killed Duvall to protect the Navigators?" Aaron asked.

"No, not Theroux. He might have known about the drugs, but he couldn't have known that I had Digger's notebook. Gordo did, though. He saw it in my knapsack during our hike."

"You still had it after the hike, though?"

"Right, I transferred it to my shoulder bag. But Gordo could have followed me from the Batter's Box over to Yesler Field and taken it while I was out on the concourse with Nelly." I kneaded the back of my neck and sighed. "If only I still had that notebook. It's the one link between Gordo and steroids. So now I've got nothing to show the police, and tomorrow Rose might be marrying a killer!"

"But we don't know for sure . . ."

When he's thinking really hard, Aaron can't sit still. He began to circle the room, drumming his fingers on whatever surface he was passing, bookcase or door frame or window. Any other time I'd have asked him to quit, but now I could tell he was cooking up an idea—something I was fresh out of. I watched him and waited.

"Are you certain the notebook was stolen? It's not possible that you lost it somehow?"

"Well, maybe." I had an uncomfortable recollection of the torn lining in that pocket. "Anything's possible."

"Either way, we don't know for *sure*," he said, frowning in concentration, "that the notebook is the only link between Gutierrez and steroids. There could be something else. Some witness besides Leroy Theroux, some evidence that a reporter could track down."

"But Digger didn't find anything else."

Aaron gave the bookcase a final rap with his knuckles and turned toward me, his face alight. "He's not the only reporter around, is he? I don't usually cover sports stories, but who's to know I'm not following this one?"

"You're losing me," I said. "The wedding is tomorrow. How are you going to find evidence against Gordo so quickly?"

"I wouldn't have to find it, just make it seem that way. Remember the time I leaked the idea that I'd found a secret source about bribery in the governor's office? Once that got around, I had informers coming out of the woodwork." He gnawed his lower lip. "If I could provoke Gutierrez into saying something, or making some move, that would be enough to take to the police."

"Some move like killing you?" I crossed the room to take Aaron's arm, as if I could root him to the spot and keep him safe. "You can't—it's too dangerous!"

He gave a shout of laughter. "*You're* saying that? After running off to the wilderness with this guy, and prowling around the stadium after dark extorting confessions—"

We stared at each other, as the same thought struck both of us. I was the one to say it. "If Nelly wasn't confessing to murder, then what was he confessing to? It's really hard for me to see him as a killer, but—"

"Right." Deflated, Aaron dropped onto the couch again. "Tell me again what he said. His exact words."

I closed my eyes, remembering. "Nelly said he was sorry,

and that Digger made him do it. He kept saying 'What else could I do?' "

"But that could mean lots of things. Maybe he tried to quit drinking and then fell off the wagon. Or, I don't know, something else, something completely unrelated to the murder."

"And the blood on his shirt?"

Aaron rubbed his head briskly with both hands, leaving his crow-black hair in a mess of cowlicks. "Well, if Boris Nevsky touched the body, maybe Nelly did too. Doesn't mean he was the killer. Besides, unless you lost it, *somebody* took that notebook."

"True. But using yourself as bait isn't the way to find out, is it?"

"Guess I got carried away," he admitted.

"You sure did," I said. But meanwhile I was thinking, *Hmm . . . it's really not a bad idea . . .*

"And I don't suppose Gutierrez will be giving interviews on his wedding morning anyway," Aaron continued.

"Absolutely not," I agreed. "You couldn't get anywhere near him tomorrow."

But I could, I thought. *And since Gordo knows I had Digger's notebook, how does he know I don't have something else as well?*

To hide these thoughts, and the others racing into my mind on their heels, I opened my arms to Aaron.

"Speaking of carried away, are you spending the night?"

"Try and stop me," he said, his lips against my throat. Then he leaned back a little, smiling mischievously. "I've got my shaving kit in the car, but I was afraid to bring it while you were fuming like that. Why don't I go get it?"

Perfect. "Yes, why don't you?"

The minute the door closed behind him, I whipped out

my cell phone. The parking lot had been full when we arrived, so Aaron's car was a block away. I had to look up the number and work out how to phrase my message, but there should be just enough time . . .

"Hi, it's Carnegie," I said to Gordo's voice mail. I only had his home number, not his unlisted cell phone, but that was fine. I didn't want to reach him tonight anyway. I wanted to talk to him tomorrow, with other people within shouting distance.

"I need to ask you about something," I continued. "Digger Duvall was working on a story about steroid use, and I've just turned up a tape recording he made. It's a long story, but I was hoping you could help me decide what to do with it. Let's talk before the ceremony, OK?"

I added my call-back number, then shut off the phone. I didn't want Gordo calling me while Aaron was around. *But I'll watch him carefully tomorrow, and if he gives the least little sign that he's guilty, I'm going to raise hell and stop this wedding. I owe it to Rose.*

Aaron returned just a few minutes later, and murder was the last thing on his mind.

"Now, where was I?" he leered, guiding me back to the couch. "I think it was right around *here* . . ."

We picked up where we'd left off, so enthusiastically that an hour or so later we were both deep asleep among the cushions. My couch isn't all that roomy, but we didn't stir at all until the muffled but relentless sound of a cell phone disturbed us sometime near morning.

At first I tried to keep dozing, while Aaron fished around in the pile of clothes on the floor. Then I came full awake in a panic. If that was Gordo—

"Gold," Aaron croaked into the phone. I held my breath,

then let it out in relief as he said, "Izzy? Izzy, it's barely sunrise here! Yes, I know it's breakfast time where you are."

Smiling, I kissed Aaron on the temple and headed for the bedroom with my own phone firmly in hand. I set it on the bedside table along with the ruby ring and its chain, then crawled under the covers to stretch my cramped legs and sink back to sleep.

But not for long—I can't sleep properly without brushing my teeth. I tiptoed down the hall toward the bathroom, so quietly that Aaron must not have realized that I was up again.

"Like my life, Grandpa," I heard him say softly from the living room, taking care not to wake me. "I love her like my life."

I halted, eavesdropping shamelessly, while Izzy replied. Then Aaron spoke again.

"Well, you tell Frankie she can get over it. Carnegie's the best thing that ever happened to me, and I won't put up with . . . No, I'm sure she didn't mean to be rude . . . Uh-huh. Just tell her this is my wife she's talking about, OK?"

I hurried back into bed, and when Aaron slipped in next to me, I held him tight to my heart.

Chapter Thirty-two

Directing a large formal wedding is hard work. Assisting a bossy Frenchman to direct one is even harder. But if you add attempting to determine whether or not the bridegroom is a murderer, what you've got is an exercise in insanity.

I started the day off-balance, because Aaron and I overslept. We reviewed the coming day hastily, gulping breakfast as we talked.

"So can I hang out with you at this wingding," Aaron asked, "or are you on duty every minute?"

"Most minutes," I told him. "The ceremony's at noon on the pitcher's mound, so I'll be back and forth between the diamond and the rotunda until around eleven. After that I'll be up in the owners' suite helping Rose and Sheila get dressed."

I didn't add that at some point I'd be having a private conversation with the groom—which might lead to shocking news for the bride.

"Where will you be during the ceremony? I'll look for you from the press box."

"Oh, somewhere on the fringe of things." If things went as I expected, there wasn't going to be a ceremony. "Want the rest of this bagel?"

"Thanks." Aaron was looking adorably tousled and unshaven, and I suddenly wished we'd awakened extra early. "Who helps the groom get dressed, anyway?"

"Beau will, but it's just a little tie-straightening. If anything actually goes wrong, like a button needs sewing, he'll call me."

Aaron grinned. "And for this he gets the big bucks?"

"Well, he did design the whole event." I put our empty cups in the sink and dried my hands before lifting the ruby ring from my throat to gaze at it. *Thank you, Izzy. Thank you, Bella.* Then I noticed the clock on the stove and snapped out of my reverie. "I've got to run. See you at the stadium."

Ten minutes later I was up in the Made in Heaven office, explaining the situation—or rather, an edited version of it—to Eddie while reviewing my bridal emergency kit. Talk about insanity.

"You're giving up?" he asked in disbelief, chomping so hard I thought he'd bite his cigar in half.

"I told you, with the notebook gone I'm stuck." I stared at the items littering my desk. These were a mix of standard supplies and a few special items I'd added after one wedding mishap or another. "Let's see, emery board, bobby pins, lint brush . . ."

"I thought you were worried about the McKinney girl marrying a killer."

"I am, but there's only so much I can do." I was nervous as hell about what I'd already done, but no way was I going to tell Eddie about that. So I tried to distract myself from the risk I was running by diving deep into wedding-day mode. "Where's that nail polish?"

Clear polish is the best fix for runs in stockings, but I'd spilled mine the last time I used it. Eddie, still grumbling, yanked open the file drawer where we keep such miscellany, extracted a fresh bottle, and tossed it to me. I fielded the toss almost without looking and continued with my inventory. Moist towelettes, spare panty hose, moleskin for tight shoes...

The mini–first aid kit seemed to be complete, from antihistamines to aspirin to ammonia capsules for fainting spells. And I'd remembered to collect the spare buttons that came with Rose's gown. I tucked them into my sewing kit along with some black buttons for the gentlemen's tuxedos.

"Can't you bring the cops in?" Eddie demanded. "It's a hell of a thing to let that little girl—"

"No evidence, remember?" *Not unless I come up with some today.* "Now where's the chalk?"

Technically a tux should only be worn after dark, but at least Gordo and Rob wouldn't be sporting Navigator uniforms, as Leroy Theroux had suggested. Next to the sewing kit I set a little can of black polish for their dress shoes and a stick of chalk to hide any scuffs on Rose's white pumps.

I also had a Baggie of spare earrings and earring backs and even a pair of "gold" rings. I'd bought those after one dreadful occasion when the moronic best man had tried to juggle the wedding bands, and they'd rolled merrily into a gutter.

Eddie was still fulminating. "You know, it's all fine and good that Nevsky's off the hook now, but I should think you'd want to—"

"Could you just *drop* it, Eddie!"

I threw up my hands in vexation. One was filled with rolls of antacid and breath mints, the other with a pair of black socks. You'd be amazed at how many groomsmen show up in navy. I put the socks down and sighed.

"Sorry. I'm just anxious about—about the arrangements for today."

I picked up the big yellow identification badge that Beau insisted all his minions wear, so that interlopers could be spotted and barred from his domain. As I slipped the badge's lanyard over my head, I thought how odd it must look beside the ruby ring. But I could tuck the ring inside the neckline of my jade silk—which reminded me that I still had to polish my own leather flats.

"I've got to go get dressed. Tell me what I'm forgetting here."

Eddie came over to my desk—he can even walk indignantly—and surveyed the litter of stuff on it.

"Toupee tape," he growled.

"Right."

Double-sided carpet tape works in a pinch on slipping hems and bra straps, but toupee tape is a lot easier on the skin. I threw a roll of it into my bag, followed by the rest of the supplies—including a special spool of medium-blue thread. Sheila, Rose's bass guitarist and maid of honor, had demanded a black dress instead of the "lame" pastels she was originally offered, but we'd compromised on the blue of the Navigators' logo.

"I guess that's everything," I said. "I'll call you if—"

My phone chirred then, and I jumped. But it was only Beau, hounding me already.

"The *chocolat*, where is the *chocolat*? The machinery is here, the supplies are not! This was your responsibility, and you—"

"I'll be there in half an hour, Beau, right on schedule. And I'll call Justin before I leave."

Justin, a tall curly-haired youth, was our attendant for the chocolate fountain today. The fountain itself came by delivery truck, with the attendant bringing the edibles separately.

Justin was easily flustered but not flustered enough to forget the chocolate. Or was he? I thumbed in his number with one hand while opening the office door with the other.

"Hi, Justin?" I trotted down the outside stairs as I spoke. There was a chill in the air this morning—Indian summer couldn't last forever—but the sun was gaining strength already. "You've got all our supplies, don't you?"

"Well, there's a little problem."

I froze with my key in the front door lock. "I don't want to hear this. What kind of problem?"

"My car won't start. I think it's the battery, so I called a towing service, and—"

"Cancel it! What's your address?"

I didn't make the half-hour I'd promised Beau, but within the hour I was at Yesler Field helping Justin unload his delicacies, including the apricots, from my van. Then some of the caterer's men came out to help us, so once I'd confirmed that the bulk chocolate was Valrhona and not some cheap substitute—I can tell—I left them to it and entered the rotunda.

"Oh, wow." I turned in a slow circle to take it all in. "Oh, *wow*."

Beau Paliere was arrogant and volatile and a pain in the butt to work for, but I had to admit, the man was a genius with decor. Although he was famous for his after-dark affairs, the kind that use hundreds of lanterns or thousands of candles, he was no slouch in daytime either. Even partway decorated as it was now, with caterers and florists and electricians scurrying everywhere in a sort of orderly chaos, the rotunda was transformed.

Along the walls, tiered banks of blue and white hydrangeas

curved around the serving tables. One table held a special sort of pedestal affair for the cake, which hadn't arrived yet, and another bore the tall stainless-steel chocolate fountain. All the tablecloths were Navigator blue and green, and each table was flanked by old-fashioned lampposts festooned with ivy and hung with baskets of gardenias and stephanotis.

The centerpiece of the huge round space was an ivy-twined latticework gazebo beneath the chandelier of bats, surrounded by a raised ring-shaped dance floor guarded by a low railing. One of Boris Nevsky's Sergeis, the tallest one, was attaching a garland of greenery and white roses to the railing, and the overall effect was as cheery and wholesome as baseball itself.

"It makes an improvement, *non*?"

As Beau approached across the rotunda, he was trailed by one of the videographers I'd hired to take documentary-style footage. And Beau was certainly photogenic this morning. Next to his hand-tailored Italian suit, my good old jade silk dress felt provincial.

"It's phenomenal, Beau." I tried not to look at the camera or fidget with my hair. "You've done wonders."

"Of course I have." He favored the future audience with a profile, then waved the videographer away and snapped, "You brought the *chocolat*?"

"It's unloading now. Is Gordo here yet? I need to talk to him—"

"Later." Beau made a haughty gesture toward the gazebo. "First you will coordinate with the electrical crew. The sound system, it has too many cables, and— Who is that person? He has no badge!"

"It's OK, Beau, I'll take care of it."

The person in question was JD, Digger's son and Rose's

lovelorn bandmate, who had apparently slipped in through the loading dock. He wore the same black leathers I'd seen him in at the engagement party and also at NocNoc the other night. But unlike his hangdog demeanor on those occasions, JD came marching across the rotunda toward me now with his eyes ablaze and his goateed chin held high, a man on a mission.

"Where's Rose?" he demanded. "I've got to see her. I've got to!"

He leaned in close to me as he said it. That's when I saw that his breath was coming short and fast, and his pupils were the size of salad plates. I'm no expert on controlled substances, but it was clear that young JD had snorted his breakfast this morning.

"She's not here yet," I said brightly, slipping my arm through his and moving toward the exit. "Let's go talk about this, OK? Then I can tell you all about today's schedule, and we'll work something out. Rose will be glad to see you . . ."

Like hell she will, I was thinking, but I kept up a relentless flow of words as we walked. All I wanted was to get JD outside the main doors, where one of the stadium's security guards could take over. I had enough to worry about today without heartbroken druggies cluttering up the scene.

"You see, Rose will be busy getting dressed for the ceremony, and of course with everything going on, it'll be quite some time before she's available, but I'm sure we can arrange a few minutes for you and the rest of the band to say goodbye before she leaves—"

My tactic almost worked. But at the sound of the word "goodbye" JD exploded.

"I'm not saying goodbye!" As he tore his arm away, his

voice rose to a scream. "I'm never going to say goodbye to Rose! She's mine, she has to be mine, it's our destiny!"

"Maybe it is, JD, but you have to face facts and—"

"Don't you talk down to me!"

We were almost at the door by then, and the guard stationed there heard the shouting and burst inside. A nasty little scuffle ensued, but the damage was limited to a pot of hydrangeas toppling over and my cracking a nail when JD's flailing arms sent me stumbling into the door frame. Within three minutes he was pinned tight between the guard and a Sergei, who seemed to be enjoying the break from his floral duties.

"I'll get you for this!" JD howled, but not at the guards. As they hustled him away, his wild eyes were glaring only at me. "I'll kill you, you bitch. I'll *kill* you!"

Chapter Thirty-three

Up in the owners' suite, the atmosphere was chaotic but cheerful—and I didn't darken it by mentioning JD's outburst. Rose would soon have enough to deal with without that.

She was certainly in good spirits this morning, giggling with her friends over coffee and pastries and the traditional bottle of champagne. The suite's curtains were drawn to give the ladies privacy, and both Rose and Sheila were already down to their underwear.

Sheila, a tall and busty blonde, was making most of the noise as she flung her bouquet in the air and caught it again, over and over. Three other girls, whom I recognized from NocNoc, sat at the bar making faces at themselves in the lighted makeup mirror that I'd had delivered the night before.

"Hey, Sheila, show us your new tattoo!" one of them called out.

Sheila obliged by turning her back and bending over. She wore a black lace thong, so the artwork was clearly visible: a full-color "USDA Prime" shield low on one cheek. I'd also had a full-length three-way mirror set up, and she turned to admire the view herself. Silently, I applauded myself for banning the photographers from this particular dressing room.

"I'm gonna get one on the other side next," she announced. "A big sign saying 'Exit Only.'"

As the girls shrieked with laughter, I set down my tote bag.

"Good morning, Rose. Sheila, it's too late to replace those flowers, so if you wouldn't mind—"

"Whoops!" she said. "The chaperone's here. Beat it, you guys."

The three friends trooped out, and Rose surprised me by rushing over to give me a hug—even though she was sober. Her lingerie was a bit more decorous than Sheila's, and she'd gone with all-black for her hair, no spikes or neon streaks. Her eyes were clear and glowing, just like a bride's.

"Hey, Carnegie. Everything OK down there?"

"Everything's fine. How about you? No last-minute nerves?"

"Nope." She frowned a little. "Gordo's sure edgy, though."

I kept my voice neutral. "Oh, really?"

"Yeah, he was fine at first this morning, and then all of a sudden he got real quiet and tense."

"Any idea why?"

Rose looked at me curiously. "Well, duh, he's only getting married today. Why do you think?"

"Of course," I said, feeling pretty tense myself. I fingered the phone in the pocket of my dress, willing Gordo to call and get this over with. "Of course that's why. Um, shall we do your makeup?"

Some brides have beauticians and hairdressers standing by for the big moment, but Rose had requested only a little help from me. She took her place before the mirror, I adjusted its lights to mimic daylight, and together we accented her large, dark eyes and dusted blush on her cheekbones.

It all felt like such a charade to me, when any minute now I might be accusing the groom of murder and the bride might be spoiling her mascara with furious tears. Rose reached for a lipstick, but I shook my head and offered her a different tube.

"Try this," I said. "Lipstick always photographs dark, and if you wear that one, it'll show as practically black."

"Cool!" said Sheila, breathing over my shoulder. "We gotta do something to jazz this up, instead of looking like a couple of Barbie dolls. I'm telling you, these dresses are so lame—"

"Enough about the dresses!" I snapped. "The dresses are lovely."

"Temper, temper," Sheila taunted. She reached for the champagne while Rose applied the paler lipstick. "Have a drink and chill, why don't you?"

I gave her my sternest frown. "No, thank you."

She set the bottle down again. "Guess I've had enough myself. For now, anyway. I've got a bitch of a headache. Rosie, have you got something I can take?"

"I do." I pulled out the first aid kit and removed the little white package of aspirin. Sheila reached for it, but I put it quickly on the bar and stepped away.

"What, you're afraid to touch me?" she asked hotly. "Like I got cooties?"

"It's a liability issue," I explained, almost glad of the distraction from waiting for my phone to go off. It was like having a bomb in my pocket. "We never give drugs to anyone, we just make them available. That way if someone has an allergic reaction, or—oh!"

I snatched the phone from my pocket and saw that the

caller ID said UNKNOWN. I moved to a corner of the room. "Hello?"

"Carnegie, it's Gordo Gutierrez." His voice, normally so laid back, was oddly formal and self-conscious. "Could I talk to you for a minute? Alone."

"Sure," I said. My heart was hammering. "Where?"

"How about the interview room? You know where that is?"

"Give me five minutes."

I excused myself to Rose with a vague comment about checking on something in the rotunda. But at the door of the suite, I hesitated. Gordo wouldn't dare harm me this morning, I was sure of that. But there was no sense in being foolhardy.

"I'm going to stop by the interview room as well," I said. "To talk with Gordo. I guess he's pretty nervous."

"Should I go?" said Rose. Then she grinned. "But he's not supposed to see me, right?"

"Right. You two stay here, and I'll be back shortly."

I felt myself perspiring as I strode along, and at one point I stopped to take some deep breaths and fight off some second thoughts. *Maybe I should have brought a tape recorder, in case he incriminates himself. Maybe I should have brought a security guard, in case he has a gun. Why don't we screen for weapons at these big weddings, anyway?*

Maybe . . . maybe nothing. Just go. So I went and saw no one along the way, though I could faintly hear the noise of the gathering crowd down in the rotunda.

To steady my nerves, I deliberately imagined the scene. People would be streaming through the stadium's main entrance by now, and the press would be gathering up in their gallery. Soon the gates to the stands would be flung open, and the fans would pour in. They'd see the flower-decked pergola set up on the pitcher's mound and hear the Dixieland band tuning up in the home team dugout.

Soon the Reverend Francis Cornwell, an old friend of the bride's father and a major baseball fan, would take his place beneath the pergola. All the Navigators, in full uniform and bearing regulation bats, would line up in double file to make an aisle leading to the mound from home plate.

The fans would be given a wedding program—designed to resemble a baseball program, of course—which described each phase of the celebration. Including the fact that after the ceremony the bride and groom would return along the aisle under an arch of bats held aloft by Gordo's teammates. Given the way that Digger died, I'd objected to the bats, but Beau had overruled me.

All too quickly I had reached my destination. *Still time to chicken out ... No! You've come this far ...*

I entered the interview room with a nasty sense of déjà vu. But instead of Nelly Tibbett ranting, there was the bride-groom sitting quietly in the front row of folding chairs. He was gazing at the wall of Navigator logos, looking large and dignified in his tuxedo. But when he turned toward me, the round brown face above the bow tie was young and anxious.

I made myself approach him, though my pulse was thud-ding in my ears. "Hi, Gordo."

"Carnegie." He rose, and I fell back half a step. The man was huge. *The minute he says anything I can use, I'm out of here.*

He took a step toward me, and I made myself stand my ground. *What a phenomenally stupid idea this was. Why did I do this?*

Gordo came even closer—and then went past me to the doorway, to peer up and down the corridor.

"Listen," he said stiffly, his voice strange and unfamiliar. "Did you tell anybody you're talking to me?"

Don't tip him off. Make him commit himself.

"No," I said through sandpaper lips. "No one knows I'm here."

"Good." He reached behind him and shut the door.

Chapter Thirty-four

"It's my lawyer," said Gordo.

I looked at him blankly.

"Y-your lawyer?"

"Yeah. He says this has to be real confidential." Gordo heaved a vast sigh, and I realized that the expression on his face had shifted, not to anger or menace or guile but to *embarrassment*. "I want to help you out, I really do. But see, if anybody knew that I knew anything about . . . about what you said in your message . . ."

He shook his head in frustration. "This is crazy, but Bernie told me not to even say that word."

"Bernie?" I felt like a parrot.

"My lawyer. He said I shouldn't talk to you about . . . you-know-what, that begins with S. But you been so nice to me and Rosie, I didn't want to be rude."

"Rude." The air was leaking out of my big balloon of a drama. "I don't understand."

"Bernie says, if you have any information about anything illegal, you got to take it to the police right away." Gordo forced the words out in a rush, as if he'd rehearsed them. "Don't tell me about it, or tell anybody else in the Navigators, 'cause then we could get subpoenaed."

"But—"

"Por favor!" he pleaded, looking very young indeed. "I don't want to get in trouble and mess up my honeymoon. Rosie would kill me."

I almost laughed aloud, as relief flooded through me like warm brandy. Thank heavens I never voiced my suspicions to anyone but Aaron!

"Digger tried to interview me about drugs," Gordo was saying. "But everybody said not to talk to him."

"Everybody?" I asked quickly. "Do you think anyone else on the team was using steroids?"

"No way! Mr. Theroux makes a big deal about that, every season, and he's always doing drug tests." He grinned. "On the Navigators, you get good at peeing in cups."

This time I did laugh. There was still the chance that Gordo was bluffing, but I didn't believe it. He was transparent in his innocence. Suddenly my whole edifice of suspicion and theory and guesswork came tumbling down upon itself like a house of cards.

Of course Nelly Tibbett had killed Digger Duvall. Being back in this room only served to confirm it. Why else had Nelly confessed to me right here on this spot, and why else had he ended his life? Boris was free, Gordo was blameless, and Rose would have a wonderful wedding day.

"Don't worry," I said warmly. "I'll take . . . my information to the police, and we'll pretend this conversation never happened. You were nervous about the ceremony, and I reassured you. All right?"

"All right." He grinned. "Thanks, Carnegie. How's Rosie doing?"

"Just fine. In fact, I have to go help her get dressed. You look very handsome, Gordo."

"You think so?" He squared his tuxedoed shoulders and

puffed out his substantial chest. "I thought it would feel weird, but special clothes for a special day, right?"

"Right. Off you go, then, or Beau will be frantic."

The grin grew wider. "That guy's a real character, isn't he? Like in a movie. Thanks again."

And off he went. As his footsteps faded down the hallway, I heard the bridegroom whistling "Take Me Out to the Ballgame."

"*There* you are," said Sheila, when I returned to the suite. "Isn't it time to suit up?"

"I suppose so," I said absently, preoccupied with my thoughts. Once again I'd made a murderous mountain out of an accidental molehill. I'd have to explain to Aaron that—

"Carnegie?" Rose had put her jacket on over her underwear. She looked chilly and nervous. "Carnegie, it's eleven-fifteen."

"What?! I mean, yes, of course, let's get you both dressed. You first, Sheila."

Once the maid of honor saw herself in the three-paneled mirror, her fashion objections died away. The royal blue of her gown suited her coloring beautifully, and so did the wrapped-V neckline.

"Am I hot or what?" she crowed, swaying this way and that before the glass. "Can't I open up the front to go lower? If you got it, flaunt it."

"No," I said hastily. Sheila's left breast bore the tattooed image of a death's-head skull with a dagger through it, and the dress barely covered it now. "No, you can't. Ready, Rose?"

Even Sheila gave a wondering sigh at the vision of Rose in her wedding gown. She helped me fan out the gleaming curves of the fluted skirt, and then I lifted the veil from its special Le Boutique box and stood on a chair to let it fall free. As I set the headpiece on Rose's dark curls, the yards and yards of silk tulle floated down around her like a blessing from above.

"Beautiful," I said, my voice breaking and my thoughts adrift. *Should I wear a long veil? Should I hire a planner to help me with it, as Joe suggested? And do I really have to wait a year? It seems like forever.*

Rose smiled shyly at her reflection, her eyes showing huge and dark behind the filmy tulle. "Am I really?"

"Really and truly."

I was so transfixed, I almost fell off the chair when my phone rang again.

"*Eh bien,*" said Beau. "The bride is ready?"

"Ready, willing, and—"

"Very well. You will come downstairs at once."

Downstairs, near the archway leading out to the diamond, Walter McKinney awaited his daughter. Daylight penetrated the shadows of the hallway where he stood, glinting on his glasses and lighting up the white shirtfront of his tuxedo. The black jacket disguised the hunch of his shoulders, and the gratified smile on his face took ten years off his age.

"Rose," he said. "Oh, *Rose.* Your mother would be so happy."

I half-expected her to bristle, but instead she lifted the veil and held aside her deep-blue bouquet so that she could embrace him. He pressed his lips delicately to her cheek, careful not to muss her lipstick.

"Thank you, Daddy," she whispered. "Thanks for everything."

God, I love this job, I thought. Then, more pragmatically, I looked around for our chief sound technician. As he hurried forward to fit Rose with her wireless mike—where on earth had he come up with a white one?—I gazed out at the diamond, shielding my eyes from the brighter light.

The backstop behind home plate had been removed, and I could see all the way to the far end of the double file of ballplayers. Gordo stood wide-eyed on the pitcher's mound with Rob Harmon beside him. *Charmin' Harmon,* I thought appreciatively, *was born to wear a tux.* Then I caught a flicker of movement closer to the archway: Beau, waiting impatiently in the on-deck circle, had put his fists on his hips. I waved to him that we were all set.

Beau lifted his hand. The Dixieland band played "Here Comes the Bride," surprisingly well. I sent Sheila out into the sunlight, counted out the interval, then nodded at Rose and Walter to proceed. As they stepped across home plate, the eager crowd broke into a storm of applause.

Once again I had to admire Beau Paliere's expertise. His marketing slogan was "Beauty and Perfection in Every Detail," and for the McKinney/Gutierrez nuptials he delivered exactly that. Gordo and Reverend Cornwell were miked as well, so every word of the ceremony was carried into the stands with nary a hiss or a crackle. The soloist was excellent, the videographers and still photographers worked briskly and inconspicuously, and even the arched bats seemed like a good idea after all.

I watched from my hidden vantage point, attempting as always to maintain my professional distance and analyze the logistics of the event. But then, as always, I gave way to sentiment and blinked away tears when the reverend said, "You may now kiss the bride."

Only this time, as my clients embraced, I caressed the ruby ring on its gold chain. I'd have it resized Monday, then ask Aaron to slip it on my hand. Meanwhile the kiss was over, and I gasped and cheered along with everyone else when Rose Gutierrez suddenly turned into Honeysuckle Hell.

"All *right*!" she shouted, pumping her fist—and then she leaped into her husband's arms.

Even drug free, Gordo was a powerful man. Without the slightest sign of effort, he carried his wife the entire length of the arch of bats. Rose's veil lifted and rippled in their wake, to trail teasingly across the faces of his grinning teammates.

Rob and Sheila followed the happy pair, laughing gaily. This unorthodox recessional continued across home plate and on through the archway, where Gordo set his bride down right in front of me.

"Congratulations!" I gave them each a heartfelt hug. "You're amazing, both of you."

"*Vite, vite!*" Beau appeared and flapped his hands at us. "To the gazebo, at once!"

"All right, we're going," I told him, as Rose and her father embraced. Then, because I was happy for my bride and feeling generous, I added, "You're a master, Beau. It was a lovely ceremony."

"Of course it was, except for this—this prank at the end," he muttered venomously. "I make precise plans, and then this bizarre little 'Oneysuckle ruins them with her—"

"You know what, Beau?" Still giddy with relief about Gordo, I threw caution to the winds. "You know what I think?"

"What?"

"I think you're a freakin' drama queen."

Chapter Thirty-five

As Beau stared at me, astonished, I turned my attention to the bridal party. Rose and Gordo were lost in each other's eyes, and Sheila had seized the moment to plant a big wet kiss on the best man. Rob looked startled at first, then returned the favor with interest—so much so that when they broke the clinch, her skull was showing. Then Rob smiled at me invitingly, and I briefly considered following Sheila's example. *After all, I missed out on that kiss at Snow Lake . . .*

No. I'd had enough trouble with Charmin' Harmon, I decided. So I confined myself to a firm handshake—which he used to pull me quickly toward him and deliver a chaste but impudent peck on my cheek. I felt his breath across my earlobe, caught the musky scent of sandalwood—and had to pull myself together before my knees gave out from under me.

With my eyes on everything and everyone but Rob, I escorted the wedding party up the elevator and along the corridor to the owners' suite.

"Bathroom break, everybody," I announced. "And then you're on stage again for the duration. Rose, let's hang up your veil, and Sheila, let me fix your hair. You're a little tousled."

When everyone was sorted out, I ushered them out to the gallery above the flowery, festive rotunda. The crowd had poured back inside, and another round of applause and camera flashes greeted the foursome as they descended to the main floor and then mounted the steps of the gazebo. Beau, I noticed, was busy chatting with the governor's wife—who just happened to have a marriageable daughter.

"Welcome, guys and gals, welcome!"

Today's master of ceremonies was a popular local DJ named Drive Time Tony, a tiny fellow with an enormous voice. As he boomed out his greeting to the crowd, I retreated and checked my watch. I had a few moments to myself before starting my rounds of the serving tables. Beau, of course, would stay in the spotlight, while I kept track of the food and drink supply.

The press of people was getting denser by the minute, but I pushed my way through to the escalator and rode it upward, scanning the faces below for Aaron. I was bursting to tell him about Gordo's innocence, hopefully without admitting to the risky method I'd used to confirm it. Beau saw me ascending above him and nodded graciously, so either he'd forgiven my rude remark or—more likely—he hadn't understood it.

"Kharrnegie!" There was Boris at the head of the escalator, resplendent in a three-piece suit and flinging open his bear-like arms. "You left restaurant so quickly last night, I did not say proper goodbye."

Naturally, the Mad Russian's definition of *proper* involved a rib-crunching embrace and a lengthy kiss. His beard smelled like vodka.

"Is wonderful party, no? You like my flowers?"

"They're as fabulous as always, Boris. I especially love the gazebo. Although I wish they'd turn down the microphone."

Down in the gazebo, Drive Time was loudly introducing

Rob Harmon, Seattle's own soon-to-be Hall of Famer, three-time winner of the Cy Young Award, a man with a remarkably long and brilliant career, a pitcher of deadly accuracy and astonishing speed, blah, blah, blah . . .

He concluded with an off-color quip about the effect of Rob's movie-star looks on what he called "all the broads." Nearby I saw Leroy Theroux, the general manager, scowling fiercely.

"What a stupid thing to say," I protested.

"But true," said Boris, pursing his lips. "Rob Harmon looks good, even smells good. Women like that."

"Mm-hmm," I murmured. "Sandalwood."

"*Nyet.*" The Russian shook his head with authority. "Musk, amber, with midnote of lavender and leetle jasmine."

"You would know," I said, amused. "You've got the nose for flowers. Maybe you should find out his brand and wear it yourself."

Boris surprised me by hoisting his shoulders in a shudder of revulsion. "*Beh.* It would remind me of finding corpse. Deeger, he wore this same cologne."

"Really? I thought—" Someone tapped my shoulder, and I turned. "Aaron! Listen, I have to tell you something—"

But Aaron was making up for his ill-tempered departure from Canlis last night.

"Congratulations, Nevsky. Welcome to the free world."

Boris pumped the hand he was offered. "Thenk you! And my congratulations to you too. You will be good husband to my Kharnegie, no?"

"I'll certainly give it a shot." Aaron straightened his tie, dislodged by the force of the Russian's handshake. "Got a minute, Stretch? We need to talk."

"We sure do. See you later, Boris."

Aaron and I took a spot at the gallery rail directly above the chocolate fountain. From there I could keep an eye on the proceedings, and we could converse privately under cover of the general noise.

"So, what's the big news?" Aaron asked. "Swell party, by the way."

"Thanks. The news is that Gordo didn't do it."

He cocked an eyebrow. "You're certain of that?"

"Positive. I, um, happened to discuss steroids with him—"

"You *what*?"

"It just came up."

"Of course it did." Aaron's disbelief was obvious. "You know, you are the most—"

"Never mind, just listen." The clamor of voices all around us, combined with the band's upbeat background music, created a sense of seclusion. I described the way Gordo had reacted to the mention of steroids, and how convinced I now was of his innocence. "So I guess it must have been Nelly Tibbett all along."

Aaron listened solemnly, but I could see him suppressing a smile. "You think so, do you?"

"Yes, I do."

"Well, thank God for that!" He snorted with laughter. "The more I thought about it today, the more nutty your theory sounded. Here I've been trying to figure out a way to convince you to drop the whole thing, and now you saved me the trouble."

"But what about last night?" I protested, feeling strangely let down. "You were so into the whole idea."

"You have that effect on me, Nancy Drew." He nodded at the ruby ring. "That's why I gave you that. C'mere."

Aaron hugged me to his side, and as the heady aroma of warm chocolate wafted up to us, I forgot all about murder and hugged him back. Then, highly contented, we leaned over the railing to peer downward. Justin was doing a nice job down there, handing out little plates and instructing guests on how to dip their chosen goodies.

A chocolate fountain is basically a heater for melting the chocolate with a big stainless-steel column on top. The column has a corkscrew-shaped blade inside that draws the thick liquid upward and releases it in a slowly descending flow of delectability. I watched a little boy poke a pretzel stick into the glistening brown curtain and then pop it in his mouth. My own mouth watered.

"Should we have a chocolate fountain?" I said.

"What, in our living room?"

"No, idiot, at our wedding reception."

"Is this what you want, Stretch?" Aaron glanced around the rotunda with narrowed eyes. "Something as fancy as all this?"

"Well, not quite on this scale, but—" I turned to face him. "What about you, Aaron. What do you want?"

"What else?" He kissed me lightly. "All I want is you."

"And you shall have me," I said, "but not until later. I've got to go."

"Me too. Now that we're not snooping today, I'm heading over to the office. But tell me something first." Aaron paused, looking ill at ease. "Um, was that all right last night about asking Dree and Kimmie to be bridesmaids? I was trying to get involved, like you wanted, but you didn't look too happy about it."

"Happy? About being preceded down the aisle by the Bitch Sisters?"

He winced. "Sorry. I just thought, since they're going to be your relatives soon—"

"I'll handle it," I said, though I had no idea how. "Maybe they'll love Belize so much they'll never come back."

"There's a thought. Call you later."

We parted at the bottom of the escalator, Aaron for the exit and me for the cake table. Juice's giant baseball was deliciously witty—and even bigger than I'd expected, at least a hundred pounds of cheesecake waiting to be devoured. Just as I'd planned, the pedestal arrangement prevented anyone from touching it, but lots of folks were snapping pictures. I checked in with the designated cake-slicer and moved on to the other tables.

"Hey there, gal!"

Buck Buckmeister tipped up his bag of Cracker Jack to get at the last fragments, smacked his lips over them, and gave me a big smile. Beside him little Betty was working on a hot dog as long as her forearm. They both wore Navigator caps, Navigator jackets over Navigator T-shirts, and for all I knew, Navigator underwear. No half-measures for the Killer B's.

"Having fun?" I asked them.

"You bet!" Buck bellowed, that being his normal volume. "This here's almost as good as the wingding you put on for our Bonnie. Hey, we just got some news from her!"

I looked from him to Betty, and from the sparkle in her shoe-button eyes I guessed right away.

"She's expecting?"

"Due in April," said the proud grandma-to-be, and took another bite of her wiener. "In fact they might name her April, only that doesn't start with B, does it?"

As I agreed that this was an issue to be considered, the band swung into a salsa beat, and the three of us turned toward the dance floor. Time for the wedded couple's first dance, which, in honor of Gordo's birthplace, was to be a merengue.

"Ain't they something?" Buck marveled.

They were indeed. For all his size, Gordo moved deftly through the intricate pattern of steps, while he and Rose undulated their shoulders and hips in rapid but sultry harmony. The crowd whistled and stamped as he spun his bride around and around, then gathered her to him in a sudden twining of arms.

"Bravo!" I called out. "They must have practiced for—"

"Jiminy *Christmas*," said Buck. "What's that young feller up to over there?"

He nodded toward the chocolate fountain. I followed his gaze and groaned: JD was back, arguing heatedly with the same security guard who'd removed him the first time. Justin had backed away in concern, and the guard looked baffled, as well he might.

Loud and distraught, JD was already drawing stares. But frog-marching him out of the building would cause a sensation, and not a good one. At least most of the guests were focused on the dancing. I darted through a gap in the crowd, pulling out my cell phone as I went and speed-dialing the other guards.

"Trouble at the chocolate fountain. Get this guy out of here, quietly and *now*."

As I arrived at the scene, things suddenly got worse. Much worse. JD tried to push past the guard, they grappled, and then JD fell back and pulled a small black pistol from his jacket. He didn't point it at anybody, but that didn't help much.

"If Rose won't talk to me," he said grimly, "I swear to God

I'm gonna blow my head off. It's loaded too, don't think it isn't. I'm not kidding, you bring Rose over here."

The guard froze, and so did I, but my brain didn't. *A gun! The crowd could panic, jam the exits. Not another suicide, not after Nelly. Not after Digger's bloody corpse. Oh God, a gun.*

Behind me the salsa tune speeded up, rose to a climax, and ended with a blare of brass and a burst of applause. JD hesitated, his attention wavering, and as he did, a black-clad figure stepped in front of me. Rob Harmon strode quickly up to JD, spoke a few words I didn't hear, and slid the gun into the pocket of his tuxedo.

Just like that.

Given the events of the past week, my nerves weren't too steady to start with. I sagged back against the fountain table, pressing cold fingers to my trembling lips and trying to remember how to inhale. Rob and the guard took JD by the arms and began to move him toward the nearest exit. As they passed, I watched JD's face. The fight had gone out of him, but his eyes were still wide and staring, and—

"Bitch!"

JD lashed out at me with one booted foot. His captors wrenched him aside and hustled him away, but only after he caught me right on the kneecap. It hurt like hell, and as I leaped backward my feet flew out from under me and my full weight came down on the table edge. The table teetered, its cloth dragged forward as I slid to the ground, the fountain rocked on its moorings . . . and the rest was a foregone conclusion.

I wound up on the floor, surrounded by gawking guests, with a lap full of apricots and a stream of warm Valrhona pouring down my hair and over my chest to join them.

"What the blue blazes are you doing down there?" Leroy

Theroux, as bad luck would have it, hadn't seen JD at all. But he'd caught the first candy-dipped wedding planner in history, and he was not amused. "Things are getting crazier and crazier around here! First it's Duvall, and then it's Lionel Goddamn Tibbett, and now it's *this*!"

"I can explain," I said, struggling to get up. Justin reached out a hand to help me, while one of the less charitable onlookers took a flash picture. "You see—"

"Never mind explaining!" Leroy snapped. "Just get yourself gone!"

And so I did.

Chapter Thirty-six

"You washed it *off*?" Aaron sounded inconsolable. "No fair! I always wanted a chocolate-covered girl."

"Very funny." I tilted my wet head away from the telephone and scrubbed at my hair with a towel. "Leroy Theroux was furious, and so was Beau. He told me not to come back, but of course I have to—to—"

My lips kept moving, but no sound came out. I dropped the towel and clutched at my throat in horror.

"Are you there? Hey, Stretch? Hello?"

I shook out the towel and then opened my robe. No gold chain. *No ruby ring.*

"Um, gosh, I just noticed the time." Frantically, I checked around the floor of my bedroom. Nothing. "I have to go back to the stadium, Aaron. The reception must be almost over. Talk to you later, OK?"

"All right. Just stay away from kids with guns."

The moment he said goodbye, I tossed the phone aside and dropped to hands and knees to peer under the bed. Then I checked the bathroom floor, the bathtub drain—with its fine-meshed strainer, thank God—and all my chocolate-stained clothing. No sign of Grandma Bella's ring.

Swearing breathlessly, I jumped into jeans and sweatshirt and backtracked my way through the houseboat. Then out to the parking lot, where the sun was still shining but a chilly wind licked at my wet hair. I patted down Vanna's front seats and pulled out the floor mats. Nothing, nothing, nothing.

As I drove downtown, I mentally backtracked my way through the wedding. When did I last notice the ring? I'd touched it during the ceremony, that was definite, and then Aaron had said something about it. I'd meant to show it to the Buckmeisters, but Buck had spotted JD and—

"Oh, *shit*," I said aloud, and barely made my turn onto Aurora Avenue. "The chocolate fountain!"

At some point in my tumble against the fountain's table, the chain must have come loose or even broken. With all those liquefied calories oozing around, and the cleanup that followed, the ring could have easily been scooped into the garbage.

I drove faster, trying to reconstruct the details of the incident. The tablecloth bunched beneath me, the apricots in my lap . . . Had I noticed a glint from the ruby, had I felt the chain give way? The crowd gathering, Leroy yelling about Lionel Goddamn Tibbett . . .

Lionel Tibbett . . . *Lionel* Tibbett? What if LT wasn't Leroy Theroux? What if he was Nelly Tibbett?

The truck ahead of me braked, and Vanna damn near ran right up his tailpipe. I slowed down and proceeded more cautiously, setting aside for the moment my fears about the ring. Nothing I could do about it till I got to Yesler Field, and meanwhile I had some thinking to do.

Because if Nelly was the LT mentioned in the notebook— and that made sense, with Leroy Theroux so adamantly antisteroids—then what was it he knew that Digger was so curious about? And was that knowledge a motive for murder? That piece still didn't make sense.

Threading through the traffic around Pioneer Square, I realized something. Despite my conversation with Aaron in the gallery, I still couldn't convince myself that Nelly, the man I'd seen feeding the seagulls, was the man who killed Digger Duvall with a baseball bat. Yet the police were convinced.

As I reached Yesler Field, I strained to remember everything I knew about Nelly Tibbett, which was little enough. His career had been mediocre, so if he used steroids himself, they didn't help him much. And he'd worked as a batting coach for the Navigators, but according to Gordo he wouldn't have seen any drug use in Seattle, at least not since Theroux came on board.

So what did LT know? Tibbett's playing days with the Red Sox seemed too long ago to use for a news story now, but I wondered what he'd done with himself between then and his job with the Navs. That could be researched, of course.

Of course, but why bother? I steered Vanna into the lot near the loading dock and yanked on the brake with a discouraged sigh. It didn't matter much now. Poor Nelly was dead, and his motives would hardly interest anyone among the living. Besides, I had my own mystery to solve. Where the hell was that ring?

The reception wasn't almost over; it was over. Inside the rotunda the gazebo was denuded of flowers and the cleaning crew was almost finished. I threaded my way through the trash barrels full of wadded paper napkins and crumpled peanut bags, praying that my engagement ring wasn't lying at the bottom of one of them. Then I reached the center of the space and circled the gazebo toward what had been Eugene's station.

It was completely vacated. The table was still in place, stripped of its cloth and scrubbed clean, and the aroma of chocolate still hung in the air. But the fountain itself was gone, along with the plates of goodies, the napkins, everything. I could have wept.

" 'Scuse me, Miss Kincaid?" Eugene, the dependable security guard, approached me with a hopeful expression on his creased old face and a platter in his gnarled old hands. The platter held a heap of biscotti, macaroons, pretzel rods, and dried apricots, mixed higgledy-piggledy in a most un-caterer way. "There was a lot of sweets left over, and I was wondering, could the fellas bring some home to their kids?"

"Sure, why not? Be a shame to waste it all." I picked up a pretzel and munched it miserably. *Might as well fortify myself. All those trash barrels to search, and probably the Dumpsters outside.*

"What the hey?" said Eugene. "Careful, there's a piece a wire or something in there. Almost looks like a—"

"A ring?" I poked frenetically into the heap. "Is it . . . ? It can't be . . . Oh, Eugene, it *is*!"

A moment later you couldn't tell who was the more amazed: me because I had Bella's ruby clutched safely in my hand, or Eugene because I'd wrapped my arms around him and was kissing him in gratitude. My gold chain was long gone, but that didn't matter. The chain must have snapped and sent the ring flying into a tray of dipping items, from which it had been dumped into the platter.

"I can't believe it!" I said, releasing him. "You have no idea how important this is."

"What's so important?" drawled a soft voice, and the fading aroma of chocolate was joined by the musky scent of Rob Harmon's cologne. He had changed from tuxedo into slacks and a windbreaker, and carried an oversize gym bag by its handles with the shoulder strap dangling. "Must be something good."

"Incredibly good," I told him. "I lost my engagement ring when the fountain tipped over, but Eugene just found it for me."

"Well, not so much found it as come upon it," said the older man. "You lose anything else, Miss Kincaid, or can the fellas take the rest of the leftovers? We're clearing out now."

"They can have them all," I said gaily. "I'll be in the owners' suite for a little, then I'll lock up."

As Eugene walked away, I turned back to Rob. "What a relief!"

"Glad to hear it."

With the ring recovered, I refocused on the rest of the world. "So what happened with JD? And thank you so much for stepping in. That could have been a nightmare."

"Your security people took care of him," said Rob in those honeyed Virginian tones. Was I mistaken, or was his accent getting stronger? "I don't think the boy was capable of much, doped up like that."

"Still, taking that gun from him was incredible."

He shrugged. "No big thing. You get some strange goings-on during road trips sometimes."

"And I suppose pitching is all about grace under pressure, isn't it?"

"Oh, yes." Rob smiled. "Yes, it is."

And at that precise moment, looking into those unblinking blue eyes and breathing in that distinctive cologne, I knew. All the odd-shaped pieces clicked together like the pattern in a kaleidoscope, and I knew who really murdered Digger Duvall. And it wasn't Nelly Tibbett. *Oh, my God.*

"Well," I said, turning aside and trying hard to keep my voice level, "I'd better get back to work."

"I'll walk with you up to the suite," Rob said lightly. "My plane's not for a couple of hours. I can help fetch and carry."

I halted. "Um, that's all right, don't bother. In fact, maybe I'll stay down here to supervise the cleaners . . ."

But when I looked around, the last of the cleaning crew was dragging out the last of the trash barrels, and the guards were nowhere to be seen. How had everyone disappeared so quickly? And how was I going to get away from Rob without tipping my hand?

". . . and inventory the equipment," I concluded, "and the, uh, rental furniture."

Just go, I told myself, and took a deep breath to steady my vibrating nerves. *No need to panic, just leave. But not too quickly, in case he suspects. And get close to that exit first. It's nowhere near the van, but there'll be people out there.*

The inventory was a pointless and imaginary task, but I did it anyway, moving along the circumference of the rotunda toward the street exit, scribbling in a notebook as I went. Rob kept me company, ever so casually.

But why should he suspect? I thought. *He doesn't know what Boris said about the cologne—or that I've figured out that Boris must have smelled Rob's cologne on Digger's dead body. But don't take the chance, just run for it the minute you can.*

I had noticed the sportswriter's cologne the night of the murder, and it was nothing at all like Rob's. Boris must have been too drunk to tell when he was sitting with Digger, but later on the shock of coming upon a corpse made him register every last detail, including that musky scent in the air. *Rob Harmon's scent.*

"It was a fine party," said Rob, slinging the gym bag over

his shoulder so he could slip his hands in his jacket pockets. "Rose said to say goodbye to you."

"I'm sorry I missed her." I forced a smile. "That chocolate took forever to get out of my hair."

He chuckled as we continued around the ring of tables, our small talk echoing back at us from the lofty vault of the ceiling. I hardly knew what I was saying, so urgent were the ideas racing through my mind.

Rob must have seen Digger's notebook in my hiking pack. He was the one who mugged me outside NocNoc, and when he didn't get it then, he followed me into the stadium the night Nelly died. Why didn't I think of him along with Gordo as a player who might have used drugs?

I knew the answer, and it was a painful one: because I'd had a crush on him since I was a teenager. And also because Rob was retired now and couldn't be fined or suspended from the game. But even retired, he still had a lot to lose. Once it got out that he'd used steroids to prolong his career, he'd be barred forever from the all-important Hall of Fame.

Another pattern piece suddenly clicked into place. Gordo said Leroy Theroux had zero tolerance for drugs—but Rob had retired the year Leroy arrived. Leaving behind Nelly Tibbett, who knew his dark secret, and Digger Duvall, who guessed that Nelly knew and planned to run a sensational exposé about it before the Hall of Fame ballots went out . . .

"Lot of pressure on the Cubs now," Rob remarked. "Do or die."

"D-die? Oh, of course, they have to win tonight to stay in the Series, don't they?" Only a little farther to the exit. I hastened my steps. "Should be quite a game."

Poor Nelly. When Digger forced the information out of him and confronted Rob with it, Rob used that laser control

of his to make an instant decision: pick up the commemorative bat and eliminate the threat. Nelly must have been re-
morseful at betraying his friend—and then terrified that he
would be next.

And now maybe I am.

"You know what?" I said, and my voice sounded stagy
even to me. "I need to talk to Eugene about something. Don't
wait for me, I'll be—hey!"

Rob had seized my upper arm in a bruising grip—and in
his other hand he held JD's loaded gun.

Chapter Thirty-seven

"Where is it?" Rob demanded, and dug the muzzle of the gun into my ribs. "Just tell me."

I played dumb. "Are you crazy? Where's what?"

But it was too late for playing.

"You know right well," he drawled. "I want that tape recording. You told Gordo about it, and he told me."

"There isn't any recording. I made it up."

"Sure you did."

The gun dug in harder, and I heard myself whimper.

"Y-you can't shoot," I said, and wished I believed it. "People will hear, they'd see you running away."

"Why would I run from an accident?"

The drowning blue eyes held mine in an unwavering stare, the stare that had unnerved so many batters—and that Digger Duvall had defied, to his cost.

"Accident?" I echoed.

"I was handing you the boy's gun so you could take it to the police, and somehow it went off. Neither of us knew to check the safety. Terrible tragedy. Now *where is it?*"

I swallowed, or tried to, and said the first thing I could think of. "In my van. Near the loading dock."

"Let's go, then."

We moved across the rotunda in tandem, Rob's left arm

around my shoulders, his right hand with the gun tight against my side. From a distance, I supposed, we might have been lovers. I walked as slowly as I dared, praying that Eugene would come back. Or would that panic Rob into shooting us both?

In any case, I was unlikely to survive once we got to Vanna and my lie was revealed. That is, if Rob Harmon was capable of killing in cold blood, not just in the heat of anger. I slowed even more.

"Rob, listen. I'm sure you didn't mean to kill Digger. He was probably provoking you—"

"Arrogant *bastard*." The hatred in his voice was chilling. "This is all his fault. I just meant to scare him, but then he was—he was . . ."

His voice dwindled as he descended once more into the bloody nightmare. Then he blinked rapidly and clutched my arm. "Keep moving."

As we walked, I tried again. "None of this is my fault, Rob. You don't want to hurt me. That's not who you are."

"You have no idea who I am," he said bleakly. "No idea."

"But I do." I groped for something that might pull him back from the edge, recall him to reason. "You're Gordo's friend. And Rose is so fond of you. You—you seemed fond of me, up at Snow Lake. At least I thought so."

Rob's breathing changed. We had reached the gazebo by then. He stopped at its plywood side and swung me around to face him. His forehead bore a sheen of sweat, and his musky scent was strong and cloying.

"Y'all thought I was going to kiss you up on that crag, didn't you? And I wanted to! But what I needed to do was push you over. You'd seen that notebook, the same one Duvall waved in my face, and I couldn't tell if you knew about me. I've been in hell, don't you understand?" He clutched me tighter, and I gasped. "I've been in hell!"

"Rob, this doesn't have to go any further. Listen to—"

"Hiya, Stretch! Whoa, Rob, am I interrupting something?"

Aaron came trotting across the rotunda toward us, a big smile on his face. A big phony smile—I'd known him too long to be fooled. *He's figured it out,* I thought. *He knows.* But Rob Harmon didn't know Aaron at all—he was just some reporter. The gun disappeared, and though Rob's voice sounded stilted, he had himself under control.

"Hey, there. Aaron Gold, right? Just saying goodbye to Carnegie here." Then, before Aaron reached us, he muttered to me, "Get rid of him."

My thought exactly. The only thing that frightened me more than harm to myself was any kind of threat to Aaron. And what could he do against a gun? If he even guessed that Rob still possessed it, which I certainly hadn't. No, I had to persuade him to leave, to summon the police.

"Aaron!" I called out brightly, and as he came closer, I widened my eyes in what I hoped was a meaningful manner. *Where's ESP when you need it?* "I, ah, still have some things to talk over with Rob. About the wedding and, and things. So I'll meet you back at the houseboat, OK? Maybe we can have dinner with Lily and Mike. I'd love to see *Mike.*"

No good. Rob shifted impatiently, and Aaron planted himself in front of us and folded his arms.

"I think I'll stick around," he said, and his smile became an icy calm. "Don't mind me."

Incredibly—insanely—Aaron was calling Rob's bluff. *Don't do this,* I silently cried. *For both our sakes, don't do this.*

"Don't be stupid, Gold." The grip on my arm tightened. "Get out of my way."

Aaron didn't move. "Oh, I'm not stopping you. But you have to go alone. Carnegie stays here."

Ever so faintly I heard Rob give a sigh, and the gun reappeared. "No."

"Two hostages, Harmon?" Aaron spoke quietly, almost hypnotically. "Now that's going to be awkward. You'll need one of us to drive the car, of course, but— *Run!*"

I ran. Maybe I should have stayed to help Aaron as he dove for the gun, but my nerves were stretched to the breaking point and adrenaline took over. Adrenaline, but not a sense of direction. I ran blindly, thinking I was heading for the street exit, but fetched up against a small door near the escalators instead. I heard gasps and grunts behind me—and then a muffled shot.

I looked back. Aaron was lying on the floor, while Rob stumbled to his feet and came after me, his face contorted, the gym bag still swinging from his shoulder. With a sob of terror, I pushed through the door, raced down a dim narrow hallway, around a corner—only to find another corridor, with rakes and other pieces of groundskeeping equipment lined up along the walls.

I was in some kind of service tunnel. I had to turn back and find an exit—but there were footsteps pounding behind me, and they were getting closer. I had to summon an ambulance for Aaron, but first I had to survive.

I flew along the corridor, squinting through the gloom for any sign of escape. Finally I spotted something up ahead, a wide set of double doors with a printed sign above it. I pushed myself faster, shoved through the right-hand door, and emerged onto a stretch of crumbly dirt with a huge grassy expanse stretching before me.

I was on the baseball diamond, at the edge of the outfield

beyond third base. And I only knew of one other door, the archway where I'd watched the wedding ceremony just a few hours ago. An eternity ago.

Rabbits must feel like I felt, exposed and panicky, scuttling to cross a meadow while a hawk comes diving in for the kill. The October afternoon was fading, and with the stadium lights turned off, the grass at my feet was dim and cool.

I sprinted toward home plate, my lungs burning and my breath tearing at my throat. My bolt hole seemed impossibly far away, and though I didn't dare look back, I heard the service door bang shut as Rob came through it.

Zzzzt!

Something hummed by my ear, so close that I cried out in alarm. But it wasn't a bullet, it was a white blur, and then somewhere on the far side of the diamond, I heard an echoing *crack*.

Startled and puzzled, I wasn't watching my feet, and when the surface changed from grass to the dirt around third base, I stumbled and sprawled flat, skidding painfully on knees and palms. I began to haul myself up, but slowly, too slowly. Behind me in the outfield, beneath the empty stands, Rob Harmon was waving his arms.

No, not waving. *Winding up for a pitch.*

That's when I knew for sure what the murder weapon had been. Not a baseball bat, though he used that afterward to disguise the death wound. The weapon had been a hundred-mile-an-hour fastball, launched with deadly accuracy down that hallway full of memorabilia. An autographed ball, like the ones in Rob's gym bag today.

These ideas flooded quickly into my mind, but I could barely move my body, barely breathe. I cowered there, eyes closed, but as I did I heard the service door bang again. My eyes flew open.

Aaron! He reached into Rob's discarded bag, he straightened up with something in his hand—and then both men moved. Another white blur came at me, and I saw only an explosion of stars and darkness.

Chapter Thirty-eight

Someone had a terrible headache. I was yearning to sleep, but I couldn't sleep because the person with the terrible headache kept moaning.

"Stop it," I moaned. "Please stop it..."

The moaning came and went, but the headache stayed. Faces bobbed above me like balloons, blurred and then harshly focused and then blurred again. Bright lights, darkness, voices in the distance, voices in my ear, memories...

"Aaron!"

I struggled in panic, trying to get up, trying to run to him. Gentle hands pressed at my shoulders, and I fell back into the pillows.

"Shhh, Carrie, it's all right. Aaron is safe, dear. You're both safe."

"Mom?"

"Shhh."

Darkness again. My headache faded into a far, dim distance. I drifted after it, into the silence, and slept. When I awoke, it was to pale morning light that filtered thinly through the curtains of a hospital room. I lay motionless, unthinking, my gaze wandering from the windows to the vacant bed next to mine to the armchair in the corner, which had someone sleeping in it. Aaron, his head tilted to one side, snoring softly. I smiled and slept again.

When I woke up next, I was alone and feeling remarkably normal except for a fair-sized lump over my right eye. In fact, I was attempting to get out of bed when a plump and ruddy woman, wearing a flowered smock and a name badge that read JANICE M., barged into the room and said, "Oh, no you don't!"

"But I'm thirsty," I said meekly.

"And what do you think that's for?"

She nodded at my bedside table, which indeed held a glass and pitcher, as well as a vase of yellow roses. Next to the vase lay a notepad with the hospital logo, and on the pad, within the penciled outline of a heart, was the ruby ring.

"He's just getting himself some lunch," said the aide, making the shrewd assumption that I knew who "he" was. "And your mother will be back shortly. She just called."

"Lunch? What day is it?"

"Sunday. You took quite a whack on the head. Mild concussion and shock, though you're supposed to hear that from the doctor, not from me. But the way she's backed up today, she won't get to you for another hour, and you'd be asking me anyway, wouldn't you? *There* now."

Bustling busily as she spoke, Janice had poured a glass of water, helped me sit up to drink it, fluffed my pillows, and twitched my sheets into order. She gave a quick brisk nod, satisfied with her handiwork.

"Want some lunch yourself?"

"Mm . . . no, thanks."

"I'm not surprised. Lots of fluids, though." She pointed at the television set mounted at the ceiling. "Your remote control is there with your water if you get bored. I don't think they'll keep you tonight, but if they do, you can still watch the game."

"Game?"

"The Cubbies tied the Series last night! Oh, of course, you wouldn't know that, would you? I'm from Chicago, you see, so I can hardly think about anything else. My husband says it was a fluke, they'll win the World Series when hell freezes over, but I think they're going to do it tonight, I truly do. I tried to get off work early so I could see the first pitch, but I already swapped one shift this week already, so . . ."

I must have dozed off again, because suddenly she was gone and Aaron was there gazing down at me. He looked the worse for wear—but then I hadn't seen myself in a mirror yet.

"What happened?" I asked, when I could bear to stop kissing him for a moment. I touched his right cheek gingerly. It was scraped and bruised, but otherwise he seemed intact. "I thought you were shot."

"Nope. The gun slid under the gazebo where Harmon couldn't get it, and I crashed into the damn thing myself. Plywood is *really* hard."

"And Rob?"

"He took off after you and—well, you know."

"No, I don't. He was throwing at me, but then you threw a ball at him? I forgot, you were a pitcher too. Did that stop him?"

"No way." Aaron grinned, but there was a shadow in his eyes. "My glory days in college were a long time ago. I just bounced a ball near his feet, and it spoiled his aim."

I shuddered. "That was how he killed Digger, you know. With a pitch."

"Yeah, Mike Graham wants to talk to you about that. He's

outside there now, but if you're not feeling up to questions—"

"Ask him to come in, would you? I want to get this over with and then forget all about it. If I can."

Mike's manner was a mix of his official and his private personas. He was doggedly thorough about learning exactly what had happened since the murder, with special attention to the contents of Digger's notebook. But he was also considerate of my fragile condition.

"That's enough for now," he said, putting his own notebook away. "I'll save my lecture for another time."

"The one about interfering with police business?"

"That's the one." He smiled. "Take care, now. Lily says she'll be here soon."

"If I'm still here," I retorted. "I want to go home. But Mike, wait. What's Rob saying about all this? Has he confessed?"

The same sort of shadow crossed Mike's face. He glanced across the bed at Aaron, who shook his head slightly. That apparently meant *I haven't told her*.

"Robert Harmon fled the scene in his rental car," Mike said, frowning at the wall behind me. "He almost collided with the ambulance that was coming for you. We pursued, but he drove to the state ferry dock and gunned his engine. Went right through a barrier and into the water. Rescue efforts were unsuccessful. It, um, appeared to be deliberate."

"Oh."

Mike left quietly, and Aaron held me for a long time.

After that Mom came, to reassure herself all over again that her darling daughter was going to survive. Then Lily brought me some clean clothes to go home in, if the overbooked doctor would ever show up to set me free. And

Owen, having parked the car after dropping Mom off, arrived with a cardboard cup of coffee for her and a two-pound box of chocolate creams from the gift shop for me.

"I wasn't sure what was appropriate," he said, his hearty executive manner a bit subdued in these medical surroundings. "But Lou's always telling me that chocolate cures all ills."

"She is so right!" Lily laughed her marvelous, contagious laugh. "You going to share, Carnegie?"

"Absolutely," I said, determined not to think about Rob Harmon. At least not today.

I opened the box, and we had ourselves quite a little party. Owen went out for more coffees, and when he returned, he had more visitors in tow: Buck and Betty Buckmeister, who had somehow learned about the situation on the Navigator grapevine. After a round of introductions, Betty was full of tender solicitude about my injury, and Buck boomed with relief at my evident recovery.

" 'Cept for that goose egg on your noggin, you look just fine," he said, tossing a chocolate toward his back teeth and chawing at it like tobacco. "Practically a picture of health."

"I can imagine," I said. "Mom, have you got a comb and mirror? Thanks, I just need to—*yikes!*" My face was recognizable, but I almost wished it weren't. The "goose egg" was a monumental bulge that contorted my expression grotesquely. "Why didn't someone tell me? I look like a monster."

"I asked the doc," said Aaron, "and she said the swelling will go down quickly. Don't worry, you're going to look fine for your wedding."

"*My* wedding?" As the chitchat continued around us, I looked up at him in dismay and whispered, "Aaron, it's *our* wedding."

"Of course it is," he blurted, with the horror-struck air of a well-meaning man who's just said The Wrong Thing to a woman. "Of course it is. It's just that all the fancy arrangements are more for you than for— Oh God, Stretch, don't cry."

"I'm not crying," I said staunchly, through the tears, "and I would marry you tomorrow if I could."

This overdramatic announcement fell into a lull in the general conversation, and everyone's eyes turned toward us. A startled pause, and then Betty Buckmeister piped up.

"Honey, you can marry him right this minute if you got your heart set on it. I been a Universal Life minister since nineteen-seventy-nine."

Everyone seemed to speak at once. Buck opined that that was a mighty fine idea and wasn't his Betty something, while Owen wondered aloud about obtaining a marriage license on a Sunday and Lily said she was pretty sure we had one already and my mother said I should probably get some rest.

Aaron, meanwhile, just cocked an eyebrow at me and grinned. There's nothing Aaron likes better than calling somebody's bluff.

"Everybody just *hold* it," I said, raising my voice above the clamor. "No way am I getting married in a hospital gown."

"But, Carrie," said Mom, "you don't have a wedding gown."

"Sure she does." Lily winked at me. "She's got the one she wore at my wedding, and she loves it."

I jutted my chin at Aaron. "Lily's right. And that's the gown I'm going to wear tomorrow, at our intimate ceremony and reception on the houseboat. If Betty can make it tomorrow."

"I surely can, honey."

The Killer B's were jubilant, but as the excited chatter rose around me, my heart began to sink just a little. Was this really what I wanted? No pomp and circumstance, no grand formal occasion? No engraved deckle-edged invitations and color-coordinated napkins and Dungeness crab tartlets?

On the other hand, no professional pressure, no huge expense, and no waiting for another year...

I was vacillating—until I noticed Aaron breathing a happy sigh of relief. A small celebration on the houseboat really would be our wedding. And then my mother spoke up and sealed the deal.

"You know, dear, Dree and Kimmie couldn't possibly make it back from Belize in time to be your bridesmaids."

"What a *shame*," I said. "We'll have to save them some cake."

Chapter Thirty-nine

Happy is the bride the sun shines upon, but what about the bride that the wind blows around? My wedding day was a blustery light show, with shafts of sunlight that pierced the scudding pewter clouds to kindle flares of silver on the surface of the lake.

"Just like you and Aaron," said Lily, helping me get ready in the bedroom of my houseboat. "Bright and sunny one minute, stormy the next."

"While you and Mike are permanently fair and mild?"

She chuckled. "Most of the time, anyway. If you throw in a couple of minor earthquakes for Marcus and Ethan. That color is *perfect* on you."

Even with the breeze the weather was still unseasonably warm, so I'd decided to go ahead and wear the peach-colored gown I'd worn as Lily's maid of honor. She would be all in purple, of course, a deep-hued dress with a swirling zigzag hemline. And Aaron, presently off on some secret errand, was already wearing the salt-and-pepper tweed sports jacket that I liked so much.

I learned later that the errand was to procure a pair of gold wedding bands, which he assured me we could always exchange if I wanted something different. But I was happy with the design—and even happier that he'd remembered my ring size.

"Thanks," I said to Lily now. "I love this dress. I'm so glad you . . . you . . ."

I interrupted myself with a vast yawn. It wasn't just Seattle weather that had shifted; I'd been up till after midnight watching hell freeze over. After fifteen neck-and-neck innings, the longest World Series game ever, a third-string Chicago Cubs shortstop knocked one out of the park to win the final game, for the honor and glory of underdogs everywhere.

Happily, Aaron and I had been free to watch every historic inning together—and toss around honeymoon ideas during the commercials—because our impromptu wedding arrangements had come together with such absurd ease.

The plan couldn't have been simpler. Betty Buckmeister's ceremony would take place on the floating platform below my deck, with our dozen or so guests watching from the deck itself. Then we'd all troop inside for champagne and hors d'oeuvres courtesy of Joe Solveto, and slices of something that Juice Nugent called Chocolate Extremity.

Apparently the guests had begun to arrive, because a buzz of conversation came through when the bedroom door opened a crack.

"May I come in, dear?"

"Sure, Mom. What do you think?"

Lily and I pirouetted in tandem, and my mother clasped her hands and beamed.

"Just lovely, both of you. Lily, could I have a moment?"

"Of course. I'd better make sure Marcus hasn't gone swimming."

"Oh, I hope not, dear. That water is ice cold!"

"Kidding," said Lily, and left us.

Mom and I sat on the bed, and she took my hand. The

ruby ring still didn't fit my finger, but it was back around my neck on a new chain, with the macaroon crumbs all cleaned off. Mom gazed at it and gave a little sigh.

"Carrie," she said, and hesitated. "Carrie, you know I will never forget your father. I hope you don't think—"

"I think Dad would have wanted you to be happy," I said firmly. "In fact I know he would. Is he on your mind today?"

She nodded.

"Mine too." I sighed myself. Another minute and we'd both be in tears. "So, what sort of advice would he have for me, do you suppose?"

"I'm not sure," she said, giving it serious thought. "But I have some."

I waited, curious. Mom might be less irreverent than I was, but she'd never been given to self-help homilies or greeting-card clichés.

"Marriage is ... complicated," she said. "It can be much harder than you expect, but also much sweeter, in ways that you keep discovering as the years go by. So give it your all, Carrie. Just throw yourself into it, and you'll be fine."

With that she kissed me quickly on the cheek and went to the door. But there she turned back. "Oh, and keep in mind, men are *terrible* mind-readers. Always speak up. But that's never been your problem, has it? Now don't be late, dear. Aaron is back and people are waiting. Shall I tell Lily you're ready?"

I nodded, and in a few moments Lily rejoined me bearing both our bouquets. Hers was a playful concoction of every purple flower Boris could lay hands on at such short notice. Purple parrot tulips, lisianthus, calla lilies, hellebore, even a fringe of deep-purple African violets. Floral purists would have cringed, but Lily adored it.

My bouquet was just what the Mad Russian had promised in our conversation at the jail: a waterfall design of peaches-and-cream roses with trailing strands of sweet-scented stephanotis among the glossy leaves of grapevine. Lily handed it to me.

"Ready, girl?"

"Ready."

We crossed the hallway, Lily leading, and rendezvoused in the kitchen with the gentleman who would escort me down the "aisle." Two delightful sights greeted us there: the unheard-of phenomenon of Eddie Breen in a tie, and on one of Joe's hors d'oeurves platters, a gorgeous array of crab tartlets!

"What are you giggling at, sister?" asked Eddie. He was trying for his usual irascible tone, but his eyes were suspiciously moist. "Don't go getting hysterical on me."

"Promise," I said.

"You two look bitchin'!" came a whisper from behind us. Juice, sporting a spangled silver tube top and her best lizard boots, was giving a final stir to the coffee-spiked crème anglaise sauce that would go on the wedding cake.

"So does that," I said, nodding at her creation. The single dense layer of chocolate bore an intricate and customized design: my initials twined with Aaron's, stenciled onto it in powdered sugar. "Amazing."

"Yeah, isn't it?" said Juice. "I'll be right out there. Break a leg."

Eddie harrumphed and offered me his arm. I took it with one hand, settled my bouquet in the other, and gave Lily the go-ahead. Eddie and I followed her through the living room and out along the deck, passing Mom and her Owen, Joe and his ever-so-handsome lover Alan, the proudly beaming Boris, and Buck Buckmeister, pleased as punch to have Lily's two little boys in his temporary care.

There were also a handful of other friends, including Aaron's editor Paul Wheeler, whose wedding I'd directed a year ago, and Nickie Parry, now Ishigura, a favorite bride of mine at whose home I'd first met Aaron. I smiled into every face with fondness and gratitude. Then Eddie helped me descend the ramp of worn gray planks to the little floating platform, which rocked a bit as we stepped aboard.

Betty was waiting for us, rosy-cheeked in her natty black pantsuit, and Mike Graham was there as well. But once I saw Aaron's face, my powers of observation went missing, and I slipped into a soft-edged dream. Betty's remarks went by within the dream, and I seemed to watch from a distance as Mike produced the rings and we placed them on each other's hands.

I didn't really focus until Aaron recited the paraphrased excerpts he'd woven together from his favorite book, Thoreau's *Walden*.

" 'Let us arise before the dawn and seek adventures.' " Aaron's voice was strong and eager. " 'Let the noon find us by other lakes, and the night overtake us everywhere at home. And let us walk always hand in hand, as near the water's edge as we can go.' "

I hadn't planned to recite anything, which was lucky because after that I just dissolved in happy tears, while we said our vows and then Aaron kissed me for a very long time. Everyone applauded, and the excitement was just too much for Marcus and Ethan. Instead of waiting on the deck as they'd been told, they broke free from Buck and raced down the ramp onto the platform, blessing our union at the tops of their lungs.

"Aunt Car, Aunt Car, Aunt Car, Aunt *Car*!" Marcus shrilled, while Ethan danced an ecstatic jig, his toes just inches from the lake.

"Hey there, fellers!" Buck bellowed, pounding down the ramp himself. "C'mon back to Uncle Buck!"

Right on Buck's booted heels came Boris Nevsky, always keen to kiss a bride, any bride. They were both big men, and their combined weight hit the floating platform just as I stepped out of Aaron's arms. Inevitably, the platform plunged inches deep into the water on their side, while rearing up like a panicked horse on mine.

"Whoa!" I shouted. "Whoa—oops!"

My shoes scrabbled as I tried to stay upright, and I windmilled my arms for balance. Bad move. That lofted my lovely bouquet into the air, high over my head and behind me, to land with a splash beside a Canada goose—no doubt she'd be the next waterfowl to get married.

You know the line about getting by with a little help from your friends? As my arms swept back, down, and forward, Aaron grabbed one hand and Lily the other, and together they hauled me to safety.

"Hang on, Stretch," said Aaron, laughing, as his hair flopped down across his eyes. "Not *that* near the water's edge. Who am I going to take to the Olympic if you float away?"

"The—the what?"

"The Olympic Hotel. Maybe you've heard of it? I know we're going to honeymoon in Portugal later on, but I booked us a suite for tonight. If that's all right with you?"

"Oh, *Aaron*."

I kissed him again, for another long time, and then we went off to share champagne and chocolate with our friends. Honestly, I can't wait to see what happens next.

About the Author

DEBORAH DONNELLY is a sea captain's daughter who grew up in Panama, Cape Cod, and points in between. She's been an executive speechwriter, a university librarian, a science fiction writer, and a nanny. A long-time resident of Seattle and a bloomingly healthy breast cancer survivor, Donnelly now lives physically in Portland, Oregon, and virtually at www.deborahdonnelly.org.